GRIFFIN BLADE

AND THE BRONZE FINGER

You see things, and you say "Why?"
But I dream things that never were, and I say "Why not?"
– *George Bernard Shaw*

WHY NOT BOOKS

Pacific Grove, California | www.WhyNotBooks.com

Why Not Books is dedicated to producing good books and good karma. Toward that end, we partner each title with a charitable organization and donate a portion of proceeds to the cause. The nonprofit partners for this book, the Camp Nebagamon Scholarship Fund and Camperships for Nebagamon (CNCharities.org), provide opportunities for children who experience poverty and disability and from socioeconomically diverse backgrounds to enjoy safe, joyful, and potentially transformative summer camp experiences.

GRIFFIN BLADE

AND THE **BRONZE FINGER**

LUKE HERZOG

www.whynotbooks.com
www.lukeherzog.com

ISBN: 978-0-9849919-6-9

Library of Congress Control Number: 2014953330

First Edition: November 2014

Printed in the United States of America

Cover and interior design by Tessa Avila

To Ms. Jenna Hofer
and the members
of the PGMS book club

ALASTIAN

Kni Hmun Mountains

Proudtop · Jaggeredge · Dumalar · Hare's Hop · Glory Stone

Fellgong · Bird's Gate

Minstel Peak

Twisted Summit

The Crystal

The Foothills

Zahee Forest

Quah

Marshlands

Northern Plains

Northerner Country

Southerner Country

Naran Lake

Bordertown

Cana

River Kak

River Maz

River Baj

Hellgrot

Southern Plains

Bajuru

River Cul

River Baj

Gocian Tribes

Desert of Waste

Faveos

Mocon

Firstport

Gocian Tribes

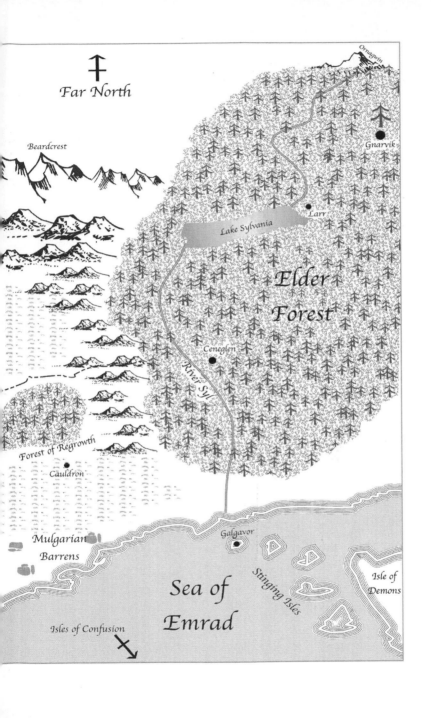

CHAPTER 1

Griffin heard shouts coming from nearby. "Curse them," he muttered. He looked down at the Hiamahu Jewel, a sparkling gem that felt at home in his hand, despite the fact that he had just stolen it. The jewel glimmered bright blue before he quickly placed it in his breast pocket. He reached back over his shoulder and readied his crossbow, suddenly wishing he hadn't used four bolts as footholds to climb to the upper floor of Scadnik's treasury. Only two bolts remained.

The shouts grew louder, as a group of guards stormed into the room. They wore leather armor and carried black shields adorned with Lord Scadnik's crest—an orange lion head, its mouth pulled back in a snarl. *How did they find me?* Griffin wondered.

As the first two guards arrived, he shot the closest one in the shoulder, careful not to aim for the heart. The second guard took a bolt through the thigh. *A shame,* thought Griffin, *but they'll survive.* He then grabbed a rope that had been attached to his belt by a hook and tossed it upward to a brass chandelier hanging from the high ceiling. The hook looped around an arm of the chandelier, and Griffin leaped, swinging across the room and landing on a narrow ledge halfway up the wall on the opposite side. Wasting no time, he shortened the rope and again leaped, this time toward a high window, as the chandelier began to creak from his weight.

Holding on with one hand as he swung, he removed a heavy dagger from his belt and hurled it toward the window, shattering the glass just before he arrived. Grabbing hold of the window sill with his fingertips, he began to climb through the open space. He turned to face the guards below, their mouths agape. Two of them rushed to a corner of the room, where javelins gathered dust on a rack. They grabbed the weapons, returned to the center of the room, and aimed them at the intruder.

Griffin glanced upward and grinned. He tugged hard on the rope that had been his savior, and the ceiling began to crumble. Just before the chandelier fell atop the unfortunate guards below, rendering them unconscious, they could have sworn they saw Griffin Blade wink.

Griffin raced through the darkened streets of the city of Quah. During the day, the city was bustling with life—merchants charging up and down the streets, practically begging customers to buy their wares; friendly travelers tipping their hats or nodding toward passing strangers; burly men boasting of their skills; and pages, usually children of noblemen, running about on errands.

At night, however, the mood of the city changed. Locals locked their doors. The Main Gates of the city were closed, and nobody was allowed in or out. City Guards were posted along the walls above the gates, staring into the darkness, waiting for invisible foes. Also when night arrived, new figures emerged. Some of them were rogues like Griffin. Others were outcasts and bandits and spies and mercenaries dealing in dark business.

After Griffin made sure he was not being pursued, he finally ceased running and began striding down a side street. A stooped man in a gray cloak, his face hidden by a hood, walked toward him. As the man neared him, he suddenly veered into Griffin, knocking him to the ground.

"Very sorry, good sir," the man whispered. "Here, let me help you up." He held out a long, calloused hand. As Griffin grabbed it, he noticed that the old man's index finger was mechanical. *Odd,* he thought, as he brushed the grime of the street from his clothes. Griffin turned to ask the old man about the finger, but he had disappeared.

Griffin walked farther until he reached a dark alley in the most questionable part of town. Attached to the wall in the alley was a small, wooden board. Griffin tapped it three times, then twice, then three times again. Suddenly, the board moved to reveal a slot. All Griffin could see was a pair of eyes staring back at him.

"Code," the eyes asked.

"Heron."

"Name."

"Griffin Blade," he replied. "I wish to sell an item to the Lord of Lies."

The eyes seemed to accept his answer. "Very well, you may pass." A stone door that had blended in with the alley wall slowly swung open.

"I don't want any trouble outta you," said the eyes, as Griffin prepared to walk in.

Griffin raised an eyebrow. "Wouldn't dream of it."

As he passed through the stone door, the air became considerably cooler. Griffin could see his own breath. He began to make out figures moving about in black cloaks. The air smelled of sewage, a scent Griffin had learned to tolerate. He remembered the first time he had visited the black market of Quah. He had been seven years old...

Young Griffin tried to keep up with his father. Ramyr Blade had dark brown hair and matching eyes that were constantly scanning his surroundings. He stood erect, one hand never far from his sword's hilt, the other gently on his son's shoulder. "Come, Griff! Business does not complete itself!"

It was dark, later than he had ever been allowed to wander the city, and Griffin began to make out shadowy figures strolling the streets. Suddenly frightened, the young boy stopped in his tracks, his hands trembling. "W-where are we, Father?"

"A place... for people like us," his father slowly replied. "Sometimes the shadows are the safest place to be."

Griffin shook the memory from his head until it began to throb. But he could never shake it completely. His memories of his father were like slowly fading embers from a fire. He feared the day when they would be mere ashes. He sighed and continued through the dark hallway. From a nearby room, he could hear a small band of men singing an eerie song, their low voices working in harmony:

> "By raven's call and deadly grasp
> he ferries us to long-earned past.
> He holds your fate,
> which he shall rate.
> He decides the path you take…"

Griffin shivered. The song only further depressed him. *Think about business,* he mused. *Business first, all else second.* He made his way to an open-air courtyard and strode up to a large, gray tent, torches flaming on either side of the entrance. He paused and peered down into a small puddle of water. Griffin always expected to see a boy with nervous eyes and a small frown. Instead, he was greeted by a smirking, bright-eyed man, chestnut hair falling across his forehead. He stepped into the puddle, sending the reflection rippling away, and took a deep breath as he walked inside the tent.

Moments later, he found himself looking at a short man with bushy eyebrows above large violet eyes, a trimmed red beard and a curly mustache that was darker, almost black. He wore light brown hunting boots and a red robe made of the finest silk. His name was Alnardo Fist, but he was more commonly known as the Lord of Lies. The man leaned back and put his feet on his desk.

"Ah, Blade. I presume your mission was a success?"

Griffin nodded. "More or less."

Fist removed his feet from the desk and sat up straight. "Less?"

Griffin grinned. "I used up the last of my crossbow bolts."

The Lord of Lies began to chuckle. "With the amount I'm paying you, you could purchase the finest bolts in Quah." He paused, and his eyes narrowed. "You do have the gem, don't you?"

"Of course." Griffin reached into his breast pocket, but was startled to find that it was empty. He mumbled, mostly to himself, "It's... gone."

"Gone? GONE! That jewel is priceless, Blade. Priceless! Your father never would have been so careless."

Griffin thought back to his journey through the streets of Quah and remembered the old man who had crashed into him. Could he have stolen it? "Sir, I think..."

"Do not even speak, Griffin. You will find that gem. You will retrieve the Hiamahu Jewel."

"But..."

"You will find it! Or I will consider our deal broken," said the Lord of Lies. "And I don't think I have to tell you what happens to people who break their promises to me."

Griffin shivered again.

CHAPTER 2

As Griffin lay in his bed in a shabby house on Quah's eastern side, a place purposely difficult to find, he imagined himself speaking with his father.

"Why did you not just do away with the guards?"
"I am not a killer," answered Griffin.
"But they saw your face. You are now a wanted man in Quah."
"I do not kill, Father."
"Good. I'll have no son of mine killing without reason."

Griffin smiled to himself, came up with a plan, and then began gathering his belongings. He was not entirely sure that he wasn't a killer, but he was certain that he was now a fugitive.

Before dawn, Griffin departed his home, packing his crossbow, some throwing daggers and a few days' worth of rations on the back of his horse, a rose gray stallion and longtime companion. His face hidden by a hooded cloak, Griffin headed toward the western section of the city, the market area. When he arrived, he stopped at a wooden building. "SILVERBEARD FORGE," said the sign. His horse neighed impatiently. Griffin hadn't named him Fuss for nothing.

He tied Fuss to a post and walked inside the building, where he encountered a female dwarf sitting behind a desk. It wasn't an entirely rare sight in that part of the world, but not a particularly attractive one either. She wore simple gray clothing and old leather gloves. Beneath braided brown hair, she had wide, green eyes.

"Welcome to our little family forge. How may I 'elp ya?"

"Well, I am looking for my old friend Roland Silverbeard. Are you a relative?"

She shook her head. "No one's actually related 'ere."

Griffin scratched his head. "Well, can you tell me where I might find him?"

"If you are an old friend, ya won't be surprised to 'ear that he's at Staghorn Tavern, as usual."

Griffin, indeed, wasn't surprised at all. It was a quick ride from the forge to Staghorn Tavern, a well-known pub in Quah. He heard laughing and singing, as he tied up his horse while Fuss fussed. Inside, he found quite a scene. A few travelers sipped ale while seated on padded stools at a bar. Arranged throughout the room were many wooden tables of various shapes and sizes, most of them occupied by wine-drinking men and women. In the middle of the room, around the largest table, sat ten dwarves, their beards stretching nearly to their toes and each a different color—white and gray and jet black, light brown and dark brown and auburn brown, blonde and cherry red and copper red. Griffin recognized Roland

Silverbeard among the group. He had a silver beard, of course, tightly braided, and long silver hair falling to his shoulders. He was the tallest of the bunch, which wasn't saying much.

None of the dwarves appeared sober, and they were singing in their deep, dwarven voices:

"Drink the ale, pour the wine.
Slurp the brandy. Mine! Mine! Mine!
Drain the rum, guzzle the beer,
chug the cider. Hear! Hear! Hear!
Finish the whiskey and the scotch.
Empty bottles! You just watch!"

Dwarves, Griffin chuckled. He walked up to Roland, as a blonde-bearded dwarf began dancing on the table. "Roland," he said, leaning forward into the light and slightly revealing his face, "it's me, Griffin."

"Wha --?"

"It's me, Griffin Blade."

Roland put his hand on Griffin's shouder. "Griffin, my boy! It's been too long!"

"I need to ask you about something," said Griffin. "It's a... private matter."

Roland opened his eyes wide and tugged at his silver beard. "Well, all right then, why don't we talk at the forge."

Griffin guided the tipsy dwarf to the door. "There's a stable out back," said Roland. "My horse, Moon, is there."

Roland's horse was a white pony with sea-blue eyes. They led Moon to where Fuss was tied, then Roland ungracefully climbed aboard him. Quickly it became clear that he was in no state to guide a pony. He veered left and right, never particularly straight. As Griffin reached out his hand to balance him, Roland shouted, "I know what I'm doin'!"

Seconds later, the silver-bearded dwarf crashed into a few street-side boxes. All Griffin could do was roll his eyes. After a much longer ride than Griffin expected, they arrived back at Silverbeard Forge. The woman was still sitting at a desk. She looked up. "Drinking too much again, Roland? Ya really should know better by now."

Roland patted his throat. "Nothing wrong with wettin' your gullet, Melendi."

"Maybe so," Melendi replied. "But there is something wrong with staggering around like a fool."

Roland waved his hand. "Don't listen to her, Griffin. Stagger around as much as you'd like." He motioned to a back room where anvils lined the floor and hammers hung from various hooks on the walls. "So," Roland said, "out with it."

Griffin explained that a man with a mechanical finger had stolen a gem of his. He didn't bother with the details about how he had obtained the gem in the first place. "Do you have any idea how that finger might have been created?"

The dwarf stroked his silver beard. "A finger made o' metal, ya say? Hmmm... what sort o' metal?"

"Bronze, I believe."

"A bronze finger," said Roland. He stroked his beard again. "I can think of only one place that might forge such a thing—Briskhammer Forge in Dunalar."

"Dunalar..."

"Yes, the Marble City, the dwarven capital, ruled by Rindivor the Almighty. Briskhammer Forge is where I trained for many years. Best forge in all of Alastian."

"That's farther than I would have liked," said Griffin. He had never been to Dunalar. He didn't even know anyone who had been there.

"Aye, it's one week to the north by foot. But only two days on horseback." He grinned at Griffin, "Actually, I was thinkin' o' headin' there tomorrow to restock on supplies."

Griffin's eyes suddenly sparkled with interest. "Could you use some company, Roland?"

"Been a while since we traveled together, eh? Of course, no human has entered Dunalar for many years, but I see no reason for ya not to come along. Although I will have to educate ya a bit about dwarven customs."

"I appreciate that, Roland."

"Whatever ya need, my boy. What's mine is yours, except what's mined, of course."

"Well, I could use a place to stay tonight, Roland."

The dwarf nodded.

"And a quiver of crossbow bolts."

The dwarf nodded once more. "That'll be six gold pieces."

CHAPTER 3

On the way out of the city gate the next morning, riding atop Fuss and Moon, they passed a pair of City Guards. Griffin winced and lowered his his hood over his eyes. They exited Quah unnoticed.

A mile beyond the North Gate was a large forest. The Zahee Forest was the only place in all of Alastian where Everwood trees grew. Everwoods were so tall that they seemed to pierce the sky. They had thick, brown trunks, and their leaves were a sunset orange. In the trees the mirds— small primates with bright white fur—sang, bird-like, while swinging amid the Everwoods.

As the travelers followed a wide, dirt trail that swerved around the massive trees, Roland imparted a few lessons about dwarven customs.

"What do ya think," he began, "is most important to a dwarf?"

Griffin thought for a moment. "Gold?"

"No."

"Songs?"

"No again."

Griffin grinned. "Ale?"

Roland laughed. "That's second on the list." Griffin shrugged.

"Beards," said Roland.

"Beards? You're saying a beard is the single most important..."

"Have ya ever seen a dwarf without one?"

"I haven't seen too many dwarves at all, besides an occasional encounter with you and your mates."

"The length o' your beard symbolizes status," Roland explained, as he tugged at his own. "I am roughly middle class in dwarven society. Ya should see some of the nobles in the Dwarven Court. They need servants just to 'old their beards up. Otherwise they would be tripping all over themselves."

Griffin laughed and then noticed that Roland hadn't been joking.

"And then there's the color," the dwarf continued. "It generally represents a dwarf's personality."

Griffin looked at him quizzically. "But isn't that just a family trait, passed down through the generations?"

Roland nodded. "Exactly. Now then, blonde generally suggests a trickster, a charmer. Black is mysterious and secretive. Brown is intelligent, but impatient. Red is courageous and friendly. White and gray are wise and humble. Gold is a leader..."

"And what about silver, Roland Silverbeard?"

"You'll just 'ave to figure that out for yourself," he replied with a wink. "Now ya know about the nine gods, don't ya?"

"Well..." Griffin was becoming quite aware that he didn't know enough about the other cultures of Alastian. His father might have educated him about it, if only he had been around to do so.

"We worship eight gods, each associated with a beard color. And of course, the ninth god is Tyzon, creator of dwarves."

"Interesting," said Griffin. "And colorful."

"That it is. I suggest ya learn more about it. Not many humans are familiar with our religion nowadays..."

"I just might do that, Roland," and he kicked his heels at Fuss, as the travelers regained their speed. They rode many more miles—dwarf and pony, human and horse—until the sun began to say farewell to the sky. They set up camp on the edge of the forest, within view of the Kni Hmun Mountains.

Roland pointed toward the highest peak. "That's where we're 'eading. But I need a rest. My backside is aching. Tomorrow, we reach the Marble City of Dunalar."

Griffin found a comfortable spot next to the fire and covered himself in a thin blanket. As he drifted to sleep, pondering his newly-learned dwarven customs, he scratched at the stubble on his chin. It was the closest thing he had to a beard. His eyes closed, and he was taken suddenly into the midst of battle...

The 12-year-old boy stood next to his father, who held a sturdy spear in one hand and a small wooden shield in the other. They were surrounded by at least a dozen members of the Southern Cavalry—at least, that is what his father said they were. One of them, a tall red-haired man atop a proud brown stallion that matched his bearing, spoke: "Our highness has accused you of two misdeeds—theft and dishonesty to the crown. What say you?"

After a moment, Ramyr Blade slowly replied, "I say that the accusations are correct."

The man eyed Griffin's father curiously. Griffin saw hatred in his eyes. "You shall be executed."

Ramyr balanced his spear. "Not without a fair fight, Seretigo Va'hou."

"Very well. I am glad that the name of your killer will echo in your head as you descend the steps of the under-realm, criminal scum!"

"Then let's fight like proper gentlemen. Remove yourself from your horse, horseman," said Ramyr, "and draw your blade."

"It would be an honor, worm." Seretigo dismounted and unsheathed a long sword.

"On three then?" asked Griffin's father.

"On three."

"One," said Ramyr, as he maneuvered Griffin behind him.

"Two," snarled Seretigo, adjusting the sword in his hand.

Griffin's father grit his teeth and barely whispered, "Three."

Seretigo charged, his sword held high, gleaming in the afternoon sun. Ramyr was able to block the attack with his shield. He then pointed his spear toward his attacker and thrust it forward. Seretigo used his quick reflexes to dodge, but only barely. He swung his sword wildly, but Ramyr avoided it with a calm sidestep. He smiled, an intimidating grin.

Seretigo stepped backward. "You find this humorous, scum? You don't deserve my blade in your throat. Let's see if you're grinning after a year in our dungeon." He shouted to his men. "Chain this man!"

"You said it was to be a fair fight, you coward," said Ramyr.

Seretigo smirked. "I say many things…"

Ramyr quickly found himself surrounded by several horsemen. He glanced at Griffin and slumped his shoulders. "I will surrender," he said, "if you spare my son."

"Very well."

Ramyr dropped his spear, which fell with a dull clang. Two horseman held him in place, while a third and fourth chained him.

"My son…" Ramyr pleaded, as he was roughly tossed onto the back of a horse.

Now Seretigo smirked. "I shall leave your grub of a son… to die of starvation."

As the horsemen turned and galloped away, Griffin stood blinking back tears. "Father!" he cried, as he stood amid the empty grasslands, watching the horses ride toward the horizon.

"Don't worry about me, Griff!" he heard his father shout. "Be smart! Be strong! Be safe!"

And he was gone.

CHAPTER 4

Griffin awoke with a start. It was early morning. The words "Don't worry about me..." still echoed in his head. He sighed. "Just a memory," he muttered. Griffin leaned over and shook Roland awake. "Wake up, Roland. Your bearded friends are waiting."

"Can't a dwarf sleep in?" Roland croaked. He stood up slowly. "Why don't ya just look around a bit, enjoy nature..." Roland took a step back and toppled over a fallen log.

Griffin couldn't stop himself from laughing. "You're right. I can enjoy nature."

Minutes later, they were riding once again. As the morning became afternoon, the vague forms of the great stone pyramids that were the Kni Hmun Mountains slowly came into view. There were nine mountains. Roland pointed toward them. "There is Proudtop. And Minstrel Peak. And Jaggeredge. And Glory Stone. And Fellgong. And Hare's Hop, Twisted Summit, and Beardcrest. And there... is Bird's Gate."

Bird's Gate was the tallest mountain by far, rising high above its brethren, four on each side.

"That is where we'll find Dunalar," Roland explained.

"Amazing," Griffin whispered.

Roland smiled. "I'm glad ya see it that way."

It was not long until they could see what appeared to be gray smoke coming from Bird's Gate. "Smoke from the forges," said Roland. "One of them is Briskhammer Forge. Maybe ya can learn a thing or two about that finger."

Soon they arrived at a large marble gate, guarded by a pair of bald-headed dwarves wearing gleaming chain mail armor. One was a bit shorter and had a long, golden beard. He carried a war hammer. The other, a chubby fellow, had a red beard that reached to his waist. He carried a wooden spear. The shorter one cleared his throat to speak. "Halt! State your name, occupation, and reason to enter dwarven lands!"

Roland began, "My name is Roland Silverbeard, blacksmith of Quah. I travel to Dunalar to restock on supplies. Oh, and to 'ave a drink of Weakbane wine with a couple o' my old mates."

"A good brew, Weakbane is," remarked the taller dwarf.

"Bruo!" said the other dwarf. "Stop babblin' on about wine, and do your job!"

"Not babblin'," Bruo muttered, but he stopped speaking.

"You, beardless one," the other dwarf continued. "State your title."

"I am Griffin Blade. At the moment, I have no occupation," he lied. "I travel with Roland to Dunalar to learn about a certain forged mechanism."

The golden-bearded dwarf eyed him cautiously. "You may pass," he said.

As they moved through the gate, Bruo nodded at Roland and smiled. But he frowned at the sight of Griffin's bare chin. A half-mile later, a short, stone tower came into view. Its bricks were cracked, like the face of an old man.

"Our oldest outpost," Roland explained. "Grinklehaim is its name." He squinted into the distance. "We should see the Crystal any minute now."

Griffin shot him a questioning look.

"You'll see in a second."

And he did. The Crystal was a translucent stream, its water as clear as the air itself. A small wooden boat was docked at the edge of the stream. An elderly dwarf with a jagged scar across his face sat in the boat, holding a paddle.

"No horses," croaked the dwarf. "Leave 'em with Krang."

Griffin and Roland handed the reins of Fuss and Moon to a cross-eyed dwarf nearby and stepped into the boat. The boatman mumbled something about extra weight, but once they were settled he began to row toward Bird's Gate Mountain. When they had reached its base, the dwarf kept rowing—toward a cavern that seemed to have eaten its way into the side of the mountain. Inside, it was dim. The only sound was the slow dripping of water. Every once in a while in the darkness, Griffin caught a glimpse of a statue of a dwarven warrior holding a sword, battleaxe, or war hammer. Roland began to whisper a song...

"Hammers hard, axes aged, swords sharp, blades caged,
    we ride upon a riverboat, amid a river wide,
    passing kings with dwarven rings, all of them have died.

Ho! There's Haltark the Vain.
　　He died of his own shame!
Ah! There be Nauth the Old,
　　the king whose heart was forged of gold!
We ride upon a riverboat, amid a river wide,
passing kings with dwarven rings, all of them have died.
Oh! He is Murok the Steel.
　　'Tis sad he could not find a meal!
Him there! Bodrauth the Third.
　　A shame he was no flying bird!
We ride upon a riverboat, amid a river wide,
passing kings with dwarven rings, all of them have died.
Alas! There be Gardnet of Khath.
　　He died within his very bath!
Finally now, made all of stone,
　　the oldest dwarf of dwarven home,
Hurverick the King, Death's Bane,
　　longest of all his reign.
He braved the fight, returned our might,
　　forever serves as guiding light.
We ride upon a riverboat, amid a river wide,
passing kings with dwarven rings, all of them...
　　have died."

The statues faded behind them, and a soft light began to emerge from the tunnel's far side.

CHAPTER 5

The riverboat pilot wiped a bead of sweat from his forehead. "We 'ave arrived," he announced, and Griffin stepped off, swaying slightly.

"This way, Griffin." Roland began to walk forward, toward a cluster of small, brown huts. On the way, they passed a few grim dwarves wearing robes of gray and brown. Their faces were caked with dirt, their beards only an inch or two long. "This is the Turnkh District, mostly farmers and miners," Roland explained.

Soon, the little huts were far behind, and Roland brought Griffin to a well-lit, marble building. Inside, the floor was also made of marble. In the center, however, was a square, five feet in length and width, made entirely of wood. Five-foot-tall metal poles rose from each corner, and a massive pole rose from the center, stretching upward farther than Griffin's eyes could see.

"A lift?" asked Griffin.

Roland smiled. "In a manner o' speaking…"

They both stepped onto the square, and Roland pulled a lever adjacent to it on the marble floor. In an instant, the silence of the room was replaced by a whirling noise. "Hold on," said Roland, grabbing one of the corner poles.

The machine quickly came to life. Instead of going straight up, the wooden square spun slowly around the center pole, quickly moving up as it did so. After what seemed like centuries of spinning in darkness, the lift came to a sudden stop. Roland stepped off, followed by Griffin, who was now a curious shade of green.

"Ugh." Griffin put his hand to his head. "Never do that to me again."

Roland simply laughed. "Better than climbing the mountain, isn't it?"

Griffin looked around. "Mountain?" It was then that he noticed the pure white snow at his feet. Looking back, he realized that they were now thousands of feet up. It would have been a nearly impossible climb. Then, looking forward, he saw a great marble fortress surrounded by marble towers, inns, butcher shops, smithies, armories, and large, fancy homes. Gray smoke puffed from many of the buildings, like dark serpents twisting through the sky. The scent of cold ale and warm mushroom stew drifted through the air. Dwarven merchants crowded the streets, shouting and gesturing.

"Welcome," said Roland, "to Dunalar."

Roland motioned for Griffin to continue forward. "It is too late to go to Briskhammer Forge. We'd best rent a room. I know a fine inn, not too expensive. It's in... pretty good shape. Good enough, at least."

Griffin was pleased to find that the inn was not far from their location, no more than a ten minute walk. The feeling quickly diminished when they arrived. Unlike most of Dunalar's buildings, it was not made of marble. Instead, it consisted of dark wood. It seemed as if the entire structure was held together by a couple of loose, rusted nails. An old sign, hammered into its side, seemed to shout "OY A SUIT." Griffin figured that some letters were missing.

"Royal Suite," said Roland. "The most... inexpensive inn in all of Dunalar."

"Not very royal," Griffin remarked, as he began to walk forward. He pulled at a wide, wooden door, which opened with a loud creak, scaring away a group of mountain birds nesting in a nearby tree. An old dwarven woman came to greet the two companions. She had curly gray hair and a noticeably hunched back beneath her dark gray cloak.

"Welcome," she said, and then she noticed Griffin's companion and clapped her hands joyfully. "Well, 'ello, Roland! I 'aven't seen you in a long while!"

"Good to see you, Algra. How is Garuf?"

Algra brushed a lock of gray hair from her forehead. "All right," she replied. "Better than when you saw 'im last, anyway."

"Good," Roland answered. "My friend Griffin and I would like to rent a room."

"Very well. That will be ten gold pieces, Mr. Griffin... Five for you Roland."

The elderly dwarven woman winked and smiled. Roland, feeling a bit awkward, quickly handed the money over.

"Second room on the left." She smiled again. "Ya 'ave a nice evening... Roland."

They quickly found their room, which was in better shape than Griffin had expected. Its walls were painted a dull beige, and on them hung small paintings of various mountain scenes. The beds were too small for Griffin, and the sheets felt a bit like a potato sack. But at least it was a place to sleep. Griffin took the bed on the right, and when he blew out the bedside candle, the room fell into complete darkness. A gust of wind shook the inn to its roots, and distant thunder roared, echoing across the mountain. *It's going to be a rough night,* Griffin thought.

It was.

Rain began falling like daggers, and the darkness of the night became even darker. Lightning blasted through the sky. Roland dozed off quickly. Griffin, however, was not as lucky. He covered his ears with his hands, but it was not nearly enough to shield the sound of the raging storm. Griffin couldn't fight it any longer. His memories of that cold, stormy night flooded back to him...

Young 12-year-old Griffin winced as he turned to his side. It was dark inside the hollow log, and the great storm outside would not allow him even a minute of slumber. He shuddered, not from the cold, but from the memory of his father's last words. "Don't worry about me, Griff. Be smart! Be strong! Be safe!"

Out of the three things my father told me to do, *he thought,* I am failing at all of them. *He had figured that the forest near the grasslands where his father had been captured would provide shelter and a fine place to spend the night. He hadn't figured on the storm. Griffin began to shake uncontrollably. He took a deep breath and calmed himself down. After a moment, he decided to venture outside the log. He slowly pushed himself out and was instantly drenched by the rain.*

Griffin's first step would be to try to find any civilization. He was a good climber, and he carefully made his way up the nearest, tallest tree. Even though the tree's trunk was slippery, he moved from branch to branch and eventually made it to the top. He immediately looked around, and hope rose in him. He saw a light in the distance...

A loud snore from Roland shook Griffin from the journey into his past. He was able to force the memory back into the deepest, darkest, foggiest part of his subconscious. He then sat up, unable to sleep, and slowly sneaked out of the room, careful not to wake the snoring dwarf.

After closing the door behind him, he headed quickly to the inn's cellar and came back with a bottle of vintage Weakbane wine. Griffin couldn't help grinning, as a plan was fast forming in his mind. He had learned long ago that information can be more valuable than gold and that the best place to find it was on the fringes of society—from the mouths of the outcasts and rogues who knew secrets and rumors.

On the inn's front desk, he spotted a map of Dunalar. On it, he was able to find a small jail, located not far from the Royal Suite. As he stepped outside, he was quickly dripping with rainwater. The map became soggy, but still readable, and Griffin soon found his way.

The building was easily recognizable as a jail, as bars were visible on the windows. The gate through its surrounding iron fence was guarded by two burly, long-bearded dwarves wearing heavy armor, which Griffin thought wasn't very practical under the circumstances. Griffin smirked. This was going to be easy.

He scanned the guards' faces. The first guard was much younger. He had a handsome face, for a dwarf anyway, and broad shoulders. His beard was blond, and he carried a mace. The other, a tall and fidgety dwarf, stood by his side. He had an aura of experience about him and was most likely a senior warrior. His long white beard was evidence of his age. In his hands he held a broad sword, a weapon built for one with great blade skills. But it seemed that he had been injured in combat. A scar ran from his forehead, through his left eye and to his left ear. Griffin could tell by the way that he tilted his head that he was most likely blind in one eye and deaf in one ear.

Using the little knowledge that he had learned, Griffin developed a plan. He picked up a small white stone and clanged it against the iron fence a couple of times. "What's that?" asked the younger dwarf, the one with better hearing.

"What's what, Lervin? Ya better not be playin' tricks on me again."

"I'm not this time, Yugmaz. I 'eard somethin'. I'll go take a look. Wouldn't expect ya to actually move, would I?"

As Lervin strode forward, Griffin crept up behind the rather dim-witted dwarf and conked him on the head with the Weakbane wine, causing him to fall over limp and unconscious. He used all of his strength to lift the unmoving guard back to his feet. He then, pretending to be the dwarf, moved the guard's legs with his own and walked back to Yugmaz, making sure to stay on his blind side.

"What was it, Lervin?" the senior guard asked.

"Oh, nothin', just my imagination, I suppose," huffed Griffin in the most dwarven voice he could muster.

"Ah, you know, you're not sounding that well, Lervin. Caught the Flauthart Flu, perhaps?"

Griffin saw an opportunity and took it. "That's just it, Yugmaz," Griffin sniffed. "I'll just be goin' inside for a moment, see if I can clear my nose a bit. Would ya mind unlockin' the gate for me?"

"All right, but if this is one of your tricks to get out of guard duty, I swear I'll report ya to King Rindivor the Almighty 'imself..."

Griffin nodded Lervin's head, still staying away from Yugmaz's good eye. With the door unlocked, he slipped into the jailyard, smiling ever so slightly.

He carefully set Limp Lervin on the floor and surveyed the interior of the jail. The walls were made of loose stone and bricks that seemed to have been slapped together decades ago, many of them covered with a gooey green moss. The floor was coated with grime and dust. Drops of water fell slowly from the ceiling, adding to the dreary effect. A rat scurried past. It seemed the size of a bear cub.

A long row of cells lined a hallway in front of him. Some were empty, but most were not. As he slowly walked down the hallway, he passed several sleeping dwarves... and several who were quite awake. They watched his every move with wild, gleaming eyes. Griffin eyed them just as carefully until he noticed a particularly nasty-looking prisoner with a short black beard that was braided into a point at the end. His eyes, even though they were brown, seemed to glow with a red tint.

"Who ya starin' at?" snarled the dwarf.

"You, I believe. But I better avert my eyes. Don't want to go blind," he replied.

"Ya think you're smart, do ya?"

"I'd say I'm a good bit more intelligent than the average individual."

The fierce dwarf ground his teeth. "Ya know that's not what I meant..." His hand curled into a ball.

"Want a present?" Griffin asked suddenly.

"I'll give ya one," said the dwarf. "A big ol' fist with your name on it."

"How delightful," said Griffin, "but gifts are really better as surprises." He unveiled the Weakbane wine that he had been concealing behind his back. Suddenly, all the rage seemed to melt from the jailed dwarf's body. He acted like a dog begging for his favorite treat.

"Oh, give me it. Give me the wine. I need some Weakbane."

"Not so fast," Griffin smiled. "Answer my questions, and you'll get your Weakbane."

The dwarf grumbled. "Make it fast."

"What's your name?" Griffin began.

"Grilkus Humva. Friends call me Grilk the Greedy."

"Friends, huh? I can't imagine what your enemies call you. What are you in here for?"

"The greedy part," the dwarf simply replied.

Griffin didn't dig any farther into the subject. He was more interested in other information. All along, he had felt like there was much more to this man with the bronze finger, something dark, perhaps something sinister. "I'm in the market for rumors. Have you heard anything," Griffin asked, "about any unusual types in the area? Strange visitors? Something far from the ordinary?"

Grilk the Greedy looked at him curiously. "My whole life has been far from the ordinary."

Griffin stood silent, and the dwarf thought for a moment. "Well, I 'ear talk of shadowy figures who ride horrible, dark beasts with piercing red eyes." Even this nasty, good-for-nothing dwarf seemed to shudder for a moment. "You ask me, them's the ones who should be behind bars."

"Do you know where they might be found?" Griffin asked.

"Well, I 'eard that someone was attacked by 'em not too long ago, out near Gnarvik, one of the gnome villages."

Griffin stared at the dwarf for a moment. The information seemed truthful, if likely useless. "Thank you," he said. "I'll be leaving now…"

"But…"

"Oh, yes, the wine. I'd nearly forgotten." Griffin placed the bottle between the bars, and Grilk eagerly grabbed it.

As Griffin walked away, he heard Grilk shout, "Got a corkscrew?"

Griffin just chuckled and shouted over his shoulder, "Use your fist!"

CHAPTER 6

"Griffin! Ya missed breakfast!" Roland was standing over him. "Get up! Briskhammer Forge awaits us!"

Griffin groaned and, still a bit addled from sleep, thought to himself, *Never bribe a jailed dwarf with Weakbane wine to gain information after bedtime.* He rubbed his eyes. He imagined his mother might have said something similar, if less specific. If he had known her.

He stumbled out of bed and prepared for a long day ahead. He ate a quick breakfast, then departed the so-called "Royal" Suite with Roland. They started off toward the other side of Dunalar, in the direction of Briskhammer Forge.

There was no mistaking it when they arrived—a huge marble edifice that puffed out great streams of dark gray smoke, causing a haze to surround the building. As they drew near, Griffin began to cough, and his eyes began to water.

"You'll get used to it," said Roland.

It wasn't any better inside. Hammers rang and sparks flashed everywhere. Griffin heard a loud voice periodically shouting things like "Keep your other hand away from the hammer!" and "You call that a sword? I thought it was a spoon!"

On one side of the room, there was a long countertop made of a hard stone that Griffin could not identify. They approached it, and Roland rang a bell that rested atop it, but no one appeared to greet them. *Probably all the noise,* Griffin thought. Roland rang it again, but once again no one came. So Roland decided to ring it... and ring it... and ring it. Finally, a dwarf arrived in a huff, his black beard streaked with gray.

"No need to make such a racket, Silverbeard!" he said.

Griffin rolled his eyes. The blacksmith noticed him and smirked, "Who brought the beardless stick?"

Griffin frowned. He probably should have shrugged off the insult, but he was no good at that. "Probably the same person who brought in the hairy potato," he said.

The dwarf opened his mouth to speak, thought better of it, and instead glared. He then turned back to Roland, who was trying to hide a smile. "Ya need more supplies, I'd wager. I 'ave 'em ready for ya in the back."

As Roland headed toward the supply room, he looked at Griffin. "Don't mind Cagran," he said. "The dwarf is all talk. Loud talk. But a master blacksmith, I'll give 'im that."

As soon as Roland was out of sight, Cagran once again glared at Griffin. His voice rang out like a cannon. "Look 'ere, No Beard. This is my sanctum. Here you abide by my rules. None o' yers or any others, ya 'ear me?"

"A little too well," Griffin murmured.

"Good. Now what do ya need anyway?"

Griffin took a deep breath and began, "A man stole something very precious to me. I did not see him very well, but I did notice that he appeared to have a bronze finger where his right index finger was supposed to be. Roland told me that the finger was most likely created here..."

Cagran nodded slowly, and Griffin continued, "Is it possible that you keep records of who your customers are and what they purchase?"

Cagran took a long look at Griffin. "What's yer name, human?"

"Griffin. Griffin Blade."

"Roland must trust you if he brought you 'ere." Griffin nodded. Cagran shrugged. "Kind of a peculiar purchase, but we've been keepin' records for more'n fifty years. Follow me."

He led Griffin to a massive wall consisting of dozens of wooden drawers from floor to ceiling. Cagran glided to the "BRONZE" row, then to a drawer marked "BRONZE, D-F." He pulled it open and began to pick through pages and pages of parchment. Griffin, his senses as tuned as always, noted that some of the pages contained different handwriting—most likely Cagran's father or even his grandfather.

"Let's see 'ere..." After a bit of searching, Cagran drew out a small pile of papers. "Should be somewhere in 'ere..." For the next few moments, he mumbled to himself. "Bronze fox... bronze forks... bronze fish..." Finally, he exclaimed, "Aha! 'Ere we are! One bronze finger! Take a look."

He handed Griffin a small slip of stained parchment. Excited, Griffin slowly scanned it:

Name: Anonymous

Occupation: Unknown

Age: 44

Race: Human

Gender: Male

Products purchased: Bronze index finger, one small silver key

Other notes: Mysterious fellow. Kept face hidden. But paid well (priority customer if he returns)

Griffin frowned. "Not much to go on. No name. How will I trace him now?"

"Not my problem," Cagran replied.

"Maybe it still is," said Griffin. "Is it possible that you still have that key?"

Cagran huffed and waved his arms. "Ya think I keep every stinkin' key I forge? If I'd kept it, I wouldn't have been paid. It's probably been melted down by now and bein' worn by some pretty elvish lady as a silver ring." There was an awkward pause, and then Cagran continued in a quieter voice, "O' course, I may still have the mold..."

Griffin grinned. "Do you think you could find it?"

"Do you think you could afford it?" asked Cagran

"Let's see if you can find it first."

Cagran examined some numbers at the top of the parchment slip and then disappeared into a nearby room. By the time he returned, Griffin was resting his weary head. With a wicked smile, Cagran startled him by loudly dropping his discovery onto the countertop. When Griffin reached for it, Cagran gripped it tightly. "Pay first," he said. "Mold second."

He held out one hand. "Ten silver pieces."

"Ten! You didn't even know this mold existed a moment ago. I just want to see..."

The dwarf raised a bushy eyebrow. "Make it twelve."

Griffin frowned and dropped the coins on the countertop. Cagran then handed over the mold, which consisted of a key-shaped indentation where the liquid metal was to be poured. But there was also an unusual indentation within the key shape itself, a deeper section, possibly forming a symbol of some sort.

"I know I'm going to regret this, but is it possible for you to forge a second key?"

Cagran smiled, showing his crooked teeth. "Of course." He held out his hand once again. "Money talks. Four gold pieces."

Griffin rolled his eyes and retrieved a few gold coins from his pouch. He slammed them into Cagran's palm.

Cagran smirked. "I'll make a mental note to put 'ill-mannered' on your record, Blade."

"Well then, we will have something in common."

The smirk turned to a frown and then a smile. "Yer a cheeky one, Blade."

Griffin watched as Master Blacksmith Cagran went to work, pouring molten hot silver into the mold. Griffin knew many things—how to turn a loose nail into a lock pick, how to climb across a rooftop without making a sound, how to perceive a person's intentions by examining facial expressions—but blacksmithing wasn't one of them. He was mesmerized enough by the process that he didn't hear Roland trudging up behind him.

"What did I miss?"

Griffin filled him in, still watching Cagran. Drops of sweat slowly dripped down the dwarf's face into his beard. His concentration was something to behold. Twenty minutes later, Cagran held an old, brown rag in his hands. "There we go. The shiniest, most pristine, most beautiful silver key in all the land." Cagran paused for a moment. "And forged by the most handsome dwarf in dwarven country."

"Looks like a rag to me," Griffin grinned.

Cagran pulled the key out of the rag. It was actually quite beautiful, and it seemed to shine with a silver glow. The most interesting part of the key, however, was the symbol upon it. It was a small flower with three petals and a curved stem. After Griffin carefully studied the symbol, he wondered out loud, "What is it?"

Cagran turned his back to them. "Don't know. Don't care. Ya 'ave fun chasin' a flower-lovin' man with a bronze finger."

With that, Cagran, Master Blacksmith of Dunalar, walked away. Roland and Griffin watched the dwarf leave and then turned to each other.

"It seems your search has hit a bit of a brick wall, my friend," said Roland.

"Or possibly, it just went around one."

"What do ya mean?"

"The symbol. The symbol on the key—maybe that is the key. I have to figure out what it means."

Griffin closed his eyes and thought for a moment. In an instant, he was once again a 12-year-old boy, drenched in rain and smiling at a faint light in the distance...

Griffin's smile vanished as he looked down from the tree. He was one of those boys who climbed like a squirrel, adrenalin pumping through his body. Going down, however, was a different story. One glimpse down caused him to shiver. He gritted his teeth. He suddenly felt trapped in place. Terror took over, and he did the worst possible thing he could do—he let go.

As he tumbled, the world seemed to slow. Rain became blue shards impaling the soft earth below. A simple falling leaf became a mighty ship out of control in the fierce winds. As gravity's sinister arm pulled him downward, Griffin understood the world a little better. When he hit the ground below, he felt no pain. But he also no longer felt weightless. He lay on the ground, his eyes glazed over, as if he were in a trance. His last thought before it all went dark was, "I hope my father can forgive me..."

CHAPTER 7

"Griffin! Griffin?!"

"Father?"

"I don't think I'm ready to adopt." Roland shifted uneasily.

Griffin blushed. "Er, never mind that. What's next?"

"Well, it seems pretty obvious to me."

"What?"

Roland shrugged. "If I find me'self unable to move forward, there's only one thing to do."

"And that is?"

"Have a seat at the local tavern." Roland grinned hopefully.

Griffin figured it couldn't hurt to get more local information. "Fine," he said. "But no dancing on the table."

As they made their way to the tavern, the pavement eventually became smoother, and the dwarves wore finer clothing. They strutted around like nobles.

"Where are we?" asked Griffin.

"The Royal District, the area surrounding where the king and his family live. This tavern is a bit on the pricey end." He saw Griffin's reaction, and added, "O' course, I gambled with the owner. Got me'self free service for a year. Friends included, of course."

Should have known, thought Griffin. "So tell me more about King Rindivor."

"Rindivor the Almighty, 47th Dwarven King of the Verkanan lineage." Roland peered around to make sure no one was listening. "I've 'eard, though, that he's been dealin' with some shady types in recent years. Just rumors, mind ya."

During the rest of the walk to the tavern, Roland recounted the 46 Verkanan rulers before Rindivor, while Griffin tried mightily to retain interest. The tavern was a white marble building with pillars supporting the roof. Fancy handwriting on an oval-shaped sign in front of the door announced it as "The Giggling Goose." Beneath the name was a small painting of a floating goose, its mouth open wide. Roland walked in, followed by Griffin. The floor was made of well-cut wooden planks. Chandeliers hung high from the ceiling, the candles emitting a dim light. There were six long stone tables stretching from one side of the room to the other. In one corner of the tavern, a handful of dwarves sat at a bar. They were either drunk, asleep or laughing so hard that ale was coming out of their noses. Roland began to walk in that direction. Again, Griffin followed.

The barkeeper was an average-sized dwarf with an unkempt blond beard. He wore a shirt that was one size too small and pants that appeared to be one size too large.

"Ah, Roland! How n-nice to see y-ya again! My w-wife is still angry at me for g-gambling with ya! F-free tavern visits f-fer a year! And for a b-bucket o' beer, too! What was

38

I thinkin'? Anyway, w-what brings ya 'ere? And who's the b-beardless fellow?"

"Whoa, slow down there, Numbti. And quiet down, too. Ya don't want to wake up the peaceful sleepers over there." Roland pointed to two dozing dwarves, one of whom was drooling on the table.

"Oh, don't w-worry about them. They come 'ere all the time. They w-wouldn't wake up if ya shoved 'em 'eadfirst into a t-tankard 'o whiskey."

To prove his point, Numbti walked up to one of them and flicked his forehead. The dwarf just gurgled something about rum. Numbti grinned and looked into the distance, thinking of memories. "I've had f-fun with these two."

"Anyway, Numbti," said Roland, "this is a friend of mine— Griffin Blade from Quah." Numbti gave Roland a blank look. "Ya know," Roland continued, "the city where I live." The blond-bearded barkeeper didn't respond. Roland tried again: "The one with Staghorn Tavern?"

"Ah, yes! S-staghorn Tavern! Not quite as great as the G-gigling G-goose, o' course!" There was an awkward pause. "Anyhoo... what'll it be, Roland."

"Alrox Ale, as always... with a roast goose special." He turned to Griffin. "And you?"

Griffin shrugged. "I'll have your weakest wine with... do you have any soup?"

"Rabbit foot soup, m-mushroom stew and b-buck hide broth," said Numbti.

"Mushroom stew, I suppose," said Griffin, immediately discarding the other two options.

The two companions sat at one of the stone tables, which was decorated with a centerpiece of sorts consisting of stones. Or maybe they were stale bread rolls. A rather sad-looking dwarf with a brown beard sat across from them. He poked his meat with his fork. Ten minutes later, Numbti arrived with their food. Griffin hungrily dove into his stew.

Halfway through their meal, a dwarf wearing a fine orange robe charged into the room, followed by two burly dwarves dressed in fur. All three of them seemed to have burn scars on their necks and faces.

"Barkeeper! Weakbane! Now!" he demanded.

"S-sir, I will need a g-gold piece," said Numbti. "I'm not allowed to–"

"Now!"

Numbti cleared his throat nervously. "S-sir, I –"

"Zurmin! Thurmin!" shouted the dwarf, and the two guards approached Numbti, their hands forming fists. The room grew quiet. The orange-robed dwarf smiled condescendingly. "Changed your mind, yet?"

"Sir p-please..."

The closest guard grabbed Numbti by the neck and began squeezing. "Y-yes, s-sir," he was able to croak.

The guard let go, but Griffin, as usual, couldn't. "Hey, you have no right to treat him like that!"

Everyone in the room gasped (except for the sleeping dwarves). Roland winced and whispered into Griffin's ear. "Griffin, that's Chief Ambassador Thrutch. Let it go..."

"I'll have you know, you beardless maggot of a human," said Thrutch, the scars on his face growing redder, "that

40

you're speaking to someone of great power in Dunalar. I don't know what it's like for you filthy humans, but dwarves treat our leaders with respect!"

Griffin smirked. "I don't know what it's like for you dwarves, but we humans don't respect fools."

Thrutch was shocked. No one had ever spoken to him that way. It took him a moment to wrap his head around the fact. "Guards!" he shouted, and his two hooligans stood at attention. "Take this filth into custody!"

The two goons grinned menacingly and slowly walked toward Griffin. "Now I'm just gonna grab ya nice an' easy," said one of them.

"No strugglin'," said the other.

If they knew what I am capable of, Griffin thought, *they would be running for their lives. Poor fools!* He looked around for a weapon, grabbing a spoon from the table. *It'll do.* Griffin quickly turned to the guards, his "weapon" at the ready.

"A soup spoon!" mocked the closest guard. "Terrifyin' weapon, that is! I'm shiverin' in my…"

He didn't finish the sentence, instead falling to the floor. While he had been yammering on, Griffin had grabbed a small stone from the centerpiece—or was it a bread roll?— and had used his spoon as a tiny catapult, taking dead aim between the guard's eyes. He then rushed to a corner and grabbed a mop and a bucket. For an instant, he imagined himself as his father, Ramyr Blade, fending off Seretigo with a shield and spear.

The second guard charged. A quick block with his shield/bucket and a jab with his mop/spear sent the guard spinning into a chair. The first guard, now on his feet, learned from his mistake. He approached Griffin carefully. Meanwhile, the second guard doubled back and jumped behind him. Before Griffin could react, the dwarf pulled a war axe from a pack on his back and took a swing. This time, Griffin had no time to block the blow. Anyway, it would have been utterly useless against a war axe in full swing. He squeezed his eyes shut, waiting for the pain...

But the pain never came. The guard was tackled to the floor—by that sorrowful dwarf who had been sitting across from them at the table. At the same time, Roland charged at the other guard. All four dwarves rolled around on the floor, as Roland was able to yell, "Get... Thrutch!"

Griffin didn't have to. Thrutch went for him.

He held a flail in his hands, and he swung it wildly as he ran toward Griffin. It would have been nearly impossible to evade Thrutch's attacks, so he did something Thrutch didn't expect—he jumped on top of the table nearest to him and ran. He kicked over bowls and plates, which clattered to the floor. Thrutch followed right behind.

The stone table was long, but it didn't last forever. When he reached the edge, he turned around, holding his mop and bucket in a defensive posture. Thrutch swung his flail, knocking the mop out of Griffin's hand. It fell harmlessly to the floor. He swung again, and the bucket flew into the air.

Thrutch snickered. "You have nowhere to go now."

"Oh, really?" Griffin replied. He then fearlessly leaped onto the table at which he had been eating. Thrutch jumped after him, a bit more cautious. At the end of the table, he caught up to him once again. He swung. Griffin dodged. "You have to work on your aim."

Thrutch, growing ever angrier, swung with more force. Griffin found himself dodging the flail without even thinking. "Come now," he told Thrutch, "you aren't even trying."

This sent Thrutch into a rage. He swung wildly at Griffin, not caring if he missed or hit—so hard, in fact, that he couldn't stop his momentum. When Griffin dodged, Thrutch's own flail landed with a *thwack* on the side of his head. Thrutch groaned and fell, his head landing right in Griffin's mushroom stew.

Just before Thrutch closed his eyes, Griffin grabbed him by the hair and lifted his head. "Needs more salt, doesn't it?" He then dropped the dwarf, beard and all, into the stew.

CHAPTER 8

For a moment, Griffin stared down at the unconscious dwarf. He then hopped down from the stone table. At first, the room was silent. Then murmuring began, which evolved into full-fledged shouting. Most of the shouts were directed at him; the others were aimed at Thrutch.

"Griffin!" a voice implored. Griffin turned toward it. "Let's get out while we still can," whispered Roland. They made their way to the door, ran out and caught their breath in a nearby alleyway.

"We're officially outlaws now," sighed Roland.

"As am I." The two companions whirled around. Leaning against the wall was the same sad dwarf who had taken on one of the guards in the tavern.

"You!" said Roland. "You're the one who—"

"Who tackled the guard, yes. Shame I couldn't 'ave a go at Thrutch, though..." The dwarf had a wide face and a tangled, brown beard. His clothing was plain, but his talk lively. He turned to Griffin. "When you taunted 'im like that... brilliant. When he fell into your stew, now that's a moment I'll always treasure, I tell ya." The dwarf began guffawing loudly. Neither Griffin nor Roland joined him.

"Really, though," the dwarf continued, "where'd ya learn to fight like that, anyway?"

"Er, self-taught," Griffin replied uneasily.

"Oh, I understand," the dwarf winked. "Not revealing your secrets just yet, are ya?"

Griffin nodded once. "But... thank you for your help." The dwarf returned the nod.

Roland rejoined the conversation. "Who are ya, friend?" he asked.

"Nice wrestlin' on your part, too," said the dwarf, completely ignoring Roland's question. "What's your lineage? Fastwikk? Crushveel?"

"Silverbeard," said Roland.

"A Silverbeard! I should 'ave known! Pleased to meet ya, Mr. Silverbeard. I'm a Kwinhollow myself." He turned to Griffin. "And you are?"

"Blade."

"Ah, a fittin' name, I'd say." Kwinhollow paused. "Well then, now that we're all acquainted, I'm sure that ya 'ave loads o' questions, and I'll answer them. But not 'ere. Follow me, if ya will."

Griffin and Roland looked at each other and shrugged. Neither could think of a better idea. The dwarf led them around the outskirts of Dunalar, careful to remain away from the inner city and keeping mostly to the shadows. Eventually, they stopped at a cliffside building, constructed out of uneven chunks of stone, that looked as if it was going to fall at any moment from the edge of Bird's Gate. Kwinhollow pulled at a small, rusted door knob. The door didn't budge. He tried once more, pushing and pulling with all of his dwarven strength. Again, nothing. "Gets me every time," he pouted. He took a few steps away from the door and then charged, ramming it with the side of his body, soon finding himself on the ground, clutching his sore shoulder. The door remained shut.

"Let me give it a try," said Griffin.

Kwinhollow chuckled and dusted himself off. "Ha! All right, give it a try."

Griffin calmly strode over to the door and slowly turned the doorknob with finesse instead of force. The door swung open with a quiet creak.

Kwinhollow blinked. "Beginner's luck."

Griffin smiled. "I have some experience in such matters."

The building wasn't much to look at. The floor, unlike the walls and roof, consisted of wooden planks, several of them warped. There was one small window in the back that let in a stream of light. In the center of the room was a cracked marble table and a few chairs. On top of the table sat the stub of a white candle. Hardened wax drippings ran down its side.

"Ya know," said Kwinhollow, "legend has it that ancient dwarven settlers led by our very first king, Hurverick Death's Bane, constructed this building as a meeting hall for a town named Duna. The town obviously became Dunalar. So King Hurverick sat in this very room!" Kwinhollow motioned to the chairs. "Please, take a seat."

Griffin and Roland sat on one side of the rectangular table, while Kwinhollow took a seat on the other. "Would you like me to light the candle?" Kwinhollow asked.

"Don't bother," said Griffin.

"Very well... I'd suppose yer wondering about my relationship with Thrutch, no?"

Kwinhollow breathed deeply. "Where to begin? I guess I should start some time ago... I 'ave to admit, I was a bit foolish back in my younger years, so much so that I wound up on the streets as a beggar... and pickpocket, if times became particularly troubling." Griffin smiled. He liked Kwinhollow already. "One day," the dwarf continued, "I was wandering the streets of the Royal District when Thrutch came upon me. 'You there!' he said. I asked if he was talking to me. 'No, the barrel behind you,' he said, typically condescending. Then he offered me a job. 'Easy work, good pay,' he said. That's all I needed to hear. So I followed him. People were surprised to see a beggar accompanying Ambassador Thrutch. Let's just say he wasn't known fer 'is generosity!" Kwinhollow shook his head. "He led me through the paved streets of the Royal District, all the way to the foot of the Marble Castle itself! Were they going to train me as a knight? Or make me a member of the Royal Council?" He chuckled and shook his head again.

"Unlikely," said Roland.

"I know, but like I said, I was a fool. But I was taken to the highest room in one of the main towers. It seemed to be some sort of royal guest room. It had a large bed and a window that offered a magnificent view of Dunalar. The most important—and I suppose I should say most valuable—object in the room was in a glass display case on one wall. Inside was a small, purple cushion, and on top of that was a gem—a red gem. I could 'ave sworn that it was as red as fire.

"Another gem..." Griffin grumbled.

Kwinhollow looked at him strangely. "Sorry?"

"Nevermind. Please continue."

The dwarf coughed. "Very well. As soon as I stepped into my new room, Thrutch locked the door and nearly began shouting. 'Protect the gem!' he said. 'You'll be paid. There are two guards outside the door.' Then he just walked out. And so I waited, stared at the gem a bit more, paced around. Two hours later I 'eard shuffling outside the door. A slot in the door was opened wide enough to slide in a large slab o' Frambolian beef on a fancy plate." He turned toward Roland. "It was topped with berry sauce. Best meal I'd eaten in years." Roland grinned. "Another hour passed, and a small pouch of gold was tossed through the slot." This time, Roland's grin was wider. "The same thing occurred every day. I woke up , ate breakfast, paced, ate lunch, stared, ate dinner, then the gold."

"Sounds rather nice if ya ask me," said Roland. "Sleep and food and gold—three essential needs. Well, besides ale, of course."

"I suppose," said Kwinhollow. "Yet I was bored almost to tears. I listened to my guards often, eavesdropping through the slot in the door. They kept murmuring things about my ancestry, how Thrutch was double-checking. Checking what, I don't know. It made no sense to me. My parents both died in the Bozargian Plague when I was a wee lad. I never knew a thing about my parents' parents. I also 'eard them mention something called the Mizzarkh. Eventually I was able to gather that they were talking 'bout the gem."

"Mizzarkh? What kind of name is that?" asked Roland.

"It's certainly not in the Northern Tongue," said Griffin.

Kwinhollow shrugged. "Anyway, I guarded—if you could call it that—the gem for nearly 'alf a year. I was never allowed to leave the castle. I was only let out on occasion to walk the grounds. I was paid more gold than I 'ad ever seen in my life. But it was strange, no? Why 'ire me as a guard when there were perfectly competent guards at the door? And if they were to 'ave a guard, why choose a beggar like me? I'm no knight, ya know."

"We're aware of that, yes," Griffin smiled.

Kwinhollow chuckled. "Finally, after all that time, I found the answer. At least, I think I did."

Griffin's eyes twinkled with curiosity.

"At one point, I couldn't take it anymore. The glass case was locked, but after several days of... experimenting, I found a way to open it. After months of staring at it, I finally held the gem. And the most peculiar thing 'appened. It glowed bright red wherever I touched it. If I squinted, I could see small red lines forming. They began to widen until nearly the entire gem was glowing. It scared me, to be honest. So I returned it to the case, fast as I could." Kwinhollow looked Griffin in the eyes. "It felt like a power that I couldn't control—or shouldn't control."

Griffin recalled hearing that dwarves were uneasy about magic. Some were downright frightened.

"Afterward, I demanded to be relieved of my job. All the gold in the world isn't worth an ounce of black magic. But Thrutch refused, that maggot! It was only then that I truly realized that it wasn't a job. It was a prison."

"But he can't just..." Roland began.

"Thrutch does what he wants." Kwinhollow sighed and continued. "The next day, he entered my room, followed by the two guards. He unlocked the glass case, not knowing that I already 'ad, and removed the jewel. 'Hold it,' he demanded. I shook my head. I saw something evil in 'is eyes." One of the guards asked, 'Are you sure he is the one?' And Thrutch silenced him with a glare. He told me again to hold the jewel. 'No,' I replied, and he was outraged. He instructed the guards to hold me against the wall, while he forced the Mizzarkh gem into my hand. Again, the whole gem began to glow. But I was able to get my other hand free. I 'eld it up in defense and... boom! An explosion of red light burst from my fingers, sending Thrutch and his guards flying against the wall on the other side of the room, unconscious I'd dare say. Served 'em right! I dropped the jewel and ran—from the room, from the castle, and from that blasted Thrutch."

Kwinhollow looked at his hands for a moment, then up at his two new companions. "That was nearly six weeks ago. I'm growing accustomed to life as a fugitive. My pickpocket skills tend to come in 'andy, I'll admit. Tonight, I used the little money I 'ad to buy a meager meal at the Giggling Goose. You know the story from there."

"Ah," said Griffin. "I was wondering why Thrutch and his men appeared to have been burned."

There was a moment of quiet, as Griffin thought back to what Kwinhollow had said about the Mizzarkh. "I have a hunch," he finally offered.

Kwinhollow scratched his beard. "What would that be, Mr. Blade?"

"Please, call me Griffin."

"Griffin Blade. Now *that* is a name. Wipes Kwint Kwinhollow right off the list..."

"That's your name?" asked Roland. "Kwint? Kwint Kwinhollow?"

"Gentlemen..." The two dwarves turned to face Griffin. "I suggest we get back to business. As I said, I have a hunch." Griffin decided it was time to explain to Roland and Kwint about the Hiamahu Jewel. Although he avoided telling them how he had obtained it in the first place, he told them how it also glowed as he touched it, and how it had been stolen from him by the man with a finger of bronze. He then suggested that the two gems were possibly related in some way.

"So," said Kwint, "what do we do now? Remember, we're fugitives now."

I've been one for many years, Griffin thought silently. "I'll tell you what we do now," he said. "We figure out what Thrutch was trying to accomplish. We discover why these gems are so important. Our fate appears to be entwined with these jewels." *And my promised payment, too,* Griffin thought.

CHAPTER 9

"**W**ell, where do we start?" asked Roland.

"We head for Gnarvik," Griffin responded. "Tree City of Gnomes."

"Gnarvik? It lies at least ten days to the east from Dunalar. Why in Hurverick's name would we travel to that lonely place?" Roland protested.

"Two reasons," said Griffin. "I learned at Briskhammer Forge that the man with the bronze finger had left a key bearing the symbol of a three-petaled flower. I didn't know what it meant until I discovered clue number two." Griffin withdrew a folded piece of parchment from his pocket. "It's a letter from the gnome ambassador, addressed to Thrutch. It thanks him for visiting Gnarvik and also asks if he would be willing to donate a few books to their Library of Knowledge. Thrutch apparently had refused before..."

"Maggot..." Kwint interrupted.

"What's interesting about the letter, however," Griffin continued, "is the letterhead." He held it up for the dwarves to see. A three-petaled flower was embossed at the top. "Apparently, it's the library's symbol."

"But Griffin, 'ow did you obtain this letter in the first place?" Roland asked.

"I grabbed it from Thrutch's front pocket while he enjoyed my stew."

Kwint grinned. "Looks like I'm not the only one with fast hands."

"There is only one more problem," said Roland. "A trip to Gnarvik would be a bit of a journey. But that's not all. Bears prowl the area. And even worse, bandits."

Griffin frowned. "This is bad news."

"Not necessarily," Kwint declared. "As you know, Griffin, we dwarves are most famous for our mining ability. And as the center of mining activity, Dunalar 'as mines that stretch for many miles—and minecarts that run through them. I believe we 'ave one ancient track, in fact, that runs directly to Gnarvik itself."

"Of course!" shouted Roland.

"It goes that far?" asked Griffin.

"They don't usually," explained Kwint. "But nearly two centuries ago, gnomes and dwarves were close allies. They were allied with the elves, as well. You see, gnomes are actually an elf-dwarf hybrid. Over the last century or so, elves and dwarves have grown apart from the gnomes—elves because the gnomes are half-dwarf and, I must admit, dwarves because the gnomes are half-elf. Officially, their territory is part of elvish lands, but they are basically an independent realm. During the Allied Age, we created a long minecart track to connect Dunalar with Gnarvik."

"There is one thing, though," Roland interjected. "The Dunalar-Gnarvik track hasn't been used in almost a century. It may not even be accessible."

"That's a risk we'll have to take," said Griffin. "But I hate to leave Fuss at the stables. Who knows when I'll be back here. Or if."

"From what I've seen," said Roland, "that horse can take care of himself."

Griffin nodded slowly. "Then you two dwarves should lead the way." He stood up. "Any ideas?"

Roland scratched his chin. "We sneak into the Main Mine, I suppose, and steal ourselves a minecart."

Less than an hour later, the trio had made its way to the Main Mine, a large bowl-shaped cavern, its ceiling decorated naturally by colorful stalactites. It looked to be something like a central station. At least three dozen minecart tracks led off in various directions. Dwarves shuffled back and forth with pickaxes over their shoulders. Occasionally, they stopped to glance at a huge wooden board on one cavern wall. The board listed each route, track number and condition. Griffin read down the list:

Dunalar-Birfic... 36... Operational
Dunalar-Dezarth... 4... Under Repair
Dunalar-Efarius... 43... Under Construction

Griffin skimmed the list until he found what he was looking for:

Dunalar-Gnarvik... 17... Closed

"Closed?" asked Griffin. "I thought it was at least operational."

"It is," said Kwint, "or was at one time."

"Then why does the board tell me that the track is closed?"

"Well, there have been rumors..."

"Rumors? Rumors of what?"

"Silly stories of a creature, a beast of some sort. Pure fantasy, of course, but they declared it defunct all the same."

As Kwint walked ahead, Roland whispered in Griffin's ear. "Best be cautious." About halfway to Track 17, they stopped at a small booth that stood roughly in the center of the cavern. Sitting inside, his bald head framed by an open window, was a dwarf who had a lengthy red beard spotted with gray.

"Distract the Trackmaster while we find a minecart," Roland whispered to Griffin.

"That I can do," said Griffin. He smiled as an idea formulated. He would act like one of the desperate merchants on the streets of Quah. Quickly, he got into character. He walked forward with a spring in his step and smiled slightly too wide. "Hello, my good dwarf!" he said, almost shouting. "My name is Mr. Gaurius Wilkson, and do I have a deal for you..."

The red-bearded dwarf squinted at Griffin, then looked perplexed. "What? A merchant? They never come down 'ere. And a human at that?"

"Well, it looks as if I am a special case then, aren't I?" said Griffin, sounding painfully cheerful. "You are very perceptive, sir."

"What do ya want?" said the dwarf, impatiently.

"It's not what I want, but what you need!" Griffin tried to imitate the many merchants who had bothered him over the years.

"Oh," said the dwarf, who had moved from impatience to sarcasm, "what would that be?"

"A dust," said Griffin, "found only in the stem of a wyoff petal. Wyoff dust is known to relieve pain, cure colds and make you immune to most known diseases." Griffin drew a grainy substance from his pocket (he had scraped it from a cavern wall) and held it in the palm of his hand for the dwarf to see.

The dwarf wasn't amused. "Get out of 'ere before I..."

"It's very inexpensive," said Griffin, who was after all talking to a dwarf. "And oh yes," he added, eyeing the dwarf's shiny head, "it is also known to reverse balding."

The Trackmaster's eye's grew wide. "I'm listening."

Griffin grinned mischievously. "It's a rare find. I'm supposed to sell it for eight gold pieces. But for you, the outrageously low price of five..."

"Five!" shouted the Trackmaster. "Out of the question."

"All right, three."

"One."

"Two."

The dwarf scratched his bald head. "Deal."

Griffin stole a quick glance behind him as the dwarf retrieved his gold. He saw Roland, who shook his head and motioned for him to buy more time.

"If I may ask, sir, what is your name?"

"Not that it's any of your business," he grunted, "but I'm Tyvin Heronhearth."

"Well, Mr.... Heronarf, was it?"

"Heronhearth."

"Baronharf?"

"In Hurverick's name, you blasted human, Heronhearth! Heronhearth! Heronhearth!"

"Oh, I'm sorry, Mr. Heronhearth! My apologies."

"Now what is it you wanted to tell me?" asked the Trackmaster.

Griffin pretended to think. "I'm afraid I've forgotten," he said, as the dwarf's face burned as red as his beard. Griffin looked back once more at Roland, who was pulling a lever and mouthing something to Griffin. It looked like: *Keep going.*

"May I have the gold please, Mr..." This time, Griffin really had forgotten his name, but the dwarf handed over two gold pieces anyway. Griffin sprinkled the dust into Heronhearth's hands, and the Trackmaster immediately smeared it all over the top of his head.

"Now," said Griffin, "let me warn you about some potential side effects..."

"Side effects?"

"Only a few, including itching, acne, headaches, fevers, uncontrollable flailing of the arms, joint pains, rashes in strange places, abnormal fingernail growth, a frequent need to urinate, cough, runny nose, intermittent belching, and short-term memory loss."

"But…"

"Oh, and have you had any ale recently?"

"Of course, but…"

"Then be prepared for extreme diarrhea…" Griffin looked behind him, and Roland gave a thumbs-up. "But," he told the Trackmaster as he backed away from the booth, "you'll have a lush head of hair!" He turned and ran, shouting over his shoulder, "Thank you for buying from Darius Milton!"

"I thought ya said yer name was…" But by now Griffin was gone.

CHAPTER 10

Roland and Kwint were waiting beside a minecart that was six feet long with four sides that were each three feet tall. He would have liked it to be a bit taller, but it was made by and for dwarves, after all. In the center of the cart was a wooden hand lever. Kwint quickly explained how he and Roland were going to maneuver the cart by alternately pushing each side of the lever down. "Just enjoy the ride!" he said.

Griffin hopped in behind the dwarves and looked over the side at the rusty wheels. He wasn't sure it was going to be so enjoyable. Roland and Kwint began pumping the lever, and the minecart started to move slowly. Within a few minutes, it was moving as fast as a horse. They soon left the Main Mine behind, as they entered a dimly-lit, stone tunnel. The ceiling looked to be only about ten feet high, and hanging from it were stalactites, some of them precariously low. The tunnel was wide enough for two minecart tracks—one for departures and one for arrivals, Griffin supposed. In fact, one minecart came speeding past toward the Main Mine.

Griffin was able to glimpse a massive ruby attached to its front before it passed them by. He asked Roland about it.

"Well, first ya 'ave to remember that each mountain of the Kni Hmun Mountains offers a different material for mining. It's quite remarkable," said Roland, as he continued to pump the lever. "Jaggeredge gold, Minstrel Peak sapphire, Fellgong coal, and so on. Each mountain has a Primary Mine, and each minecart sent from each Primary Mine is encrusted with a different gem or material. That one that just passed us was from Glorystone."

Griffin and the dwarves rode on for nearly two hours. As they moved, Griffin noticed slight changes in the track. It grew increasingly rusty and rickety. The nails holding it in place weren't as firm, causing the ride to become uncomfortably bumpy. The torches that lit the tunnel began to diminish, growing farther and farther apart until there were no more, leaving them in total darkness. For ten minutes, they rode in dark silence until Griffin asked, "Will it be like this the rest of the ride?"

"Surely not!" Roland declared. "The gnomes probably have lit the other side. Maybe."

The dwarves continued to pump the lever until Kwint pointed into the darkness and said, "Look there!"

Sure enough, a faint red light seemed to be coming from far ahead of them. As they moved closer, Griffin realized something odd. The light was flickering—no, pulsing every few seconds in an almost regular pattern. Moments later, he could tell that the light wasn't coming from torches at all, but glowing red crystals. Each one was set in a cluster of three.

As the minecart approached, the crystals grew brighter. Although they gave the impression of being red, they actually consisted of many colors—yellowish white where the crystals attached themselves to the wall, a shade of orange toward the center of the crystal, and a purplish red where a sharp tip protruded about ten inches from the wall.

Griffin grew uncomfortable—or, at least, even more uncomfortable. It almost seemed like the crystals could sense their approach. Then he noticed that the dwarves were pumping slower, thus slowing the minecart. Eventually, they came to a complete stop in the midst of the crystals.

"Why are you stopping?" asked Griffin, but neither dwarf replied. Instead, they simply climbed out of the minecart without explanation and shuffled toward the nearest crystal cluster, their eyes glazed over.

"Roland? Kwint? What are you doing?" Again, he was ignored, but the nearest crystals were starting to pulse faster. "Roland! Kwint!" he shouted now.

They didn't so much as glance in his direction. Roland was only a couple of feet from the nearest crystal. He raised his fingers to touch it...

"Roland, I really don't think you should—"

Roland's finger barely grazed it, and the cavern began to shake. That's when the screeching began.

Griffin had to plug his ears. He couldn't hear his own voice and could barely form his own thoughts over the high-pitched sound. The cavern began to quake violently. Then, one by one, the crystals began to shake loose from the wall. Actually, they began to *shake themselves* loose. At first, a handful of small rocks began to tumble to the ground. Next, cracks formed, and large pieces fell. Then, all at once, the crystals broke free from the cavern walls. Instead of falling, they just hovered there, slowly growing brighter.

The crystals were larger than they first appeared. When connected to the wall, the crystals seemed to be in clusters of three. But when they broke free, Griffin could see that each cluster was connected and that there were other crystals inside the walls. He realized that they were basically large, spiked, crystal spheres.

The screeching soon became less high-pitched and slightly quieter. It was then that the crystals truly awakened. Two yellow, glowing, rectangular eyes appeared on each crystal sphere. As the strange shapes shook the last pieces of stone from their bodies, Roland and Kwint began to shake themselves from their trance. Roland blinked a few times, then he stared with astonishment. "Per'aps they're friendly..."

The crystals answered with a deafening screech and began to move around the tunnel, slowly at first, then faster and faster. Wisps of red seemed to be coming from every direction, as the two dwarves struggled to make their way back to the minecart. One wrong move and they would lose an ear.

One crystal grazed Griffin's shoulder, and he staggered in pain. He looked frantically for any sort of weapon that he could use. His crossbow seemed useless, but his eyes settled on a low-hanging stalactite that one of the crystals had jarred loose from the tunnel ceiling. He pulled it free, then expertly swung it back and forth, striking one crystal after another. But when he struck a particularly fast crystal, his stalactite flew in the opposite direction and shattered against the cavern wall.

As the dwarves ducked and flinched and finally dove into the minecart, Griffin noticed that a shard from a broken crystal had fallen into the cart. It was barely a foot long, smaller than the stalactite, but it would have to do. *Too small for a club or sword,* he thought. *Maybe a throwing dagger?* He looked up to see that all of the crystals had gathered to his left. He aimed for the center, and his aim was perfect. The shard flew straight and true into the center crystal, which shattered on impact, its shards shattering the other crystals around it. Strangely, the shard that he had thrown amid the chaos flew back into his hand like a boomerang. Griffin didn't have time to wonder about it.

"Start pumping!" he shouted to his companions. "Let's get out of here."

But Kwint merely pointed to the cavern floor, where the crystals were now a collection of broken shards. "I'm not sure what that was," he said, "or how you did that. But that was amazing."

"I don't know," Griffin said, eyeing the shards. "I'm uneasy."

Kwint and Roland both shrugged. "Looks like we have nothing more to worry about," said Roland, as slowly, ever so slowly, they began moving the minecart once more.

But just then, Griffin looked back at the crystal shards, which began shaking and sliding toward one another. They began to form a figure—first feet, then legs, then torso, arms, finally a head with two glowing yellow eyes. Out of its left hand, a large shield formed from the broken crystals. Out of its right hand emerged a deadly crystal flail.

"Oh no," Griffin said, quietly, and the dwarves turned to look back, too.

Roland's eyes grew wide with fear. "I stand corrected."

"Go!" Griffin shouted, and the dwarves pumped the lever wildly, as the crystal knight charged forward.

Griffin threw his shard at the knight, but it just glanced off the crystal shield and flew back into Griffin's hand. The mine-cart began to move faster, but the knight was gaining ground. Griffin attempted to throw the shard a second time, this time aiming for the knight's head. His aim was true, and the shard slid through the knight's neck. It popped out the other side and then doubled back to Griffin's outstretched hand.

The monstrous crystal creature seemed unfazed, only angrier. His stride grew longer, the ground crumbling beneath his mighty feet. With only about ten yards between the cart and the knight, Griffin made a final, desperate attempt. He aimed not for the head this time, but for where he figured the heart might be. As the knight lunged forward, the shard struck him in the chest. This time, it didn't slide through. The shard turned white, and yellow cracks formed in the knight's chest around the point of impact. The cracks grew until they covered his torso, his arms, his legs, his entire crystal body.

Finally, the knight shattered into thousands of pieces. Griffin pushed Kwint and Roland to the floor of the mine-cart, as shards flew everywhere, and the cavern collapsed behind them.

CHAPTER 11

The cavern was pitch black once again. The three companions did not speak for several minutes. Finally, Roland broke the silence. "Well, that wasn't exactly what my 'eart needed."

"What was that creature?" Kwint wondered.

Griffin looked at them. "You dwarves don't know anything about this monstrous thing in your mines?" he asked, as he rubbed his injured shoulder.

Roland shrugged. "I've 'eard stories, but I never put much stock in 'em. Ancient myths. Creatures awakened long ago by our race. Made of the mountains, they say."

"My guess is that anyone who knows more than that," said Kwint, "didn't survive to tell the tale."

No one felt the need to speak any longer, so they rode in silence. It seemed like hours, but soon Griffin felt a dampness in the air. The light seemed to go from dark to dim, and he was able to make out thick, brown roots poking through the ceiling. A familiar scent came to him. *Pine?* he thought. *How can I smell trees this far down?* He drifted off into a memory...

Pain, along young Griffin's left side. That's what he felt. And rain, pounding hard against a roof somewhere. That's what he heard. He opened his eyes halfway. He was lying on a soft bed with a blue quilt draped over him. Griffin's eyes wandered from the bed to a figure cloaked in black, a man it seemed, who was tending a fire with a poker. The man's face was hidden by a hood. He wore black pants and leather boots, as well as a thick, black belt that held a knife on one side and an elegant short sword on the other. Griffin tried to speak, but no words would come out of his mouth. He couldn't stay awake any longer, and he slowly drifted out of consciousness.

It was the absence of sound that awakened Griffin hours later. The rain had stopped. The fire had long burned out. He heard voices coming from a small side room. One was a man's voice. The other was a woman's.

"You know what he would want," the woman whispered, though still loud enough for Griffin to hear. "Griffin cannot learn any information whatsoever."

They know my name, he thought.

"I am going to speak with him, just for a moment."

The woman sighed. "Very well, but please… do not tell the boy anything that might endanger him."

Griffin heard footsteps coming his way. He closed his eyes, then opened them as the man in black approached, his hood still pulled down low.

"How are you feeling?"

"Who are you?" Griffin asked. His voice was hoarse.

"I'm afraid I should not tell you that."

"Then… where am I?"

"That I can answer. You're in Vi Celen Ve Pellentiri, as they call it in the Southern Tongue—The Forest of Regrowth in the Northern."

"How did I get here?"

"I was… patrolling in the forest when I found you unconscious beneath a tall pine. I lifted you onto my horse and rode with you to Miss Flamentari's cottage here, not too far from where I found you."

The light, Griffin thought. "And you're lucky he brought you in time!" said the woman, as she stood in the doorway. She stomped into the room. "You could have died of hunger, or you could have made a hungry wolf a fine meal!"

The man in black shook his head. "Not exactly comforting words to a boy who just broke his ribs."

"Well, he should know better," she said, shooting a look at the man.

The man chuckled. "Yes, he should." He headed for the doorway. "I must be going. I'll be seeing you, Miss Flamentari." He bowed slightly to the woman and glanced toward Griffin one last time with a strange expression on his face. And then he simply walked out the door.

Clang! Startled, Griffin rubbed his eyes and peered ahead. The minecart had come to a full stop. They were in a wide cavern. It was dim and difficult to see, but Griffin could make out random, tangled roots growing through the walls and ceiling. So the smell of pine wasn't just a memory, he thought. The three companions climbed out of the cart and stretched their tired bodies.

"Looks as if we're here," said Kwint. "Gnarvik at last."

In the center of the cavern was a stone, spiral staircase leading upward. Griffin and the two dwarves began to ascend the stairs. As they climbed, the route became steeper and steeper. At some points, they literally had to climb the stairs—especially the dwarves.

"Old architecture," Roland muttered. "I'd guess sometime around the middle of the Allied Age."

"Well, the dwarves of the Allied Age sure 'ad long legs," Kwint grunted.

It was slow going, but eventually they arrived at the top. They then strode down a long passage, though an archway and into the open air at last. It was as if they had entered an entirely different world. They were surrounded by a grove of the thickest trees that Griffin had ever encountered. The sky could barely be seen, as massive canopies of leaves blocked the view. Everything was coated in a soft blanket of pure white snow.

"If I'm not mistaken," said Roland, "this is the Elder Forest."

Griffin looked at him blankly.

"You know, the Elder Forest, the one that covers much of eastern Alastian."

Griffin shrugged.

"In Hurverick's name, Griffin, where did you learn your geography?"

"I only learn what I need to know," said Griffin. He didn't feel a need to explain how his childhood education was more about learning the best way to steal a loaf of bread without detection.

"Well, we're traveling across Alastian. A little knowledge of places goes a long way." Roland shook his head. "You need to know about the world around you Griffin, not only the world right in front of you."

"Go on then," Griffin grinned. "Teach me."

"Well, the Elder Forest is the largest forest in Alastian, stretching for scores of miles. The area inhabited by elves is only a small portion of the larger forest."

"Why don't people inhabit the rest of it?"

"Legend tells that horrible beasts dwell there from ages untold. Of those who have ventured there, few have returned. And those who have returned have either gone mad or refused to speak."

Griffin nodded his head. "Judging by our recent encounter in the mines, legends tend to spring from fact." He turned to face Roland. "Wait, you said that elves inhabit the forests. Don't gnomes, as well?"

"Yes, of course they do, along with the Dark Elves and Light Elves," Roland replied, as the group continued deeper into the forest.

"I've always wanted to meet a gnome. I hope they're welcoming."

Kwint shrugged. "Dwarves and gnomes are not exactly on friendly terms anymore."

As the group walked on, Griffin began to notice changes in the forest. The trees grew taller and thicker, and the path seemed to be leading them uphill. An hour passed, and they came upon what seemed to be a clearing. Griffin moved a leafy branch that had been blocking his view and gasped at the most amazing sight he had ever beheld—Gnarvik, Tree City of Gnomes.

CHAPTER 12

They were standing on the edge of a very tall cliff. Below them was a valley filled with gigantic trees, the largest rising several hundred feet, all of them with bark of gold. Large wooden ramps circled around the trees and between their enormous trunks. If Griffin squinted, he could make out small figures—very small figures—making their way up the ramps toward the tops of the trees. In some of the trees, he could see windows carved into the thick bark. And in the middle of Gnarvik stood a colossal tree, far more massive than the rest. It was nearly 400 feet tall and three times as thick as the others.

"What's that over there?" asked Roland. The dwarf pointed to a thick, green rope of sorts stretched from the trunk of a strong tree toward the valley below. Firmly attached to the strange rope was what looked like a giant, wooden bowl. As they moved closer, Griffin noticed a sign affixed to the tree. It read, "LIMIT: SIX PASSENGERS AT A TIME."

"What in Hurverick's name do ya think that means?" Kwint wondered.

"Well, it would seem that this is our ride."

"Then what?" asked Roland. "We fling ourselves off the cliff?"

"Exactly," said Griffin, as took the green rope in his hands. "Interesting. Woven out of some sort of vine."

"And are we going to depend on 'some sort of vine' to carry us into Gnarvik? No thank you."

Griffin shrugged. "Feels strong. Plus the sign says it can hold six passengers..."

"Six *gnome* passengers," said Roland. "They're nearly half my size! I could carry six of 'em on my back!"

But Griffin just climbed into the oversized bowl. Kwint climbed in after him. Roland stood for a moment, grumbling, then followed them both. A metal hook attached the wooden bowl to the tree. As Griffin reached for it, Roland murmured, "Did I mention that I 'ave a fear of heights?"

Griffin smiled, as the bowl creaked under the weight of the travelers. "Didn't seem to bother you on top of Bird's Gate." And he detached the hook.

Cool wind whipped past their faces, as they glided toward Gnarvik at a downward angle. It seemed as if they were close enough to touch the giant trees that moved past them in golden blurs. Once they were under the canopy of the forest, the light grew dimmer, except for the occasional sliver of sunshine that made its way between the leaves like rivers of illumination pouring from the sky. The bowl continued to pick up speed until the rope's angle gradually lessened, eventually becoming almost horizontal. They were now well into the valley. Griffin could see deer frolicking in the fertile grass and exotic birds darting from branch to branch. After a few minutes, their ride came to a slow stop. Roland, his face now the color of the grass below, sighed with relief.

They had stopped at some sort of unloading station on one of the wooden platforms that circled the trees. Before they disembarked, a figure walked up to them. He was, indeed, quite short, being half the height of a dwarf, with skinny arms and legs and tiny hands and feet. He wore an olive green tunic fringed with gold on the sleeves and along the waist, as well as a lime green cape. The little creature had curly, brown hair bookended by long, pointed ears. Unlike a dwarf, he had no sign of facial hair whatsoever.

"Two dwarves and—what's this? A human, as well? My, oh my," said the gnome, whose face featured a short nose, large hazel eyes and a smug expression. "What is your kind doing here, may I ask?"

"We are here," said Griffin, "on our own business."

"And that business is?"

"We would rather not say," Griffin replied.

"And I would rather not unclip you from the rope and send you plummeting to your death."

Griffin knew the ill-mannered gnome didn't really mean it. But he didn't want to take any chances. "We wish to visit the library."

The gnome chuckled. "Hah! The library! Well, I expect you'll likely fail miserably."

The group looked at one another curiously and stepped out of the bowl. "Fail?" Kwint wondered. "Fail at what?"

The gnome smiled condescendingly. "The riddles, of course. Few outsiders make it inside." He pointed to an archway carved into the tree. "It will take you down to the ground level."

They followed his instructions. The dwarves had to duck their heads slightly. Griffin had to crouch low to make it through. The inside of the giant tree was hollow. A ramp, similar to those that circled the trees, spiraled downward. Griffin walked slowly down the wooden ramp. The path was narrow, and a single misstep would have resulted in a long fall.

The companions made their way to ground level, and another archway led outside. *Gnome culture and architecture is vastly different from that of their half-kin, the dwarves,* thought Griffin, as he stepped into the filtered sunlight. Looking up, he spotted several tree houses scattered among the thick branches and connected by wooden bridges. Gnomes who couldn't afford tree houses lived in small, wooden huts with thatched roofs, which were nestled between the trees. Young gnomes chased each other on the ground and across the bridges above. Soft music emanated from a lute and a lyre, drifting through the crisp air.

A very small gnome sat playing in the dirt. Griffin walked up to him and asked, "Would you possibly know where I can find the..." Before he could finish, the little gnome looked up in shock and ran into a nearby hut.

A gnome woman tended her plants a few steps away. Griffin, followed by the two dwarves, strode toward her. "Excuse me, ma'am, I'm hoping to find the library." She didn't even acknowledge Griffin's presence.

"Not the nicest welcome," Roland muttered.

As the trio wandered through the village, Griffin tried several more times to obtain information, always receiving the same response: Nothing. After a long while, they stumbled upon it themselves—a small signpost that nearly whispered the word "Library" along with an arrow pointing to the largest tree in Gnarvik. Griffin recognized the tree as the one he had seen from the cliff. The tree seemed surreal, like something from one of the folk tales about giants that Griffin's father had whispered to him many years earlier. There was a small, closed door at the base of the tree. It had no knob. Griffin tried to push it open, but to no avail.

There was some writing on the door in a language Griffin had never seen before. He did recognize a few words and parts of words here and there, but most were a complete mystery.

"Looks to be Ancient Northern Tongue," said Roland. "Haven't either of you attended school?"

Griffin glanced at Kwint and then back at Roland. "I think Kwint and I had other things to do."

Roland did his best to translate:

In birth and death I am often there.
Pick me. That will show you care.
I always rise, but sometimes rose.
Two lips, no mouth.
What am I? Who nose?

Kwint shook his head. "What a bunch of gibberish."

"The gnome mentioned a riddle, didn't he?" said Griffin. "This must be it. If we solve it, perhaps the door might open."

"Well, for a start," said Roland, "that last word is a strange one. It implies seeking a scent, rather than seeking knowledge."

"Speaking of body parts, how can ya have two lips, but no mouth?" questioned Kwint.

Roland's eyes lit up. "That's it!" he cried. "It's another play on words. It's tulips. And *sometimes rose*... You can pick it, and it's often present at birth and death. Don't you see?"

Griffin smiled. "A flower."

As soon as the word left Griffin's two lips, the symbol of a three-petaled flower glowed blue above the words on the door, which dissolved into dust that was blown away by a breeze moments later. The two dwarves stepped uneasily forward, as dwarves are not overly fond of magic. Griffin followed, and as soon as all three were inside the massive tree, the door magically re-formed behind them.

Inside the tree, a long wooden ramp spiraled up toward a ceiling, which held a chandelier bearing not flickering candles but rather fluorescent blue flowers. Small, hand-carved statuettes of meditating gnome monks protruded from the thick trunk. Besides the occasional statuette, shelves and shelves of books covered nearly every inch of the walls.

A gnome sat on a brown mat in the middle of the room. He wore a green cloak and simple leather sandals. Thick books were piled at his side, and he was engrossed in one of them. He looked up as Griffin and the dwarves walked in.

"Visitors! Oh, and unusual ones. Welcome! Welcome!"

"Finally, a friendly one," whispered Kwint.

"You're the librarian?" asked Griffin.

"I am, indeed," the gnome replied. "How can I be of service?"

"Well," Griffin began, "we aren't exactly sure. We have only a single clue that led us here." Griffin removed from his pocket the key bearing the three-petaled flower and handed it to the gnome, who inspected it from all angles. When he returned his gaze to the three travelers, his expression had changed.

"I know what it is you seek," the gnome finally said.

"How can ya know that," Roland asked, "if we ourselves don't?"

"This symbol on the key means many things," said the librarian. "You see, this is the bottom level of the Library. There are three in all. You will find what you seek at the very top."

The odd gnome handed the key back to Griffin and returned to his book as if the conversation had never occurred. Griffin shrugged and began to climb the wooden ramp, the dwarves close behind. As they did so, the gnome stole one last, curious glance at them.

There were handrails, but they were built for gnomes, meaning they reached only as high as Griffin's kneecaps. He made sure to stay as close as he could to the wall. As he slowly ascended, Griffin studied the books he passed. Most were coated with a thick layer of dust. Some were covered in cobwebs. Many were written in the Northern Tongue, Griffin's language, and quite a few were written in what he assumed was the Southern Tongue. Every once in a while, Griffin noticed a language that he couldn't identify. He was so preoccupied with the books that he wasn't watching where he was going as closely as he should have.

"Griffin! Stop!" Roland shouted.

Griffin did, and just in time. In front of him was a large gap in the ramp. One more step, and he would have plummeted dozens of feet. As he steadied himself, a scroll appeared in front of him, hovering above the gap between the two sides of the ramp.

"These gnomes and their magic..." muttered Kwint.

Griffin reached for the scroll, took a quick look at it and handed it to Roland. "What does it say?"

Roland read silently to himself for a while, then said, "Looks like we 'ave ourselves another riddle."

You can turn me, burn me,
learn from me, earn from me.
Alas, my days are numbered,
but letters are the key.
Until I came into existence,
I was but a lonely tree.
What am I?

As soon as Roland finished reading, the ramp they were on began to rumble. The gap before them was widening, as they ramp slowly dissolved, the empty space approaching quickly. As they turned around, they found that it was dissolving behind them as well.

"Quick!" exclaimed Kwint. "Solve the riddle before this ramp dissolves to nothing!"

"Money!" Roland shouted. "Firewood!"

"No, a book," said Griffin. But nothing happened.

Then all at once, the trio shouted in unison, "A page!"

The rumbling ceased. Golden dust gathered behind and in front of them and solidified into the wooden ramp. Griffin breathed a sigh of relief. Roland closed his eyes and rubbed his temples. Kwint cursed under his breath.

"Well, no sense in waiting here," Griffin smiled. "The tree could fall over for all we know."

Moments later, the ramp led them through a large hole in the ceiling. They had reached the second level. There, they encountered another gnome on another brown mat. He looked nearly identical to the first librarian gnome, except he wore a yellow cloak instead of green and appeared to be a decade or two older. He wasn't sitting. He wasn't standing either. He seemed to be doing a handstand.

"Excuse me, sir," said Griffin.

The gnome was startled and fell over. Griffin winced. "Sorry."

Picking himself up and wiping dust from his shoulders, the gnome grumbled, "Humph! You should be. I've had very few visitors, even fewer so inconsiderate."

"Wait a minute here..." Kwint started, but Griffin motioned for him to stay silent.

"I'm very sorry," he repeated.

"You should be," said the gnome.

This time, Kwint couldn't keep quiet. "You're the one who should be sorry! We almost fell to our deaths!"

The gnome chuckled. "Hah! The only thing you fell for was the ramp test! Don't be ashamed. Everyone does."

"What do you mean by test?" asked Roland.

"You wouldn't actually have fallen. Seconds before the ramp fully disintegrates, it solidifies and starts again. Very clever, if I do say so. The point is to make you think fast... and also for us librarians to have a good laugh. Hah!"

"Well, if you'll excuse us, we'll just be moving on," said Griffin.

"To the top level?" asked the gnome. "I doubt it. Very few have solved the riddle to reach the library's loftiest chamber."

"We will see about that," Griffin replied, and the companions left the gnome, who was by now back in a handstand once more.

CHAPTER 13

What will we find on the top level, if anything? Griffin thought. *Something that will lead me to the man with the bronze finger, perhaps. The Hiamahu Jewel seems to be of more importance than I originally thought. It must be related to the other gem, the Mizzarkh. It just must be. But how?*

"I hope whatever we find up there," he said out loud, mostly to himself, "gives us information to unravel this mystery."

His companions grunted in acknowledgment, as they once again climbed the long, twisting wooden ramp that circled toward the top of the enormous tree. At last they came to the third floor.

"No riddle?" Roland wondered.

This room was different from the others. Here, not a single bookcase decorated the walls, and there was no gnome librarian to greet them. In fact, the room was almost completely empty save for a tall stone statue of a gnome knight with his sword on his hip and his hands on his waist. With nowhere else to go, the travelers strode toward it. At the base of the statue, there was a small indentation in the shape of a hand. Griffin assumed someone had to press a hand against it. His was much too big, but Kwint's barely fit.

At first, nothing happened. "Ugh," Roland began. "Maybe we could—"

The silver-bearded dwarf was interrupted by the cracking of stone. Griffin looked up to see the statue turning its neck and moving its shoulders, as if awakening from a long sleep. Its once blank, emotionless eyes seemed to become more life-like as they turned toward Griffin and the two dwarves. It raised its stone eyebrows, opened its mouth and said in a voice that seemed to surround them, "I suppose you wish to reach the third level."

For a moment, the three companions stood stunned and speechless. "The third level?" Kwint finally said. "Aren't we already there?"

"In a manner of speaking," was the statue's cryptic answer. "I warn you: It has been quite some time since a visitor solved this riddle." The statue paused, an uncomfortably long pause, and then continued:

In the beginning. That is always the start.
Ask why in the end. That is the last part.
I offer tea for two and have two eyes.
I am always true and tell no lies.
What am I?

The companions glanced at each other. This riddle was indeed more difficult than the others. "You have no time limit," said the statue. "Only a lifetime."

Griffin thought for a moment. "Could you repeat the riddle," he asked, "one line at a time?"

"Yes," said the statue. "Here is the first: In the beginning, that is always the start."

"A puzzling first line," said Roland. Griffin and Kwint silently agreed.

"In the beginning... in the beginning..." Griffin murmured to himself.

"Go on," Kwint told the statue.

"Ask why in the end, that's the last part," said the deep voice that seemed to come from all angles of the room.

The trio stayed silent, thinking. "I don't suppose ya might give us a hint," said Kwint finally, as he was becoming frustrated. The statue did not need to answer.

"And the next line?" asked Roland.

"I offer tea for two and have two eyes."

"Two T's!" Griffin exclaimed. "Not the liquid, but the letter."

"Oh, and two I's, as well!" shouted Roland.

Griffin kneeled down and began moving his finger across the dusty floor. "It's just like one of the word games I used to play with my father when we traveled around the Northern Plains," he said. This was the first time Griffin had mentioned his childhood or his father to the dwarves, who stole a glance at each other. "All right," Griffin continued, as he wrote in the dust. "We know the word has two T's and two I's in it. What else?"

"Well," offered Kwint, "the why at the end might actually be the letter Y instead of the question."

Griffin traced a Y to the right of the other letters. "Anything else?"

"In the beginning..." said Roland. "Maybe he means it literally—that IN is the beginning of the word."

Griffin nodded and added an IN to the left of the other letters. It read: I N T T I I Y

"Wait," said Kwint. "Only two I's, right?" The dwarf used his foot to erase one of the I's, and the trio stared at the floor.

I N T T I Y

"Are there any words, if indeed this is a riddle meant for the Northern Tongue, that have IN at the beginning, Y at the end and two T's and another I in the middle?" Griffin mumbled.

Roland closed his eyes and leaned his head back. Kwint twirled his brown beard. Griffin simply stared at the letters on the floor. "What is the last line?" he asked.

Looking directly at Griffin, the statue replied, "I am always true and tell no lies."

"Can't be honesty," Kwint remarked.

"Truthfulness doesn't work either," added Roland.

The words echoed in Griffin's subconscious. Truth. Honesty. Qualities that Griffin always felt he lacked. But slowly, a smile crept onto his face. "I know it," he whispered. And then he looked into the statue's eyes. "Integrity."

"Well done," the stone gnome declared. The statue then began to rise, a large stone pillar pushing it upward. As it did so, a hole opened in the ceiling above it. The statue rose through the top of the tree, its base now part of the ceiling. A door appeared at the front of the pillar. Smiling, the companions squeezed inside. As soon as the last of them entered, the stone door closed behind them, leaving Griffin and his friends in complete darkness. Soon, with relief, they felt a sensation of movement, as if they were rising through the pillar. When the movement stopped, the door opened, and they found themselves outside. Blinking at the new light, Griffin realized they were standing on a small platform at the very top of the great tree.

A small figure with a dark green hood sat in the exact center of the platform, his back toward them and his face obscured. Surrounding the figure were small piles of light-colored strips of wood. The figure's hands moved back and forth rhythmically. In one hand, he held a sharp knife with a primitive wooden handle. In the other was a piece of wood that he was carving, strip by strip. From where they stood, the companions could not see what he was creating. Nestled in a pile of leaves in front of him was a single bookcase.

"You have arrived at last," he said in a raspy voice without turning to face them. He moved a hand quickly and a large strip of wood fell to the platform. "They say patience comes with age," he added, as he continued to remove strips of wood. "Quite the opposite. Time goes on forever, but people find themselves waiting for time to pass. Answer me this: If time goes on forever, why wait for time to pass?"

The travelers were unsure if this was another riddle. Griffin decided the best course was to ignore it. "We search for something to unlock with this key," he said, holding it up in front of him.

The strange gnome dropped his knife and picked up a smaller one. He began notching shapes into the wood. "I am still at work. Speak not to me until you unlock the book." The gnome made a quick gesture to the bookcase and returned to his carving. All this he said without revealing his face.

Griffin's gaze landed on the bookcase, and with a sigh he walked forward, carefully stepping around the loose strips of wood. On the top shelf, a thick, white book stood out from the others. A picture of the same key that Griffin held was delicately painted on its spine.

No lock? Griffin thought. *Maybe the key is just a symbol of sorts.* He carefully removed the book from the shelf and opened to the first page, which contained only a single sentence: *A true scholar looks beyond the pages.*

"Another riddle," Roland grunted, as he stood on his tiptoes and looked over Griffin's shoulder.

Griffin flipped through the rest of the book and sighed. "All of the other pages are blank."

"What kind of joke is this?" Kwint asked the mysterious gnome. He did not reply—or even look up for that matter.

"Beyond the pages..." Griffin muttered. He reached his hand onto the shelf where the blank book once stood. "Aha! It's not a riddle at all."

"What is it then?" asked Roland.

"It's literal. Beyond the pages. Beyond the book. Behind the book." Sure enough, Griffin pulled out an old, brown book from behind where the white book once rested. It had blended into the bookcase perfectly. Like the first book, it had no title, no author. There was a thick leather strap that

prevented the book from being opened, but there was a key-
hole in its center.

Griffin took a look at the key and tried it. Click.

CHAPTER 14

The strap released and the book seemed to open on its own to the very first page, which was yellowed with age and contained an unfamiliar style of handwriting. The book began with a message from the anonymous author:

I should not be writing this, yet here I sit, quill in hand, revealing thoughts that truthfully should not be put on parchment. As a scholar and a scribe, the need to put knowledge on paper is just too great for me to ignore. Forever more, I shall be guilty of transferring knowledge into physical being. I should not be writing this.

With Roland and Kwint reading from over each shoulder, Griffin turned to the next page. Here there was a chapter titled "A Brief Explanation of the Gems."

The gems, referred to as the Gems of Power or the Sister Jewels, are great quantities of power contained in four different jewels. As of this writing, their origins are to me unknown. They will likely never be known. The gems are as follows:

The Water Gem, *known as the Hiamahu Jewel. A direct translation of hiamahu to the Northern Tongue is "water soul." The Hiamahu Jewel has a very troubled history, as it has changed hands many times over the ages.*

Griffin allowed a hint of a smile. Indeed, he thought.

The Fire Gem, *commonly called the Mizzarkh. In the Northern Tongue, it means "fist of fire." The Mizzarkh, too, has been a source of conflict and bloodshed dating back to its very origins.*

Kwint raised an eyebrow. And Roland raised an eyebrow at Kwint.

The Dark Gem, *the Ungornem Gem, ungornem meaning "darkness everlasting." By most accounts, this gem has remained in the same general vicinity for many an age, although its exact location is unknown.*

The Light Gem, *the Anoelmenoh, translated as "grasping light." It has been so difficult to find that some have begun to suspect that it has been destroyed or lost.*

Griffin eagerly turned to the next page: "Associated Races and the People of Power."

Each gem has a race associated with the source of its power. For the Hiamahu Jewel, humans are bound to it, possibly because of their tendency to irrationally change their minds or shift their allegiances, altering course the way a stream adjusts its direction. The gem of the dwarves is the Mizzarkh, possibly related to their blazing forges, their fiery hearts, and their enflamed passions, for better or worse. The Ungornem Gem is the gem of demons, of darkness. Demons themselves represent sinister intentions, although intentions can be interpreted in multiple ways. The jewel to which they are bound has equally ambiguous properties. Finally, the elvish gem is the Anoelmenoh. The perfection of elves has no equal. Their light can blind a man with perfect sight, as can the gem of their race.

In each race, only one specific lineage has the ability to release each gem's power. With few exceptions, this ability is passed down to each succeeding generation, a fact known to most but not all who are part of the Families of Power.

To release the power of a gem, it must be held in the palm of the wielder's dominant hand, its power emanating from all five fingers. Any descendants among the Families of Power may have the ability to wield the gems, but any mingling of blood between the power races immediately negates that power to succeeding generations.

The Families of Power have changed their surnames countless times over the ages, often in an attempt to lessen the chance of being discovered by those who would wish to either abuse or remove their abilities. I considered giving an *account of the known names of the Families of Power, but decided against it because it would endanger their safety and likely mine as well.*

"Well, these gems sound like more trouble than they are worth," said Roland.

"It depends," Griffin replied, "how much they're worth." He flipped forward, scanning the text, until he arrived at a chapter titled: "Arkhaen Thrine ki Wen Ungor."

This is the part of the book that I most regret having to write, but I must all the same. In the Northern Tongue, this chapter translates as "Flame Web and True Shadow." These are the names of two organizations that seek the Sister Jewels.

Flame Web: *This organization attempts to achieve the gems in an effort to keep them from the wrong hands. The ultimate goal of Arkhaen Thrine is to keep the balance of power from shifting too profoundly in one direction. The "Flame" signifies illumination of shadow, and the "Web" represents their vast network of spies spread throughout Alastian.*

True Shadow: *A sinister organization, it has weaseled its way into power over the years through intimidation and bribery. Its goal is purely power, generally for malevolent purposes. Unlike most villainous people of Alastian, Wen Ungor does not merely understand the fact that they are evil; they embrace it.*

Although these two groups have waged war over the gems for centuries, one clearly leaning toward goodness and the other wickedness, they often are mistaken for one another by blissfully ignorant residents of Alastian. There is some truth to the confusion, however. At times, Arkhaen Thrine can be just as stealthy and deceptive as Wen Ungor. But one must remember: Flame Web always fights for justice and True Shadow for power.

Griffin quickly skimmed through the next section, the longest by far, called "Various Battles and Movements of the Gems." After a few minutes, he came to the final chapter: "Recent Gem Sightings."

"This should be interesting," said Roland.

Please note that by the time this account is read, perhaps decades or even centuries from now, the location of each gem will likely have changed. The Sister Jewels rarely remain stationary over time. As of this writing, the best information about their locations is as follows: The Hiamahu Jewel has been under the protection of Arkhaen Thrine for decades. It is kept in the possession of young Lord Scadnik in the human city of Quah.

Not any more, mused Griffin. *And here I thought it was a simple jewel heist.*

The Mizzarkh has moved frequently lately. Its exact position is unknown, although evidence suggests a location somewhere in the Kni Hmun Mountains. The Ungornem Gem hasn't so much as touched the hand of a member of

Flame Web for centuries. Long ago, it is said that it was entrusted to the care of a high-ranking general of True Shadow, Tynalussi Nanda, a cunning demon pirate, captain of the sea vessel Cyclops. The Anoelmenoh, as a gem of the elves, is assumed by most to reside somewhere in the Elder Forest. As I have mentioned before, many question whether it actually still exists.

In the long history of Alastian, nobody has ever had possession of all four gems at once—indeed, never more than two at a time have ever been held by an individual. This is a most fortunate fact. The myths have long said that possession of all four jewels will confer ultimate power, regardless of family lineage. Such power can only lead to destruction. It also has been said, but never confirmed, that if a person possesses one of the gems, he or she will be led toward the others in some manner. Some have described it as "the Sisters reaching for my soul."

CHAPTER 15

Griffin slid the book back onto the shelf. *All of this information about Arkhaen Thrine and gems and demon pirates,* he thought, rubbing his temples. *More than I bargained for.*

The hooded gnome still did not look up or reveal what he was carving. He grunted, "Almost done... there." The gnome remained concealed. "I suppose you are wondering who I am."

"Among other things," said Kwint.

The gnome examined the wooden handle of his knife. "I am sure you have heard of me, at least... a form of myself. I am the veiled hunger that burns in every sentient creature. I am the embodiment of curiosity and the pursuit of knowledge. You know me. I am Know."

The three travelers glanced at each other. "Ya look like a regular ol' gnome to me," muttered Roland.

"Oh, I am very much a gnome still," he replied. "Just old, though. Nearly as old as the trees. But very irregular, I'm afraid, a rare breed. I am a Curio, one of the handful of gnomes that received a genetic trait from the light elves of old. Some call it immortality, but I seem to be the only one left." He returned to examining his blade.

"Why have you shown us this book?" Griffin asked.

"Because of your destiny, Griffin Blade. And yours, Kwint Kwinhollow. And yours, as well, Roland Silverbeard."

"Ya know our names?" asked Kwint.

"Oh, I know more than that. I see the flow of time emerging from you like great branches growing from an oak. And your destinies are coiled together like strands of elvish rope."

"Our destinies?" Griffin moved closer.

"Indeed. You will travel far across the land in search of the Sister Jewels."

"And why would we do that?" asked Kwint.

"Because your fates are inseparable from the fates of the gems. And anyway, the more difficult question is not why, but how. I suggest searching for darkness first."

"The Ungornem Gem," Griffin mumbled.

"Yes," said Know. "The gem of darkness may light the way."

Griffin had spent a lifetime avoiding such soul-searching. He felt... something. Yet part of him remained unconvinced. The mysterious gnome seemed to read his mind.

"You think I am mad, do you not?" he said.

Griffin's face reddened slightly. "Well... no."

"You think I am a crazy, old gnome rambling about fate and time. Do not lie to me, Griffin Blade. Do not lie to me like you did to your two companions. It is time they know, Griffin, and I will not be the one to tell them."

The Curio placed his knife on his carving and made one final slicing motion. Then he finally revealed his face. Pulling back his green hood, he tilted his head towards them, showing two sightless eyes.

Roland gasped. "But... how?"

"Carving with no eyes? You will find I can do many things." The blind gnome seemed to turn to each companion, as if studying their faces. "I sense that you wish to leave. I will grant your request. But first, a gift."

Know opened his hand to reveal his carving. It was a very life-like, wooden creature with the head of an eagle and the body of a lion. There was a "K" carved into its head.

"A griffin," Griffin murmured, and his eyes began to glaze over, a memory resurfacing.

Five-year-old Griffin walked beside his father in the courtyard of Castle Quah. Instead of the courtyard, however, Griffin saw a miniature forest, lush with life. Shrubs and dandelions decorated the ground in the shadows of tall trees boasting the pink blossoms of spring. The flowers danced in the breeze. The walls of the courtyard were covered in colorful murals portraying great events and battles of long ago. Ramyr Blade pointed at one of them.

"Look there," he said. The mural showed a particularly fierce battle between two human armies. There seemed to be no clear victor. Beyond the battle loomed a steep, snowy mountain. Atop it, a strange creature was perched. It had the feet, body and tail of a lion, yet the wings, head and beak of an eagle. Its wings were spread wide, and it gazed toward the battlefield. "Do you know what that is, Griff?"

Griffin shook his head.

"It is the symbol of justice, luck and victory—a griffin. It is the source of your name. And, perhaps, the course of your destiny."

Griffin blinked the memory away.

"May it serve you when the need is great," said Know cryptically, as he handed Griffin the wooden statuette. Griffin mumbled a thank-you and carefully placed it into his pack.

"I suppose we will be leaving now."

The Curio nodded slightly. "Goodbye, Griffin Blade. Tell your friends the truth, for a lie is a truth within itself." The gnome then turned away and began to carve once more.

CHAPTER 16

The stars twinkled, as the three companions sat around a campfire in the forest. Gnarvik was just out of view. They had hardly spoken since their encounter with Know a few hours earlier. Roland broke the silence.

"What 'ave ya been keeping from us, Griffin. What was Know talking about?"

Griffin was quiet for a moment. "Know was wrong. I have never lied and would not lie to either of you."

"Oh, I see," said Roland, twisting his beard.

"I simply avoided the truth," Griffin continued.

A spark flew from the fire. "What?" asked the dwarves simultaneously.

"I never told you a lie. I told you half of the truth."

"I've 'ad enough riddles for today," said Kwint. "Out with it."

Griffin sighed. "All right. I did have possession of the Hiamahu Jewel, and an old man did steal it from me. What I haven't told you is how I obtained the gem in the first place." Griffin then explained how he had been hired by Alnardo Fist to pilfer the jewel, how he had accomplished the feat, and how it was by no means the first time he had been contracted for thievery.

"I knew ya dealt with some shady figures in the past, Griffin. But a thief on behalf of a criminal like Fist!" exclaimed Roland. "So ya did lie!"

"Correction. Avoided the truth."

"Don't play games with me, Blade. A liar is a liar. And you, sir, are a liar beyond measure."

"Oh, let it be, Roland," said Kwint. "Did you 'ear what he did to retrieve that gem? Liar or not, I'd like to find out more about his adventures."

Roland's face turned crimson. "This man is more than a liar. He's a criminal, a burglar."

Griffin shrugged. "Not bad, but I prefer rogue or—oh!—master thief. Sounds more intimidating."

Roland pointed at Griffin. "See! He's perfectly content with who he is. I have half a mind to turn him in to the Imperial Guard right this instant!"

Kwint rubbed his hands by the fire. "I think ya may 'ave forgotten, Roland. I was once a 'criminal' myself."

Roland closed his eyes for a moment. "I am going to bed." He crouched down and rolled up his bedroll. "And I'm not sleeping near you two." He walked a ways and placed his bedroll just behind the thick trunk of a tree. "Don't want ya cutting my throat in the dead o' night," he mumbled.

Griffin gazed at Roland for a while as he stomped away, then laid himself down between a stand of oak trees and the blazing fire. He slept fitfully that night until he was jolted awake by a rustling and what sounded like muffled voices toward the bushes where Roland had slept. He quickly sat up. It was a moonless night. The fire had diminished to glowing embers. Griffin could just make out the figure of Kwint sleeping on the other side of the fire pit. He scrambled over to the dwarf and shook him awake.

"Kwint, did you hear that?" he whispered.

Kwint rubbed his eyes and turned to face Griffin. "What?"

"Something. Over there," said Griffin, pointing toward the bushes. "It sounded like voices."

"Probably Roland talking in 'is sleep." Kwint yawned. "Now that I mention it, so am I—"

"Be quiet," Griffin hissed.

"What now?"

"Shhh." There were voices coming closer. "Follow me," he whispered.

They hid behind one of the large oak trees. A dozen hooded figures came into view, their faces concealed by the dark of night. One of the taller figures, who seemed to have the bearing of a leader, spoke. "There's the dwarf. Get him." His voice was gruff and demanding. The others were quick to obey, as they moved toward Roland.

Griffin took a step toward the figures, planning to defend his dwarf friend, when a war cry echoed from the forest. It was difficult to make out just what was happening in the darkness, but it looked to Griffin like at least ten more hooded figures arrived. To Griffin's horror, they were riding atop what appeared to be giant eight-legged beasts and wildly swinging long flails as the creatures rushed forward. *Reinforcements perhaps,* Griffin thought.

A spider-rider grabbed Roland, hoisted him onto the back of his beast and rode off, quickly followed by his fellow riders. As the group faded back into the shadow of the forest, Griffin could hear the protests of Roland fading into the distance, too. The original figures—those not riding enormous arachnids—remained behind.

"Come on," said the leader, and motioned for the rest of his band to follow the riders.

When they were sure the hooded figures were gone, Kwint spoke. "Who are they?" There was fire in his words. "And where did they take Roland?"

"I don't know," said Griffin, "but they have him all the same." He wondered if Kwint could hear the concern in his voice. "Let's go." Griffin began collecting his supplies. "It looks like they went west."

"Wait," said Kwint. "Griffin, you can't possibly believe we can catch up to those beasts. And we have no idea where the riders went. I have a feeling in my gut, and my gut is usually right, that this is about the gems. Let's find the Sister Jewels, Griffin, like Know said. Hopefully, we'll find Roland in the process."

Griffin hesitated for a moment, then sighed. "You're right. I must admit, I have that same feeling. I guess we're seeking the Ungornem Gem..."

"Darkness everlasting..." added Kwint in a near whisper. "But where are we going to find it?"

Griffin placed his pack on the ground. "We'll need our rest if we're going to do this right. In the morning, we set out for the sea."

"The sea," Kwint repeated.

"Ever been there?" Griffin asked, as Kwint shook his head slowly. "Neither have I."

"Ya think we'll encounter a demon pirate?"

Griffin took a deep breath. "I just hope we encounter a Cyclops."

CHAPTER 17

Young Griffin's ribs were almost healed. Twelve-year-olds can be remarkably resilient. He could walk around the cottage now with almost no effort. Occasionally, he felt a stab of pain, like a dagger thrust into his ribcage and twisted slowly. But only occasionally. Miss Flamentari insisted he stay in bed most of the time. Boredom soon took over, and he wanted nothing more than to rush outside and search for his father, wherever he might be.

Don't worry about me. The words echoed in his head like the vibration of a gong. He worried about his father constantly.

Griffin noticed that Miss Flamentari left the cottage for hours at a time. Sometimes she returned with food and supplies. But sometimes, there was a secretiveness about her. Lying in his bed, Griffin pondered the possibility of grabbing some food, sneaking out, and returning to Quah.

I've had enough wondering, enough thinking, to last a lifetime, *he decided.* **It's time to act.** *He quickly climbed from the bed, wincing slightly. He collected some supplies, including a small pack of food, and stepped outside for the first time in what must have been weeks but felt like years.*

"Sorry, Miss Flamentari," he said, as he turned his back toward the cottage. "Thank you."

Trees, trees and more trees for miles in every direction, as they trekked through the Elder Forest. Griffin missed the flat, green plains of the human lands. He missed his friend Roland, too. Upon awakening every morning, it was his first thought. Finally, four days into their travels, Griffin and Kwint came upon a wide river.

"Ah! River Syl, I believe," said Kwint. "This leads south into the Sea of Emrad."

"Perfect. If we follow this river, we'll be there in no time."

"Well, yes, I suppose. As long as we make it through the swamps of dark elf country."

Griffin looked at him quizzically.

"Roland was more of the geographer, but I'll tell ya what I know about dark elves," said Kwint. He cleared his throat and began to speak as if educating a child. "Like the gnomes, the dark elves like to keep to themselves. However, unlike the gnomes, they are particularly... aggressive toward those who cross into their lands. Regarding the swamps, I don't know much. But there is an excerpt from the *Kiladuna* that I remember."

"The *Kiladuna*? What is that, a book?"

"A dwarven poem, actually, written by Duna in his final years. Kiladuna simply means 'words of Duna.'" Kwint looked at Griffin. "Ya don't know who Duna is, do ya?"

Griffin shook his head. "I had... an unusual education."

"Ya sure must've. Duna was an ancient dwarven traveler, who was alive even before Hurverick was born. He was one of the first dwarves to migrate to the south from the

Far North. He finally settled in Mount Ornagwin, but not before traveling across most of Alastian. The *Kiladuna* is the collection of poems that Duna wrote during his travels. It's a very special book, almost holy to most dwarves. When he was in the land of the dark elves, he wrote..." Kwint closed his eyes, trying to recall the words. "A mirror that echoes the moon... that casts away darkness from the marauders... that cleanses the great bog... Omai."

"What was the last part?" said Griffin. "Oh my?"

"Omai," said Kwint, "is a dwarven word, difficult to translate. It means something like this: Shadow's light, light's shadow."

Griffin was silent for a moment and then muttered, "I'm trying to decide if the poem suggests if we're heading into trouble or not."

"Either way," said Kwint, "it's sure to be interesting."

The pair soon stopped for the night, then awoke early the next morning and followed the river for several hours—the great waterway on their right, a series of swamps on their left. "Smells like my Great Aunt Mygra's feet," said Kwint, nodding toward the swamps. He began mumbling about taking a rest.

"Just a bit more," said Griffin. "We should able to—"

Splosh! Griffin found himself in a pool of mud and sinking rapidly. By the time he realized what had happened, the mud was already waist-high.

"Kwint! Find something to pull me out!"

Kwint looked around frantically and spotted a fallen tree branch. "Grab on!" he yelled to Griffin, who was now chest deep in the mud and struggling to free his arms. He reached for the branch, and Kwint pulled as hard as he could. But Griffin barely moved.

"Pull harder!" he shouted, neck-deep in the sludge.

"I'm tryin'!" Kwint yelled, and then he saw that Griffin had become completely submerged in the muck, except for one hand that was slowly losing its grip on the branch until it, too, was submerged. "Griffin? Griffin!"

Kwint moved as close as he dared to the mud pit and reached as deep as he could with his short dwarven arm. He felt nothing. He saw nothing. "Griffin! Grab on to me hand! Please, Griffin..."

Mud splattered on Kwint's face, as Griffin's hand emerged, taking a firm grip onto the dwarf's arm. Kwint pulled mightily, and Griffin's head appeared. He spit mud from his mouth and labored to breathe. Moments later, after Kwint had pulled him completely from the mud and Griffin had shaken off the grime, he noticed that his pack was still on his back, but he suddenly realized that he was missing something. "My crossbow!" he said, as he gazed into the sludge pit.

"At least that can be replaced," Kwint replied. "And yer welcome."

Griffin placed a hand on his shoulder. "Thanks."

The pair walked on for a few more hours before setting up camp for the evening. As they tried to sleep that night, Kwint noticed that even a brief dip in the river didn't completely erase the smell. Early the next morning, as Griffin and Kwint walked alongside the river, among great strands of eucalyptus trees and beneath a hazy pink sky, the smell of the swamp slowly disappeared and was replaced by a sweet smell that they couldn't identify. Griffin parted two branches in front of him, and a beautiful lake came into view, perfectly reflecting the sky.

"Must be Lake Sylvania," said Kwint.

Griffin was tempted to jump right in, as if he were hurtling himself into the clouds. The water was very clear from up close, clear enough to offer a view of the smooth rocks below.

"Shadow's light, light's shadow," Griffin muttered.

"Indeed," said Kwint. "I think if we were to go around the lake, we should find the river on the other side, as well, and then we can follow it out to the sea."

"If we only had a boat..." said Griffin.

The universe seemed to hear his plea. At that very moment, a boat came into view, skimming across the lake. The boat had triangular, black sails that were silhouetted against the morning sky. The hull of the vessel was made of dark wood, and a large oar protruded from each side.

"Maybe they're going where we're going," said Griffin. "Or at least somewhere close."

"Over 'ere!" shouted Kwint, temporarily forgetting his reminder that dark elves don't take kindly to visitors. There was no response, and the boat soon disappeared from view as it slowly glided around a bend in the lake. Griffin and Kwint ran after it, rushing along the lakeshore. Eventually, they, too, rounded the bend and came upon a wooden dock; the boat was tied to its end. Griffin was careful not to let them get too close to the vessel, as he noticed a distinct lack of activity.

There didn't seem to be anyone onboard at all. His sixth sense suggested that something didn't seem right. Given what he had heard about the dark elves, he smelled an ambush. But how? *The boat,* he thought. *They expect us to inspect it. When we do, they'll jump out from wherever they're hiding.* It was time to act quickly.

"Kwint," he whispered. "I don't like the looks of this. I want you to slowly walk up to the boat. I'm going to swim around to the back and climb up the other side."

"Griffin, I don't think you'll be able to do that. Without being seen, anyway."

"Just do what I said. I'm about to prove you wrong."

Griffin slid into the lake. It was cold, but the water—having arrived all the way from the melting glaciers of Mount Ornagwin—was refreshing. He swam underwater, so he wouldn't make a sound, and resurfaced at the edge of the boat. A damp rope hung from its side. He grabbed it and quietly hoisted himself upward. As Kwint slowly made his way forward along the dock, Griffin glanced around the boat and spotted a very large fishing net. *Large enough to hold some elves,* he thought. It hung from a rope attached to the stern of the boat. Griffin hid behind a pile of crates, some of which were half-open, revealing various valuables, obviously stolen from somewhere. *Bandits,* he thought. *We're dealing with bandits.* He peeked out from behind the crates.

Kwint was drawing near. *That's one brave dwarf.* Kwint stepped onto the boat. "Hello? Anyone there?"

Just as Griffin suspected, a door suddenly opened from the floorboards, and four elves emerged. They quickly blocked Kwint's exit from the boat.

This was the first time Griffin had ever laid eyes on dark elves. Their skin was, indeed, dark, as the name suggested, but he could see that it had a bluish tint, as well. Their ears were long and pointed and pierced by various golden studs and hooped earrings. The bandits wore rough leather vests that looked as if they had been torn and patched a number of times. Most of them held daggers or brandished short swords.

"What do we have here? A dwarf?" said one of them.

"More like a sitting duck," said another. They laughed and moved closer.

"Let's skin him and eat him for supper!" offered a third.

Kwint's face lost all its color. "Oh, don't worry," said the first elf. "We're not savages. We'll just take everything you own and drown you instead."

"Griffin!" Kwint couldn't help himself. "I could use some assistance!"

"Griffin?" said the lead bandit. "You want a magical bird to swoop down and save you?" He looked up at the sky and grinned wickedly. "Empty," he said. "No griffin."

While the bandits had been talking, Griffin had crept over to where the heavy net was hanging. He unhooked one end and stood tall. "You're wrong about that," he said, as the bandits spun around in surprise. With perfect timing, Griffin tossed the net on top of the bandits and then gave it a strong tug to pull it tightly. The elves struggled and fell to the floor in a heap of twisted bodies.

"Hurry!" yelled Griffin. "Don't let them escape!"

Kwint grabbed one of the oars and began pummeling each of the bandits in turn. Every time one of them found his footing, he was down a second later. "Who's the sitting duck now?" Kwint shouted, as Griffin tied the ends of the net, fully capturing them. For the next few minutes, the duo dragged the netted bandits from the boat, eventually tying one end of the net to a tree.

"They have daggers. They'll eventually cut themselves free," Griffin said. "But they won't have a boat. It's ours now."

CHAPTER 18

Although Kwint and Griffin were not exactly experienced sailors, they were able to embark rather quickly, using the oars to make their way to the river. There, the current and a stiff breeze allowed them to hoist the sails and make quick work of exploring the cabin of the boat (which Griffin decided to name *The Flamentari*). It was dark and cramped, full of bedrolls, discarded food, empty jugs of wine, and a few dusty maps of the river and coast.

"Nothing much 'ere," said Kwint, as he tilted a wine jug and waited for a single drop to land on his tongue. "I think we should return to the deck."

"In a moment," Griffin replied. "I'd like to study these maps." He picked up a map and blew off the dust. "Looks like we may be the first one to actually use them. My father always had a funny saying about maps—that they were 'the giant's eye.' For some reason, I always remembered that."

"What in Hurverick's name does that mean?"

Griffin shrugged. "Maybe he meant a better view of things. My father didn't always make sense to me."

"C'mon let's head back to the—"

"For the love of Droma, get me out of this thing!"

The companions, startled, turned to the darkest corner of the room, from where the voice seemed to come. A large blanket was covering a rectangular object, but not fully. They could make out iron bars at the bottom. Griffin yanked the blanket, revealing a figure squatting in a corner of a cage, still partially in the shadows.

"Who's that?" Kwint asked.

"I'd like to ask you the same question, *remonak*. I mean... dwarf," said the female voice. "It's been a while since I spoke in the Northern Tongue. The Dromaguard adopted your language recently. Now I have two names for everything. Give your *buanov*—your names—and I'll give you mine."

Griffin hesitated. "Step into the light."

The figure stood and moved forward slightly, and Griffin saw that it was a female dark elf wearing a leather vest similar to those worn by the bandits. She was slightly taller than Griffin. Her hair was long and black, her face stern, but Griffin saw something in her eyes—a kindliness, perhaps, behind her sneering exterior. "You're one of them," he said.

"Hardly," she answered, motioning toward the iron bars. "Your names?"

"I'm Griffin Blade. This is Kwint Kwinhollow. And you are?"

"Confused. Where are the Dromaguard?"

"You mean the bandits?" asked Griffin. "We left them in a fishing net a few miles from here."

"You trapped the Dromaguard... in a fishing net?" The dark elf laughed and moved toward the bars of the cage. "You must have been incredibly brave and intelligent to have bested those fellows."

"We dwarves are naturally strong," Kwint bragged. "Knocked two of 'em out by just flexing my muscles." Griffin rolled his eyes, as did the elf.

"I was being sarcastic, dwarf. Those are some of the biggest fools on the river. A rabbit could outwrestle them. And outthink them."

"Then how did you end up in this cage?" asked Griffin.

Kwint smirked. "Was it the rabbit?"

"I was once the captain of the Dromaguard," she said, ignoring the comment. "It was a rather easy position to hold. I was better than most at most things."

"Who exactly are the Dromaguard," Griffin wondered.

"The *Eomora*, the Dark Elves, are separated into different clans. Eleven actually, one for each of the Unseen Gods—Marmraguard, Byzaguard, Foveenguard, Quillaguard, Nuelguard, Jiguard, Yeavguard, Anoguard, Dulgenguard, Vensaguard, and Dromaguard."

"Are they all bandits? Not very guard-like," said Kwint. "Or god-like."

"Your ignorance is impressive," she said. "No, not all bandits, just the Dromaguard. Droma represents the swallowing of light, ever-reaching darkness, a collective craving."

"Greed," said Griffin, and she nodded.

"As for the guard part," she continued. "That is just a matter of translation from the Southern Tongue. It is difficult to find words that explain what it means. Keeper, perhaps. No, preserver. That is as close as I can get."

"You still haven't explained," said Kwint, "why the so-called guards 'ad you in a cage."

"As I said, I was a Dromaguard captain. Captains are often overthrown, and I was confident that it wouldn't happen to me. Too confident, as it turns out. I woke up in this cage a few days ago." She rubbed a bruise on the side of her forehead. "They fed me while they decided what to do with me. Now I have told you my tale. Let me out."

"How can we trust 'er?" asked Kwint, eyeing her with suspicion. "You heard 'er. She said she was a Dromaguard herself. No better than a bandit."

"It's Droma, dwarf, and I can be trusted."

"Why is that?" asked Griffin.

"Because I told you so," she said. "And I may steal, but I don't lie."

Griffin was silent for a moment. "For now, and I hate to say this, I agree with Kwint. You may very well be lying. Until we know that you can be trusted, you'll have to stay behind bars."

"Yer first step to freedom," said Kwint, "would be to tell us yer name."

"Naymeira," she whispered and faded back into the shadows.

CHAPTER 19

Over the next few days, as they drifted downriver, they made sure to make the dark elf as comfortable and well-fed as possible. Griffin left her food on a wooden plate by the cage—without utensils, of course. He wasn't about to underestimate her ability to escape. When he returned, the food was always gone. However, she remained unresponsive and stayed in the shadows most of the time.

They made good progress in their travels, leaving Lake Sylvania long behind, sailing through the rest of dark elf country and into the lands of the light elves. Griffin sensed that they were nearing the ocean, in part because the trees of the Elder Forest were beginning to thin, but also because the smell of salt drifted northward slowly from the Sea of Emrad. Griffin and Kwint spent most of the time chatting about their former lives, Kwint as a pickpocket, Griffin as a thief. Occasionally, they tried to include Naymeira in the conversation, but she refused to participate, only mumbling, "A couple of thieves. But you don't trust me..."

The two companions found it difficult to sleep, as *The Flamentari* rocked back and forth, the floorboards creaking with every movement. Kwint's insomnia was due to seasickness. Griffin's was the result of a cluttered mind. So they turned to elf-wine to help them, and soon the two of them were nearly unconscious on their bedrolls. As sleep approached, Griffin's mind kept drifting to Roland. *Where is he? Who took him? Does he still live?* They were familiar questions.

The night. A blanket of darkness thrown across the sky. A time when all manner of things could creep unseen. Young Griffin had mixed feelings about this time. It had been two days since he left Miss Flamentari's cottage. His ribs had begun to bother him only a few hours in, but he had pushed on. The cool night wind rustled the leaves of the pines. Griffin debated in his mind whether to find a place to sleep or to travel a bit further. He felt that something was close. He had to keep going.

He noticed that he was moving downhill slightly, perhaps to a valley. Suddenly, the trees cleared as he exited the Forest of Regrowth. In a small valley below, he saw the light of lanterns that formed the outline of a village. Griffin looked up to see the stars, which had been hidden from view for days. He always thought of stars as tiny holes in the blanket of the night sky, allowing daylight to peer through...

Demon Captain Mogash grumbled and squinted his eyes. It was the middle of the night. Eventually, he sat up, grabbed his curved Jagamaurian blade and slid out of bed. Mogash smelled something unfamiliar in the sea air. He darted his yellow eyes around the cabin to make sure no one was watching. If he was mistaken about the foreign scent, he wanted to make sure none of his crew would be awake to see it.

The pirate captain sleepily shambled onto the deck of the *Bloody Rat*. He sniffed the air. It was easier to follow the scent outside, although the smell of rum from the Stinging Isles was strong as well. Mogash was almost sure of it now. Human blood. It was a very particular aroma, easily recognized by demons like himself. He was a boar-man, born at sea. Mogash's snout could sniff out a scent from a mile away on a clear day. He licked his tusks and scanned the horizon.

"You smell it, too, Captain?"

Mogash's first mate stood at the ship's wheel. He was an albino merman, scaly, with thin legs and webbed feet. He was wrapped in a dark blue cloak, which appeared black in the night, and his white-scaled head seemed to glow from the light of the full moon above them.

"Aye, Ranimus. Do you know if there are any trading ports along this area of the coast?"

The merman's blood-red eyes glared.

"Ranimus?"

"We reviewed the maps only yesterday, Captain. No, there are no ports for many leagues."

"What is a human ship doing so far south?"

"Not just human," said Ranimus. "I smell dwarf, as well."

"A dwarf? At sea? The world's gone downside-up."

"That is not the most curious part," said the merman. "Their boat is elvish-made."

"By Eag's Toe, how could you possibly know that?"

Ranimus simply pointed straight ahead. A boat was skimming the water in the distance, outlined by the full moon. Svinum, a massive ogre the color of a rotting fern, stepped out of the cabin, squinted his eyes toward the ship on the horizon, and lumbered toward the captain and first mate.

"How's about we give these travelers a proper welcome, eh?" The ogre smiled, revealing two sets of sharp, yellow teeth.

"Aye," Mogash agreed. "A *Bloody Rat* welcome, except that this time maybe the three of us can keep the loot ourselves. No sense in waking the rest of the crew." He turned to face the ogre. "Svinum, prepare the rowboat."

CHAPTER 20

Naymeira sat on the cold floor of her cage. Griffin and Kwint had offered her bedding and blankets, but she refused to accept any comfort unless it was the comfort of total freedom. Water lapped against the boat in a constant rhythm. It didn't sound at all like the River Syl. *This blasted sea,* she thought. As a Dromaguard captain, she had never traveled farther south than Ceneglen, the capital city of the light elves. The sounds of the Elder Forest usually coaxed her to sleep. The sea's only purpose seemed to be to prevent a good slumber.

She heard footsteps on the deck. They were too heavy to be human or dwarf feet. Naymeira made out three large figures entering the boat's cabin. She moved to a corner of the cage and disappeared into the shadows.

"Take anything you can," one of them whispered.

"Then we'll sink 'em!"

"Shh. Aye, they won't know what hit 'em."

Demons. Naymeira had heard stories about creatures like these, but had never encountered one up close. *They haven't seen me yet. Curse Droma, this cage.* She held her breath. The largest demon, the ogre, walked toward her cage.

"Whad'ya wager they keep in here?"

"Prisoners, I'd imagine," said the white-scaled creature.

"Maybe it's their money cage," said the ogre.

"Elves don't keep money in cages, you idiot."

"How much you wanna wager?"

"Say... half of your loot."

"Done."

"Easy money," the merman muttered, as the ogre approached the cage and drew his dagger. He slipped the dagger through the bars and poked around for an object. "Hah! I think I found something. Argh, my dagger's stuck!"

The demon withdrew his hand, leaving the dagger inside the cage. Click. The door swung open. Naymeira strode out, flexing her right hand, which held the ogre's dagger. "Now," she said. "Who's first?"

The demons glanced at each other, then snickered. "You think you can take us on, little elf?" said a boar-headed creature who seemed to be in charge. They laughed once more.

"We'll see, won't we?" Naymeira replied, and she took them by surprise. She jumped unexpectedly high and kicked the ogre right between the eyes. A trickle of blood escaped through his fingers as he nursed his nose. Another kick left him sprawled on the floor. Then she went for the boar-man, the captain. She hurled the dagger, which plunged into his leg. Mogash howled in pain, flailing on the floor. Naymeira bent down to retrieve the dagger, crouched over him and put him out of his misery.

Then she remembered: *The merman. The smart one.*

He had left the cabin and was trying to escape over the boat's starboard side. She aimed her dagger at the demon's head.

"Naymeira!" Griffin stepped in front of her, a bit wobbly. "What's going on? How did you escape your—" Seeing her dagger, he froze.

"You fool!" she shouted. She aimed her dagger once again, and it flew. It whizzed past Griffin's ear toward the merman, just missing the demon by inches. As the merman dove into the sea, Naymeira grabbed Griffin by his collar. "You let him escape! Now he'll tell the rest of his crew. There's not much time."

"I thought you were aiming for me," said Griffin.

"Maybe I should have." She grabbed an oar. "Let's get this boat moving. We're not stopping until we're far from this area."

As she spoke, lightning flashed and thunder roared in the distance. "Wonderful," she muttered. "You know how hard it is to control a riverboat in a sea during a thunderstorm?"

Within minutes, the three companions were rowing mightily. Griffin decided to trust Naymeira's judgment, realizing that she had physical and strategic skills that rivaled his own. Despite their quick getaway, both the pirates and the thunderstorm were gaining on them. The storm arrived first. Thunder drowned out all sound.

"Row!" Naymeira shouted. Although no one heard her, row they did. Water spilled over the deck, as the boat was pounded by waves from the side and sheets of rain from above. It seemed like they rowed for hours, and soon a sliver of sun began to rise in front of them. Then the thunder and lightning seemed to end abruptly, a momentary calm amid chaos. Clouds parted to reveal a sight more magnificent than Dunalar, more beautiful than the trees of Gnarvik.

"In Hurverick's name..."

"Droma's ears..."

Griffin could only gasp.

Protruding from the stormy sea was a great island with sheer cliffs rising on all sides. Countless exotic plants and trees covered the land mass, some growing straight out of the cliff faces themselves. The most magnificent sight, however, was a volcano that rose high above the dense canopy, a colossal black mountain. An orange river of lava ran down its side, and gray smoke drifted into the sky from its peak. Winding upward around the volcano toward its summit was what appeared to be a city of sorts, carved into the sides of the volcano itself.

The three companions managed only a glimpse of the wonder before the storm returned with a vengeance. The island was lost behind thick, charcoal clouds. The sound of thunder grew louder and closer until there was a deafening boom accompanied by a bolt of lightning. It struck *The Flamentari's* hull, and the poor ship exploded into burning planks, tossing the companions into the sea. The last thing Griffin remembered was seeing his belongings tumbling toward the water, his pack opening in mid-flight, the wooden griffin hurtling into the darkness.

CHAPTER 21

Kwint found himself lying facedown in the sand. Water lapped against his legs. He slowly rose to his feet and spit sand from his mouth. *Where am I?* he thought. The dwarf looked up to see a steep cliff stretching into the sky. "Great Hurverick's axe," he muttered, "I'm on the island." Kwint remembered the lightning strike and looked himself over. He smiled. "Hah. I'm alive!" His grin quickly vanished. *Where's Griffin?*

He turned to the sea behind him. The waves had calmed, and the sky was a clear blue. Kwint began walking along the shore. Large piles of seaweed were strewn along the narrow beach between the cliffs and the island's edge. Unusual orange birds with long tailfeathers scavenged the seaweed for food. As two birds searched a large pile of seaweed a few paces in front of him, a dark hand reached out of the green mass, sending the birds flying into the distance. Kwint slowly backed away.

"These blasted birds!" exclaimed Naymeira, pulling seaweed from her hair.

Kwint breathed a sigh of relief. "Thank Hurverick!" he said.

"Curse Droma, you're still alive," she said, allowing a smile as Kwint helped her up from the seaweed. "Where's Griffin?"

"I was hoping you would know," said Kwint.

"Not unless Griffin is a bird."

"Well, a griffin is... Oh, never mind ya, we have to find him."

The dwarf and the elf made their way down the beach. "Why am I helping you anyway?" Naymeira asked. "You left me in a cage."

"We had to make sure you were different from the others—the other bandits. Besides, you need us."

"Oh really?"

"Oh yes. Someone as delicate as yourself needs some protection."

Naymeira elbowed Kwint in the shoulder. "I hope you're being sarcastic, dwarf. Still, I may need an ally."

"Allies, you mean."

"Yes, if we find Griffin."

"He's alive," said Kwint.

"Perhaps, but if the storm didn't get him, the pirates..."

"He survived," Kwint interrupted. "He always seems to."

Footsteps. Guards. Patrol. One large, one smaller. Bo'cul refused to let his eyes open, continuing the illusion of his slumber.

"Is Strond asleep?" asked the large guard.

Bo'cul's ears pricked up as he heard the heavy breathing

of the smaller guard peering into his cell. "Aye, poor bull. In a few days, he won't be waking."

"Don't tell me you're sorry about the stinkin' prisoner's execution! It's long overdue. He's been rotting in that cell for months, and he hasn't said a word. Eag's toe! I can smell him from upstairs. The least we can do is give him to the gods, and leave him for them to judge."

The guards lumbered away, laughing. When he was sure that he heard no more footsteps, Bo'cul dared to open an eye, then another. He sat upright, his gleaming, red eyes welling with golden tears, staining the ground below him. He glanced around to make sure no one was watching, as if anyone would be. As if he cared. As if it mattered...

"Lad, it's very simple. You don't have the gold, you don't get the horse." With a superior look very apparent on his face, the red-haired horse master stared down at young Griffin Blade. "Sir, please. Quah is only a few days away on horseback. As soon as I have the money, I'll be sure to—"

"I'll have no more of this! I'd be a fool, indeed, if I let myself do business with children such as yourself. Be gone! Go bother someone else!"

His head bowed, Griffin left the stable, closing the door behind him. He had entered the village of Cana the previous evening, and as soon as he had awoken that morning he had decided he needed a horse. He couldn't possibly make it to Quah on foot. Griffin had tried to reason with the horse master, but he hadn't counted on the man's stubbornness.

As Griffin left the stable, a young boy who had been tending to a horse ran up behind him. "Yegir give you a hard time?" asked the stableboy. Griffin nodded. "If it makes you feel any better," the young boy continued, "you're not the first beggar to come looking for a horse."

"I'm no beggar."

The stableboy looked Griffin up and down. "Your clothes tell a different story."

Griffin was covered in mud, and his clothes were torn in many places. "So I'm a little dirty," he admitted.

"And you smell like rotten fish," said the boy.

Griffin sighed. "I guess I see your point."

The stableboy smiled and raised an eyebrow. "Why do you need a horse so badly anyway?"

"I need to get home. I need to get to Quah." He looked down at his filthy clothes. "It's been a long journey."

The stableboy's smile disappeared, and he was quiet for a moment. Then he spoke. "Meet me here in a few hours, after the sun has set. I'll take you to Bordertown. It's the largest city in the area, and you might find passage to Quah from there."

"Thank you. Thank you so much," said Griffin, shaking his hand before they parted ways. After taking a few steps, he stopped and turned around. "I'm Griffin Blade. I didn't get your name."

"Saiof," said the boy. "Saiof Kelgen."

"I'm grateful, Saiof Kelgen. You didn't have to do this."

The boy shrugged. "Maybe there are still some good people around."

Griffin awoke to find his hands tied with coarse, brown rope. He was riding in a wagon and noticed that it was being pulled by two large red jungle cats. A demon was holding the reins in front. His back looked entirely human, but when he turned to face Griffin, a sharp yellow beak was revealed.

"Ah, good!" the bird-demon shrieked in a high-pitched voice. "The prisoner is awake." Griffin turned to see that he was surrounded by exotic trees. He could hear wild and unsettling sounds coming from above him. He was on the island. The shadow of a charcoal black volcano loomed before him. Soon, the demon pulled hard on the reins, and the wagon came to an abrupt stop. They had arrived at the base of the dark monolith.

"Get out, prisoner! This is where you will be spending your few remaining days." The demon kicked him. "Stand up!" Griffin was led to a stone fort built into a side of the volcano. "Now," said the bird-man, "we don't want you finding your way out, do we?"

Griffin was blindfolded with a foul-smelling rag and led into the fort. After a long walk, his hands were untied, and he heard the sound of a door clanging shut behind him. Griffin removed his blindfold. He was in a jail cell, and he wasn't alone. A white minotaur sat hunched in the corner, surrounded by golden stains.

CHAPTER 22

"This is useless, dwarf. Griffin obviously didn't wash up on the beach like we did. We would have found him by now."

Kwint only grunted.

"Look," said Naymeira, "I see it like this: Three things could have happened to Griffin. Either he made his way to the island, was found in the water and most likely captured by pirates, or he drow—"

"He didn't," said Kwint flatly.

Naymeira sighed and sat on a boulder at the base of a cliff. "There is a myth back where I come from," she said quietly, staring at the sand. "It is said that whenever someone is born, the Eomorian god—the dark elf god, Nuel, god of fate—rolls a pair of dice. The roll determines the child's character, friends, accomplishments... and when he will die." She turned her gaze to Kwint. "What I'm trying to say is, perhaps Griffin simply had an unfortunate roll."

Kwint looked toward the sea. "What do ya think we should do?" he finally said.

"I say we climb."

They both turned toward the cliff. The endless stone wall seemed to accept their challenge.

The minotaur barely acknowledged Griffin's presence. He often sat motionless, bent over with his massive bull head in his hands, as he stared at the floor. With his head bowed, the beast's faded golden horns pointed straight at Griffin, who stayed silent until he felt safe enough to ask a question.

"How long have you been here?"

The beast didn't look up. Instead, he simply motioned— with a huge hand at the end of a muscular arm—toward the wall. At first, Griffin didn't understand, but then he saw the scratch marks. Hundreds of them. Griffin estimated that the minotaur had been living in the cell for almost a year.

"Do you know where we are?"

The minotaur thought for a moment, then nodded.

"Can you show me?"

The creature rose to his feet. Griffin noticed that they were enormous hooves—and that the beast was nearly seven feet tall. He watched as the minotaur's eyes scanned the room, looking for something. They landed on a corner of the room, where a pile of dirty rags lay, gathering dust. He rummaged through the pile until he found the item he sought—a discolored piece of parchment. The minotaur picked it up and turned it over to reveal a map of the Four Seas—the Sea of Emrad, the Sea of Lalanel, the Sea of Ye'vel, and the Jagamaur Sea. He pointed a sharp fingernail at a chain of islands in the north of Emrad—the Stinging Isles. The northernmost island was called Galgavor.

Griffin sighed. He felt no less lost than he had been before seeing the map. "Where are you from?" he asked.

The minotaur pointed toward a larger island much farther south—the Isle of Olaylador in the Sea of Lalanel—and specifically to a valley known as the Veiled Kingdom and a city called Kyne.

Griffin raised an eyebrow. "Kingdom? A minotaur kingdom?"

The minotaur nodded.

"But you're a demon..."

The beast grunted and gave Griffin a look of disgust.

"No, by that I mean... I thought demons..." He was interrupted by another grunt. "... I thought your kind was separated into tribes, not organized kingdoms."

The minotaur shrugged, as if to say, "Most are."

After a short silence, Griffin asked, "How did you end up here? Why?"

No answer came, just a deep sigh. Griffin sensed that his cellmate was also unjustly imprisoned.

"Do you miss your home?"

Now only a single tear was the reply, dripping from the beast's eye. Griffin remembered the golden stains that dotted the floor. He moved closer until he could feel the minotaur's warm breath on his face. There was something about him. He couldn't quite figure out why, but he felt as if they were joined in some way. It was as if their fates were somehow interwined. He later wondered why he so quickly felt the urge to say it, but he leaned in and vowed, "I promise you that I will find a way to get you home."

129

"If that ugly bull had stayed home, he wouldn't be stuck in this cell with you!"

Griffin whipped around.

"Remember me?" There stood the albino merman, his arms crossed, his expression amused. Griffin was too shocked to reply. "I sure hope you do. You may recall your elf friend foolishly attempting to hurl a knife at my throat."

"Where is she?" asked Griffin.

The merman smiled. "I assume she drowned."

"And the dwarf. What about him?"

"Floating lifeless, too, I imagine. A miracle you survived, actually. You're a lucky man, Mr... I'm afraid I haven't had the pleasure of learning your name."

"Blade. Griffin Blade." He figured the information didn't matter at this point. "And I haven't had the displeasure of learning yours."

"Blade? Like a sword?" The demon's eyes sparkled with interest. "Well, Blade, I just thought you'd like to know that your friend did me a favor. Since the captain of the ship was killed, I got both his portion of the gold and mine. I've now accumulated enough money to buy a ship and a crew. Remarkable vessel. Been sailing for at least a century. Bought it off a man named Maragroth Nanda. It had been part of his family for generations, so it cost me extra." The merman paused. "So you can just call me Ranimus Poratia, Captain of the *Cyclops*."

CHAPTER 23

Kwint grunted and groaned as he slowly climbed the cliff face. Naymeira, meanwhile, climbed at a much swifter pace, finding hand holds that hadn't first been apparent to Kwint. When they were nearly halfway to the top, Naymeira shouted down, "C'mon, dwarf. You live in the Kni Hmun Mountains. By Droma, you live on the tallest of them!"

"I don't climb the mountain! We have lifts!"

"Well, there is a first time for everything, isn't there?"

Kwint sighed and tried to climb faster. He came to realize there was no winning an argument with Naymeira. Kwint nearly lost his footing a few times—and then he actually did. Naymeira had just finished the climb, and he was only a few feet from reaching the top when his feet found only air. Kwint's feet dangled, as he attempted to find a foothold and failed miserably. It didn't help that the ledge that Kwint was holding onto was slippery, almost slimy. Kwint was able to lift his head enough to see the yellow goo of a bird's egg crushed in his hands.

"Naymeira!" cried Kwint, as a bird called in the distance, flying toward the dwarf as fast as it could. "Naymeira!"

The bird landed on the ledge. It looked at the ruins of its nest, at Kwint and finally at the dwarf's hands, covered in the remains of an egg. The bird shrieked, then began pecking at Kwint's left hand furiously.

"Naymeira! Help! Now!"

Kwint's left hand let go of the ledge, as he relied on all of his dwarven strength to grip tighter with his other hand. But that hand was slowly slipping, too.

"Hold on!" shouted Naymeira.

"I'm... doing... my... best," Kwint grunted through clenched teeth. The bird turned its attention to Kwint's other hand. It shrieked and began to peck once again.

"Grab my hand!" Naymeira leaned down as far as she could. Kwint let go with his right hand... just as he grabbed Naymeira's hand with his left. She pulled him over the ledge, as the bird shrieked once more and flapped away.

As Kwint and Naymeira lay panting on the ground, she said, "You're heavier than I expected."

"It's my big brain," Kwint smiled. "And the ale."

"How did you end up in this cell?" asked Griffin.

Bo'cul lifted his eyes, took a long look at his questioner, then showed Griffin the map again.

"I don't understand."

The minotaur pointed to a small ship drawn next to Lalanel.

"You were on a ship."

Bo'cul nodded.

"Are you a pirate?"

Bo'cul vigorously shook his head.

"A sailor?"

He shrugged. *Somewhat*, he seemed to say.

"Were you traveling somewhere?"

The minotaur nodded again and pointed to a town called Kalac on the coast of another island named Gongrel.

"Why were you traveling there?"

Bo'cul was unsure how to explain...

"Your new friend Bo'cul Strond was the captain of a Lalanel trading vessel called the Hardmarrow." Griffin spun around quickly to find Captain Ranimus standing behind the bars of the cell once again. "Not a bad trader either. I hear the deck of his ship was overflowing with all kinds of precious cargo. Nice ship, too, so they say. It was burned to a crisp with its crew still onboard."

Griffin could see Bo'cul clenching his fists tightly.

"He, however, survived somehow," added Ranimus, pointing to the minotaur. "Today, he's getting what he deserves."

"For defending himself against an attack?" Griffin asked.

Ranimus ignored him. "Unless, of course, our friend says otherwise. What do you say, you putrid bull? Do you want an execution?"

Bo'cul only glared back at him. Hatred seemed to gush from his body. Ranimus shrugged and turned back to Griffin.

"I don't hear any complaints."

"I'll ask again," said Griffin. "Why execute him? He's a trader, not a pirate."

Captain Ranimus's mouth widened into an evil grin. "Exactly."

Griffin had no reply.

"Strond, come with me," said Ranimus, returning his attention to the minotaur. "And don't even think about running. We have guards stationed everywhere. Unless you'd prefer a more... unofficial execution. I think it will be better for everyone if we do it in the proper manner, don't you agree? I mean, what else is a mountain of fire good for anyway?"

As two guards bound Bo'cul, Ranimus proceeded to describe in excruciating detail the manner in which the minotaur's life was going to end. As the cell door closed with a clang, Bo'cul Strond and Griffin Blade met eyes one last time, before Ranimus led the minotaur down the dim corridor and to his almost certain demise.

Griffin sat on his filthy mattress and listened to the footsteps echoing down the corridor. Then he stretched out, resting his head on an even filthier pillow, and closed his eyes. He wanted to help somehow...

"Here, put these on, and hurry," said Saiof when young Griffin returned. He tossed Griffin a green tunic and a black cloak, his other hand resting on the back of a silver mare. "We need to be quick about this. If Yegir finds out..."

The stable boy climbed onto the horse and motioned for Griffin to do the same. "Hold on." Saiof grabbed the reins. "He-yah!"

The two boys rode through the night and across the expansive plains, the silver mare speeding like a shooting star in the darkness. In the early light of morning, they arrived on the outskirts of Bordertown, where Griffin dismounted. He looked up at the stable boy who had helped a stranger.

"Thank you," he said. "For everything."

Saiof smiled. "Good luck getting home."

He waved goodbye and turned the horse. "He-yah!" Griffin heard as the silver mare sped back toward Cana.

CHAPTER 24

"There," whispered Naymeira. "If that isn't a prison, it sure should be."

The elf and the dwarf crouched low in the underbrush at the base of the volcano as they watched the stone fort intently.

"All right," Naymeira continued, "here's the plan—"

Kwint grabbed Naymeira's shoulder. "Wait. Are we just going to assume that Griffin is in there?"

"No. That would be ridiculous," Naymeira replied, and she pointed to a short goblin with a long pointed nose who was patrolling the fort's perimeter. "We're going to ask him."

Kwint nearly laughed. "Ask him?"

Naymeira nodded. "What do pirates need more than anything?"

"A bath?"

This time Naymeira stifled a laugh. "No. Riches."

"Well, that's one thing dwarves and pirates 'ave in common. But what does that 'ave to do with asking?"

"One word: Bribery," said Naymeira.

"Bribery? We have nothing to bribe the blasted demon—."

"We do," Naymeira interrupted. She reached into a pocket and pulled out something that sparkled in the sun.

Kwint gasped. "A diamond! You had that the whole time?" He looked curiously at Naymeira. "I thought Droma was the god of greed."

Naymeira shrugged. "My father once told me that the best sort of greed is the hunger for generosity. Or something along those lines. Maybe today I'm feeling particularly generous."

She looked at Kwint. What was that look on his face? Admiration? She coughed uncomfortably.

"Good for you," said Kwint, coughing himself. "But what are we supposed to do, just walk up to him?"

Naymeira thought for a moment. "You stand over there, in the open. When he's distracted, I'll come up behind him. That's when I'll show him the diamond."

After a few moments of grumbling, Kwint stepped into the open, just before the goblin rounded the side of the fort. The demon was shocked to find a dwarf in the middle of a demon island. And a dwarf just standing there, no less.

"Wh-what are you doin' here?" The goblin fumbled for a weapon and began to shout for other guards, but Naymeira rushed up behind him and placed a hand over his mouth and a sharpened stick against his throat. She held the diamond in front of his pointy nose, and his eyes widened considerably.

"You want it?" she asked, and the demon nodded. "Just answer a few questions. This is a prison, is it not?" The demon nodded again. "Does there happen to be a human prisoner?" Another nod.

Naymeira removed her hand. "What's his name?"

"Er... somethin' like Falcon Sword..."

"That's Griffin Blade," said Kwint, and the goblin nodded his head vigorously.

"Is there any way to get into the prison without walking through the front door—some way to... not be seen?" Naymeira asked.

The goblin eyed Naymeira for a moment, but then his eyes were drawn again to the diamond. "Well, there is an entrance to the cellar. It'll get you closer to the cells if that's what you fancy." The demon pointed to a small entryway next to the building. "It's right over there"

"That'll work," said Naymeira. "Now, if I give you this diamond, will you remember any elf or dwarf who just happened to sneak by the guard?"

The diamond glinted, and the demon grinned. "What elf? What dwarf?" As Naymeira handed him the jewel, he added, "What guard?" And he sprinted into the jungle.

"I'll bet you my life savings that there isn't a loyal demon on this island."

"Too late. I think you just gave that away," said Kwint, and he caught a hint of a smile on Naymeira's face.

CHAPTER 25

Griffin awoke to the sound of shuffling footsteps outside his cell. In the dim torchlight he saw the shadow of a guard rushing down the corridor. Then he heard the unmistakable sound of something blunt striking somebody's skull, followed by a body crumpling to the stone floor. A sword was unsheathed.

"What's going on over there?" It was a guard's voice.

Another sound now—a sword being plunged into a chest, then a few moments of gurgles and groans, finally a collapse to the floor.

Griffin heard the jangle of keys, soon followed by heavy breathing outside his cell. A hand slipped a key into the lock, and the door opened with a click. Into his cell stepped two familiar faces, Kwint holding the top half of a wine bottle and Naymeira wielding a guard's sword.

Kwint grinned and tilted the bottle in his hand. "Shame to waste this."

Griffin leaped from his bed and rushed to the open cell door. "You're alive!"

He grabbed Kwint in a bear hug and then instinctively turned to Naymeira, intending to do the same. She held up a hand to stop him.

"How did you find me?" Griffin asked.

"A lucky guess," Naymeira replied.

"And now that we 'ave found ya," said Kwint, "we can get off this blasted rock."

Griffin hesitated. "Not until we find Bo'cul."

"Who?" Naymeira and Kwint asked in unison.

"Bo'cul Strond. He was my cellmate—briefly. He's a minotaur, a demon, but... not really. There's something about him... They're going to execute him, and I can't let that happen."

Naymeira looked dumbfounded. "You're going to risk your life saving someone you just met?"

Griffin shrugged. "You just did."

"Even so," she replied slowly, "trying to prevent a demon execution sounds like..."

"Suicide," Kwint offered.

"I'm saving the minotaur," said Griffin simply. "You're free to go if you'd like. It has been an honor and a pleasure to know you."

Kwint clenched his hand into a fist, then grabbed Griffin by the shirt. "Blast it, Blade! You know I couldn't do that!" He paced back and forth for a few moments. "Fine! I'm with you."

Griffin gave a knowing nod. "I figured as much." He turned to the dark elf. "Naymeira?"

She took a deep breath, then exhaled. "Fine, but I better live through this." And then she rolled her eyes upon noticing that look of admiration again, this time in Griffin's eyes.

"First," he said, "I think there is a weapon storage room somewhere near here. We need to go there."

"But we took swords from the guards," said Naymeira, holding up her blade.

"If we're going to save Bo'cul, I suspect there's another weapon I'm going to need."

The three companions found the weapons room, grabbed what they needed, then exited the prison along the same route that Naymeira and Kwint had entered it—through the wine cellar. They jogged deep into the surrounding jungle and made their way to a clearing, where they stopped to consider their options and formulate a plan. Naymeira wore a dagger in her belt. She carried a long sword in one hand and a pile of cloaks in the other. Griffin had managed to find a crossbow and a short sword. Kwint wielded a two-handed axe, but he carried it in one hand because the other held a couple of bottles of wine, which he had swiped from the cellar.

"Let's return 'ere," Kwint said, hiding the bottles under a bush, "after making a mockery of this execution."

"Who exactly is the executioner?" asked Naymeira.

Griffin simply pointed toward the volcano looming above them. He then motioned to the cloaks. "Let's put these on. Hide your faces. It's a long way up, and we have a short time to get there."

Moving quickly along the road that led through the city and wound its way toward the volcano's peak, the cloaked-and-hooded trio attracted little attention. A parade of demons seemed to have the same destination in mind.

"Looks like executions are a form of entertainment," Griffin whispered to Kwint. "At least we know we're not too late."

Finally, they arrived at an entranceway that led into a great amphitheater of sorts, a semicircle of stone steps where the demons could sit and watch the spectacle. They were all standing, their faces tinted red and sweating profusely because far below them was a pool of bubbling lava. Opposite them, hovering over the lava, was a plank protruding from what appeared to be a locked iron gate. On that plank stood Bo'cul, his hands bound together. He was being taunted mercilessly by the demons.

"What in Hurverick's name..." Kwint muttered. He spotted two hideous ogres behind the iron gate, their hands grasping a very large, oddly-shaped crank attached by a chain to the plank. "They're going to pull the plank in! That'll leave nowhere for the minotaur to go!"

"Except down," said Naymeira, eyeing the boiling lava.

"We cannot let that happen," said Griffin, and he pointed to a narrow walkway that led around toward the iron gate. "Let's move. Try not to attract any attention. Act like you're supposed to be here."

Just then, a horn sounded. It sounded ominous.

CHAPTER 26

Ranimus stood on a balcony above the execution area, facing the crowd. It was tradition for newly-appointed captains to oversee executions, and he was taking particular delight in it. He motioned for the audience to quiet down and then began:

"My fellow demons, if you have come here today to watch this prisoner melt before you, to see him plummet to a fiery death, to revel in his doom, you are in the right place at the right time!" The demons shouted and jeered, then Ranimus continued, giving a dismissive wave toward Bo'cul. "This bull has been given too much mercy! Today, we correct that mistake. He is charged with—"

Ranimus was interrupted by a demon covered in matted fur with tusks protruding from a disfigured face. He whispered something in the captain's ear, then pointed wildly at three hooded figures approaching the ogres behind the iron gate. Ranimus eyed the figures with suspicion. Then, as one of them glanced to a side, his face briefly illuminated by a torch protruding from the wall, Ranimus snarled. *Blade.*

I underestimated him, he thought.

"Stop them!" he shouted. One of the two ogres turned and unsheathed a large broadsword. Kwint and Naymeira drew their weapons in response.

"Retract the plank!" Ranimus ordered. The other ogre focused his efforts on the crank. As he began to turn it, Griffin looked at his crossbow. *Can't use that yet,* he mused. Instead, he brandished his short sword and charged forward with his friends.

Ranimus looked nervously at the crowd, which shouted with glee when, a moment later, he declared, "Four executions instead of one!"

But the trio was too quick for the sluggish ogre. Naymeira dodged the demon's sword and slashed at his arms, while Kwint ducked and aimed his axe at his tree-trunk legs. Soon, the ogre dropped to his knees, bloodied. That's when Griffin aimed his sword at the demon's neck. The ogre fell in a lifeless heap.

They turned toward the second ogre, who was grunting and groaning as he poured every ounce of strength into turning the heavy crank. Griffin glanced beyond the ogre and saw that the plank was disappearing. Bo'cul had pushed himself against the iron gate, balancing his weight on only a few feet of rotting wood above the bubbling cauldron.

The ogre stopped his efforts and reached for a broadsword of his own. But Naymeira was faster. She threw her dagger, and the ogre froze and collapsed, the dagger's handle protruding from between his eyes. Kwint pounced on him and finished the job.

"Nice aim," said Griffin, as he grabbed a large key from the ogre's body and quickly unlocked the gate. He pulled Bo'cul back, cautiously stepped out onto what was left of the plank and pulled out his crossbow, as the assembled demons roared and snarled.

"Escape is impossible," shouted Ranimus from the balcony above. But then he saw Griffin load a bolt into his crossbow. There was something odd about the weapon. When Ranimus realized what it was, his eyes opened wide. Bo'cul glanced at the weapon, saw the rope tied to the end of the bolt, and grinned in understanding.

"I hope this works," said Griffin. He aimed the crossbow into a dark cavern beneath the stone steps of the amphitheater. He pulled the trigger, and the bolt disappeared into the cavern until it suddenly straightened and tightened. It had latched onto a large boulder in the darkness. As a group of angry demons began to make their way around the amphitheater toward the execution area, Griffin tied the other end of the rope to the iron gate so that it now stretched tautly above the blistering lava. He pulled out what appeared to be a very dull, slightly bent blade and handed it to Bo'cul, whose grin grew wider. The minotaur used all his strength to bend the blade further, then hooked it over the rope and grabbed each end. He nodded to Griffin, who grabbed Bo'cul by the waist. Then Naymeira wrapped her arms around Griffin's waist, and Kwint did the same to Naymeira. Just as a slobbering horde of demons approached from behind, Bo'cul pushed off and the four companions slid down the angled rope, which was starting to burn in a few places.

"It won't hold!' shouted Kwint, who was barely holding on himself, his feet nearly singed.

"It will!" Griffin replied.

"It won't!" cried Kwint.

Thwack! The foursome crashed into the boulder, Bo'cul absorbing most of the blow. As they lay sprawled in the darkness, Griffin turned to Kwint.

"See," he said, helping the dwarf to his feet, "it did."

They heard the slightly muffled sound of a crazed horde of demons in the amphitheater behind them. What they didn't hear above the din was the voice of Captain Ranimus.

"Release the lava dams!" he ordered, and then he smiled. "It's time for you to die, Blade."

"If it just wasn't so dark. I can barely see my hand in front of my face," said Griffin. Bo'cul grunted in agreement. The two of them were following Kwint, who had experience wandering through mountain caves. At a brisk walk, he led the companions though the darkness with his voice. Rather, he led Griffin and Bo'cul.

"Naymeira, don't ya go rushing ahead!" Kwint called.

"I am a dark elf, dwarf. Shadow is my friend," she said.

"Aye, but these shadows can trick ya," he said. "Ya might hit your—"

Just then, Naymeira cried out in pain. Moments later, Kwint bumped right into her as she stood in the darkness, rubbing her bruised scalp. The four of them paused.

"Let's try to think this through," said Griffin. "Kwint, do you think they use these caverns for anything in particular?"

The dwarf shrugged, though it was too dark for anyone to see it. "I'm not sure, but as we hovered over that volcano—too close to it, I might add—I did notice a sort of ramp leading down from the molten rock. I think I saw a smooth wall at the top of the ramp, to hold in the lava, I suppose, probably some sort of—"

All at once, the four of them noticed that the darkness of the cave was now only a dimness, and it was growing ever so brighter by the second. Kwint realized it first, and his eyes nearly popped from his skull.

"A lava dam! They must have opened it! Run!"

The four of them raced through the dim light of what they now knew was a lava tube through the mountain. The light continued to grow brighter and brighter, so they could see the way in front of them. However, that brightness was caused by a river of lava fast approaching behind them.

They continued to sprint forward, yet still it gained on them, and soon Kwint began to tire.

"Look! An exit!" shouted Naymeira, pointing to an opening through which daylight was pouring.

"Go on without me!" yelled Kwint, lagging behind.

The dwarf closed his eyes, preparing to be engulfed in liquid death, but then he felt himself being lifted onto the shoulders of a minotaur. The exit grew closer, as did the lava. When it was right at their heels, they reached the opening and leaped forward.

And they fell.

CHAPTER 27

As they plummeted, each of the four had time to notice the water toward which they were dropping, and each was smart enough to formulate the same plan. Upon splashing into the deep pond, each dived deeper in attempt to escape the heat of the lava pouring onto the surface of the murky water. Once they were deep enough, they swam toward the water's edge as hard as they had run. Naymeira made it first and crawled onto the sandy shore. Griffin was right behind, and they lay panting in the sand.

Griffin lifted his head. "Where are the others?"

Suddenly, a large mass of wet hair that only vaguely resembled a minotaur's head broke the surface of the water near the shore. Moments later, a dwarf popped up, his drenched beard stuck to his forehead. After Bo'cul and Kwint reached the sand, Kwint struggled to his feet.

"Ya saved my life. I will not forget this," he said, and he bowed to the minotaur.

Bo'cul shook his head and replied with a slight bow of his own to each of them, as if to say, *Neither will I.*

"We did it," said Naymeira. "We actually did it."

"Of course we did!" said Kwint, slapping Griffin on the back. "What now, my boy?"

"We should—" Griffin was interrupted by a loud hissing, as clouds of steam rose from the pond while lava continued to pour in. "We should get somewhere safer."

They ran deeper into the jungle until they found their way to the same clearing where they had stopped to plan Bo'cul's rescue.

"The good news is that Ranimus surely thinks we're dead," said Griffin. "The bad news is that I'm rather certain we need to find Ranimus."

His three companions looked at him, speechless.

"I'll explain," said Griffin. "But first, we should set up camp for a while, build a fire, find some food. I don't think we'll be spotted beneath this jungle canopy."

When the fire was burning high, the group sat around it, nibbling on a small supply of berries they had collected. Griffin began to speak. First, having learned his lesson about keeping secrets from friends, he described to Bo'cul their adventures so far and what they had learned about the four Gems of Power.

"The Sister Jewels," he said. "I don't quite understand it myself, but I feel as if I'm being called to find them—to find the one that was taken from me—and I feel like... I was drawn to the three of you in that attempt." He shook his head. Words failed him.

"I think I understand," said Kwint. He looked at Naymeira and Bo'cul, and both seemed to nod in agreement.

"I think we were drawn to this island, Galgavor, by the black jewel, the Ungornem Gem, the gem of darkness," Griffin continued. "And I think I know where it is. I believe we'll find it on a ship called the *Cyclops,* and Ranimus, that foul merman, happens to be the new captain of that vessel."

His three companions were silent. Kwint twisted his whiskers and stared at the ground. Naymeira rubbed her temples. Bo'cul peered into the fire. Then all three looked back up at Griffin.

"So what's the plan?" asked Naymeira.

Griffin thought for a moment. "I'm going back into the demon city. I'm going to find out where the ship is located."

"You'll be seen!" said Naymeira.

"Trust me. If I don't wish to be seen, I'm invisible. I'm going."

Naymeira rose to her feet. "Not without me, you're not."

"You need to stay here. Um, protect Kwint and Bo'cul."

Now Kwint shot to his feet. "Protect us! We can protect ourselves, thank ya very much," he snorted.

"See?" said Naymeira. "They'll be fine. And besides, I'll bet I'm even better at hiding in the shadows than you are."

Griffin held up his hands in surrender. "All right, all right." He turned to the dwarf and the minotaur. "Stay safe. Naymeira, let's go."

The human and the elf were soon swallowed by the darkness. Kwint plopped back down next to the fire and then noticed something shiny under one of the bushes. He pulled out one of the wine bottles that he had stashed there. Kwint stared at it in his hands and then noticed that Bo'cul was doing the same. They looked at each other and grinned.

CHAPTER 28

Naymeira and Griffin trudged through the jungle, their cloaks gradually drying off as they moved through the tropical air. "So let me make sure I understand you correctly, Griffin. We're looking for a ship called the *Cyclops*..."

"We are."

"And it's captained by Ranimus..."

"It is."

"And you think that's where we'll find the black jewel..."

"I do."

"And you believe this gem will lead you to another gem, which was stolen from you..."

Griffin nodded.

"And you learned all of this from an ancient—"

"From an old book protected by a blind gnome who can whittle, yes."

Naymeira placed a hand on Griffin's shoulder. They stopped walking. "Tell me why these gems are so important."

"I can't say for certain," said Griffin, "but I think they can shift the balance of power in Alastian."

"And you want this power for yourself?"

"Well... no. I wanted the jewel—for the money. At least, at first I did. But now... I'm not sure anymore. Maybe it's just curiosity. Maybe it's something more."

Naymeira stared at him for a moment. Then she shrugged and continued walking, shouting over her shoulder, "Well, that's good enough for me. Let's go find a ship."

They soon arrived at the edge of the jungle, where they took a deep breath, hid their faces in the darkness of their hoods and strolled into the city.

"Where are we going?" Naymeira whispered.

"To a tavern, preferably the first one we see. Alcohol makes one loose of tongue."

They heard the tavern before they saw it—bursts of chaotic shouting and laughter and the clinking of glasses. The building was brimming with demons of all kinds, from massive ogres to mangy boarmen. An ogre lay sprawled across a wooden table, unconscious. A goblin was in a heap in a corner, either passed out or dead. A couple of trolls were arguing, spitting and drooling as they did so. All reeked of alcohol and trouble.

"Just keep your face hidden. Stay inconspicuous," said Griffin. "Let's see if we can draw any information out of them."

Naymeira wandered toward a handful of ratmen, while Griffin moved in the opposite direction, finding a stool between a sitting goblin and a standing centaur.

Between hiccups, the goblin was rambling. "I'm tellin' ya, if them mainlanders aren't already melted puddles o' flesh, they will be soon!"

The centaur absent-mindedly took a swig of ale, half of which ran down his face. "You saying something?" he belched. His eyes looked as empty as his glass.

Griffin, his face hidden by his hood, muttered under his breath, "What about Captain Ranimus?"

The goblin called for more ale. "What about him?

"Captain! Captain, my backside..." The horse-man released a short burst of gas.

"Got 'im a real beauty of a ship, too, I hear," snorted the goblin. "Sigh... sigh something..."

"*Cyclops,*" muttered Griffin, hunched over a glass of ale that he was pretending to drink.

"Well, whatever it's called," said the goblin, thinking the centaur was speaking, "she's a good 'un."

"Wonder where he keeps her..." said Griffin, barely moving his lips.

The goblin snorted. "Ya don't know, horse-man? The merman ain't exactly secretive 'bout it. Keeps it in some cove on the Fang."

The centaur spat on the floor. "'Course I knew that, you stupid pile of muck, why wouldn't I?"

"Thought you was the one who asked, you scabby half-breed!"

Griffin slowly slinked away, leaving the demons to their squabbling. He met up again with Naymeira in a corner of the tavern.

"It's at a cove on something called the Fang," he said. "All we need now is a map."

Naymeira glanced over Griffin's shoulder. "I think I just found one, but you're not going to like it."

Griffin turned and spotted a bare-chested ogre standing in the middle of the tavern. A very precise outline of the Stinging Isles was tattooed on his back.

"All right," said Naymeira, taking a deep breath, "all we need to do is find an island in the shape of a fang, I suppose. How hard can that be?"

At that moment, in walked a rhinoman—a stocky, gray skinned creature with a massive yellowing horn protruding from his snout. One of his broad shoulders brushed against the tattooed ogre, who roared, "Hey, watch it, horn-nose!"

The rhinoman whirled around. "Who you calling horn-nose, you green load of lard?" He spat in the ogre's direction—with perfect aim. A blob of yellow spittle ran down the ogre's cheek.

"I'm going to rip that horn from your nose and stick in your ear!"

The ogre picked up a wooden chair and hurled it toward the rhinoman, who ducked. The chair smashed into the bar, sending splinters flying in every direction and patrons scattering. Griffin and Naymeira shared a glance. *Of course, why should this be easy?*

They tried their best to stay behind the ogre, searching the map on his back for a semblance of a fang. But the rhinoman rushed at the ogre, his horn aimed at the beast's chest. The ogre sidestepped the charge and grabbed the rhinoman, as both fell to the floor. While the two demons traded punches on the floor, rolling around in a blur of green and gray, Griffin and Naymeira were unable to get a glimpse of the tattooed map for any longer than a few seconds at a time.

Finally, the bloodied rhinoman staggered to his feet and backed up against a wall. The ogre rose and marched toward him, never realizing that a couple of cloaked figures were trailing intently behind. When the ogre cornered his opponent, he stood there for a moment, grinning and drooling, just enough time for Naymeira to notice something.

"There," she whispered to Griffin, "near his right shoulder blade."

Griffin squinted and nodded, just as the ogre balled his massive hand into a fist. The two cloaked figures slowly backed out of the tavern, leaving behind an unconscious rhinoman and a badly bruised ogre in a foul mood.

Upon slipping back through the jungle, they returned to find Kwint laughing on the ground and Bo'cul dancing around the embers of the campfire with a wine cork stuck to each of his horns.

"Griffin, my boy!" Kwint exclaimed. "Just in time. I think we 'ave a drop more of Gongrelian Red if you'd like to try some" The dwarf motioned toward one of the empty wine bottles scattered in the dirt.

"It looks as if you've already had that," said Naymeira flatly.

"Oh, that I 'ave. Great stuff it was!"

"From one drunk to the next," said Griffin to Naymeira. "Are we the only sober ones on this island?"

"What were you thinking, Kwint?" asked the elf through gritted teeth. "We're stranded on a demon island, fugitives from some sort of horrific form of justice, and you think this is the time to dull your senses?"

Kwint rose to his feet, slightly unbalanced. "Given what you just explained," he said, "I think dulling my senses makes some sense after all."

Griffin rushed toward Kwint, looking as if he were going to strike him. The dwarf flinched and raised an arm in defense. But Griffin stopped, breathed deeply, and put a hand on his friend's shoulder. "Kwint, I appreciate your support throughout this, and you don't have to be a part of it if you don't want to. You know that. But we found out where the *Cyclops* is located, and if we're going to take that ship, you need to be at full strength." He turned to Bo'cul. "We all need to be."

As the minotaur sheepishly removed the wine corks from his horns, Kwint placed his hand over Griffin's. "I'm sorry, Griffin. My apologies, Naymeira. I suppose I needed a distraction from all we've been through. Bo'cul, too."

Griffin straightened. "A distraction, huh?" He looked again at Bo'cul. "I think a minotaur is a fine distraction."

CHAPTER 29

On the northeastern shore of the island of Galgavor stood a rickety pier surrounded by a few dirty old buildings on the outskirts of a fishing village. A handful of boats were docked in the area, most of them fishing vessels, although two pirate warships were among them. Very few demons walked about, and those who did avoided making eye contact with anyone else. From their perch high on a cliff above, the four companions studied the lonely pier down below.

"Please don't tell me I 'ave to climb down that again," Kwint groaned, having sobered up enough to have an aching head. "I nearly died the first time."

"No need," said Griffin, and he pointed to a narrow, stone stairway carved into the cliff and leading downward on a diagonal slope. Even with the stairs, the journey down took a while, in part because the steps were so steep at times that a step down was more like a climb down—at least for the dwarf. Bo'cul seemed to be at ease.

"Have a lot of high places like this where you come from, Bo'cul?" asked Griffin.

The minotaur nodded slowly.

"Well, we'll find a way to get you home," Griffin added.

Kwint looked up from below them, as they continued their descent. "About that," he began. "Bo'cul and I kind of talked about it. That is, I talked and Bo listened. Well, he didn't just listen. He—"

"I know what you mean, Kwint."

"Well, anyway, Bo wants to travel with us. He's had enough of a life at sea, isn't that right, Bo?""

The minotaur nodded once again.

Griffin smiled. "We could use someone like you," he said. "Welcome aboard!"

Bo'cul began to laugh at Griffin's unintentional joke, and soon they were all laughing. The traveling band of misfits had grown one minotaur larger.

The group hid behind a massive boulder on the edge of a pebbled beach. Griffin brushed away enough pebbles to create a flat, sandy area. "All right," he began, "here's the plan."

He grabbed a twig and drew a couple of lines in the sand. "This is the pier." He drew a much larger, fang-shaped island. "This is the island. We should find the *Cyclops* in a cove somewhere around... here. When the sun begins to set, we'll borrow one of those smaller fishing boats—"

"Borrow?" asked Naymeira.

"He's being polite," Kwint grinned, and Bo'cul chuckled.

Griffin continued, "Bo'cul, you're going to board the *Cyclops* first. Distract the crew as best you can." The minotaur nodded, and this time Kwint chuckled. "While their attention is diverted, Naymeira and I will board and find the gem..."

"What about me?" Kwint asked.

"Oh, Kwint. You have the most important job."

"And that is?"

"You're our lookout."

Kwint sighed, and now Naymeira let out a little laugh. "That's your brilliant plan? Sounds rather simple to me."

"Oh? I suppose I forgot to mention how I was planning to sink Ranimus's ship."

"How?" Kwint and Naymeira asked in unison.

"Well, I forgot to mention it because I haven't quite figured it out yet."

And so the companions waited in silence as the sun slowly disappeared into the sea—all except for Kwint, who kept muttering, "A lookout! A blasted lookout!"

When evening came, four figures—including one who was small and one who was unusually large—found their way onto a fishing boat and quietly set sail for the Fang.

Standing on the Northeast Pier, Ranimus scanned the darkening horizon and spotted a fishing boat that appeared to be heading straight for the Fang. "What are they doing there?" he muttered. Then louder, so that the assorted crewmen around him could hear, he announced, "Those are restricted waters! No one goes on that island until the *Cyclops* sets out." He looked around in frustration. "Give me a boat. I'll teach them a lesson myself."

"You can take my ship, Captain!" a scaly humanoid with the head of a viper yelled from the deck of a boat docked nearby.

Ranimus looked at him distrustfully. "How much do you want?" They were pirates, after all.

"What do I want? Why, it's reward enough to serve a pirate captain like ye'self—"

"Enough false flattery! I'll ask once more: How much?"

The viperman shrugged. "A quarter of any loot you get, that'll do."

Ranimus laughed dismissively. "One-tenth."

"One-fifth?"

"One-tenth. You are giving me a ride, not a treasure map."

The viperman hesitated, then sighed. "Yes. Deal."

"There's a smart demon," Ranimus muttered sarcastically, and then he yelled to the handful of crew members nearby, "Come on, fellows! Let's show those pathetic fishermen what happens to those who wade into pirate waters."

As the crew boarded the viperman's borrowed ship, Ranimus noticed its name: the *Predator*.

The cove wasn't exactly hidden. It was merely difficult to find if you didn't know what you were looking for. Griffin only remained in the line of sight of the *Cyclops* long enough to peer through a small brass telescope at the ship.

"I don't see much activity," he said. "I'll bet most of the crew hasn't boarded yet. There may only be a handful of demons aboard."

"Then that's a stroke of luck for us!" Kwint exclaimed.

Griffin simply stared toward the cove. "We shall see."

Naymeira and Bo'cul approached. "How are we to get Bo'cul onto that ship?" asked the elf.

"Given the darkness and their small crew at the moment," Griffin mused, "I suppose we can try to maneuver our way alongside them."

Bo'cul grunted and shook his head.

"You have a better idea, Bo?" asked Kwint.

The minotaur nodded and made a wave motion with his massive hands.

Naymeira was puzzled. "What is he trying to say?"

"Isn't it obvious?" said Kwint. "He wants to swim."

"All the way there?" Naymeira looked skeptical.

"Can you make it?" Griffin asked. Bo'cul actually looked offended, and Griffin shrugged. "Sounds like a good plan to me. It'll add to the element of surprise."

After Griffin maneuvered the boat a bit closer, Bo'cul strode to the side of the boat and peered down at the choppy waters.

"Bo'cul?" The bull turned to Griffin. "Still tipsy?"

The minotaur simply smiled and dove.

CHAPTER 30

Yalf Seabreath, ratman and first mate of the vessel, waited impatiently at the bow of the *Cyclops*. He exhaled and muttered, "Where is that Ranimus?"

At that moment, a goblin ran up to him and pointed sternward. "Sir! You should see this."

Yalf's jaw dropped, as he spied what seemed to be a wet mass of hair swiftly climbing a rope attached to the ship's anchor.

"Is that... is that a...?"

The goblin squinted into the darkness. "Looks like a minotaur, sir."

Bo'cul rolled onto the deck of the *Cyclops,* rose to his feet and pounded his chest. He roared at the sparse demon crew, spittle flying in all directions. As the goblin stepped backwards, Yalf drew his sword.

"Intruder! To arms, demons! To arms!"

Two goblins were the first to attack with pathetic bronze daggers. Bo'cul managed to pluck the first goblin off his feet and hurl him toward the rest of the demons, scattering them.

He simply kicked the other goblin, his hoof crushing the demon's chest and sending him flying as well. The goblin landed in a small galley, knocking over a pot filled with embers. The deck quickly caught fire, and the blaze began to spread.

Bo'cul roared once more, this time into the moonless night sky. The flames grew behind him, transforming him into an imposing shadow with glowing red eyes. The crew, too distracted to notice a small fishing boat approaching in the darkness, grew braver, attempting to corner Bo'cul. They inched forward, while the minotaur inched backward toward the fire.

A daring but dim-witted ogre lunged toward the minotaur with his broadsword. Bo'cul easily parried his attack, just as Naymeira hopped aboard the *Cyclops,* followed quickly by Griffin. A series of clangs followed as iron bit iron. The sluggish ogre was no match for the fast-moving elf. She jumped, twirled and struck his oversized forehead with the flat of her blade, knocking him unconscious.

"I've got your back," she said to Bo'cul, who grunted an acknowledgment as the two of them charged forward.

Griffin glanced around the ship. *Now, where would they keep a gem on the* Cyclops? His eyes widened. *Of course!* The growing flames aboard the ship illuminated the ship's prow, a fearsome design that showed the bald head of a giant Cyclops... with one black eye. Carefully, cleverly, he maneuvered his way across the boat, avoiding the fire and the swordfight.

As he headed toward the bow of the ship, Griffin heard a loud crack. He looked up to see the ship's burning mast falling toward him. It collapsed onto the deck, narrowly missing Griffin. A troll wasn't so lucky. A cloud of sparks flew into the night air, and a wall of flame arose that could not be passed. Griffin's options were quickly dwindling.

Meanwhile, aboard the fishing boat, Kwint was impatiently gripping the wooden handle of his axe and watching the battle unfold. "A blasted lookout," he muttered to himself. "As if there is anything else to look out for..."

For a second, he turned his attention once more from the fiery activity aboard the ship to the darkness of the surrounding sea. But it wasn't all dark this time. "Look out!" he shouted, as he spotted a pirate warship slicing through the water. "They can't even 'ear me," he muttered. He gripped his axe more tightly and boarded the *Cyclops*.

By now, Yalf Seabreath was the only pirate still conscious aboard the ship. In front of him was a wall of flame. To his left stood an angry minotaur. To his right, an elf pointed a blade in his direction. He turned, sprinted as fast as he could, and jumped into the sea.

"Smart one," said Naymeira.

Kwint came running up. "Bo, Naymeira, a pirate vessel is coming this way! Where's Griffin?"

The trio spent the next few moments avoiding the flames and searching the ship. Kwint finally found Griffin clinging to the bow. He had a dagger in his teeth, and he was making his way toward the Cyclops's eye.

"Griffin!"

"A little... busy... at the moment... Kwint." He grunted and slowly kept climbing.

"Another boat is approaching! What are ya doing?"

"Gem… is in… Cyclops… eye," Griffin said, the dagger in his mouth muffling his words.

"Ah, why didn't I think of that?" Kwint said. "But what about—"

"Stop… bothering… me!"

Griffin arrived at the cyclops's eye, held on with one hand and used the other to grab the dagger from his teeth. He began to pry the black gem from its socket. "Stick to the plan!" he shouted to Kwint.

"But what if you can't—"

"Just do it!"

Kwint ran to Bo'cul and Naymeira, who followed him down into the ship's hold, which was starting to smoke as the deck fire continued to grow. The dwarf lifted his axe, aimed for the floorboards, then turned to face his companions. "Are you ready to sink this evil ship?"

Ranimus, seething with anger at the sight of his ship awash in flames and his crew unconscious or missing, was the first to board the *Cyclops*. A crew of eleven demons followed him, one of them daring to ask, "What do we do now, Captain?"

The merman whipped around, wild-eyed. "The ship is lost," he said through clenched teeth. He pointed to the fishing vessel. "But the traitors who destroyed her remain. Find them! We will return to the mainland with their heads mounted on spears! We will hunt them down—to the bottom of the ocean if we must!"

"No need," said Kwint, emerging from the bowels of the ship, "although you'll be there in a few moments."

When Naymeira and Bo'cul came into view, Ranimus's jaw dropped.

"You! You're alive? How is that poss—"

Before he could finish the thought, Bo'cul took a great leap forward, landing just in front of Ranimus. He threw a punch that landed squarely in the demon's albino face, knocking him to the deck.

"Let's go!" shouted Naymeira.

The *Cyclops* began to creak as water gushed onto the deck from below, and the ship began to sink into the sea. As the pirates tried to aid their fallen captain, Kwint, Naymeira and Bo'cul leaped overboard. And not a moment too soon. With a great *crack,* the *Cyclops* split nearly in two. The stern went down first, quickly disappearing beneath the waves. As it did so, it caused the bow to rise vertically, spilling the pirates into the water.

"Where's Griffin?" asked Kwint, as he treaded water alongside Naymeira and Bo'cul. All looked frantically around them, seeing only darkness and a quickly sinking ship.

"There!" shouted Naymeira, and she pointed to the burning ship as the bow made its last gasp before falling below the waves. A shadowy figure seemed to be clinging to the prow of the *Cyclops* with one hand. The other hand was clutching something.

CHAPTER 31

Just before the ship went down, Griffin dived into the water and made his way to his companions.

"What now?" asked Naymeira, as the four of them treaded water.

Griffin spat out some salt water. "Let's see if we can get to the ship that Ranimus and his crew sailed here. Then we'll get as far as possible from this place."

By now, the wreckage of the *Cyclops* and the remaining pirates were drifting away from the *Predator,* which was closer to Griffin and his mates. They made their way to the boat and managed to climb onto the ship's deck. It was empty, save for a terrified ratman at the wheel who dove into the sea at the sight of Bo'cul coming aboard. As the few pirates who were still alive—some injured and all disoriented—splashed around in the water a short distance away, the four travelers worked feverishly to prepare the boat. Bo'cul pulled up the anchor. Kwint and Naymeira set the sails. Griffin gripped the wooden-spoked wheel. As they set off, they heard a low groaning sound that seemed to be echoing from the water.

"What in Hurverick's name is that?" Kwint asked.

The groaning sounded intense, almost desperate. It soon became clear that it didn't come from one source. A dim green light began to shine from the water where the pirates flailed about, and the light grew brighter by the second. Griffin watched as the pirates began to shout in confusion and panic. Then the creatures surfaced—scores of giant jellyfish transforming the cove into a nightmare of an otherworldly shade of green.

"By Droma..." Naymeira muttered.

"Why did they come now?" Griffin wondered.

Bo'cul noticed a full bottle of wine that had been left on the boat and stomped on it, creating a pool of red liquid. He then bent down and took a good whiff of it, as if to say...

"The jellyfish. They sense blood in the water," Kwint translated. "Bo, you could have saved the wine..."

Screams echoed in the darkness as some demons were stung in dozens of places, while others were pulled under the waves after being ensnared by jellyfish tentacles.

The foursome continued to navigate away from the horror, wincing as they heard cries of pain behind them but sailing in silence. It wasn't until the lights of Galgavor were only tiny dots in the distance that Kwint finally muttered, "I hate the sea."

The water was a jumble of colors—the blue of the sea, the green of the jellyfish, the red of blood. Ranimus could only see through one eye; the other had been swollen shut by a jellyfish's sting. He had been lucky that only a smaller jellyfish had attacked him and lucky, too, that he was so comfortable in the sea. He had managed to free himself from the creature's grasp and made his way to the surface some distance away.

With his one good eye, he spotted the fishing trawler that Griffin and his friends had... borrowed. Unlike the sinking *Cyclops,* it was surrounded by only sporadic and smaller green creatures. He swam toward it, and when he reached the hull, he heard a gurgling and felt a thrashing beneath him. He looked down, and there was the viperman who had given him his ship for a price. He was struggling with a jellyfish, clawing toward the surface in an attempt to free himself and find air. Ranimus just smiled malevolently and stepped on the viperman's face, pushing him into the murky depths below while gaining the foothold he needed to climb onto the boat.

As he sailed from the cove, leaving his crew to their fate, he thought of the *Cyclops* resting at the bottom of the sea and the interlopers who had caused it to sink. His smile faded.

"Look there!" shouted Naymeira. "Land! The mainland!"

"Oh, thank Hurverick!" Kwint cheered, the green of his face already diminishing.

The first night, they had slept, letting the wind take them farther west. The companions had awoken to find Griffin standing at the prow, the wind blowing his hair, his eyes closed. In his hands he held the Ungornem Gem.

"Feel anything, Griffin?" asked Kwint.

His eyes opened. "Actually, I think I do. It's a very slight shift in balance. Hard to explain, really."

"In which direction?"

"West."

"And you think the Hiamahu Jewel is in that direction? Somewhere?" asked Naymeira.

"Yes. I think. I hope, at least."

"Well, that'll have to do," Kwint shrugged.

The wind was with them, and only two days later they spotted the mainland, although it was not particularly inviting. It was a bleak landscape of gray and brown rocks with only the occasional shrub emerging. Griffin studied the land and frowned.

"Bo'cul, can you fetch that map you found in the weapon hold?"

The minotaur, who was standing next to Griffin and eyeing the black jewel curiously, nodded and returned with a map of the coastline. He pointed to a specific spot beneath two words in bold demon handwriting: "Mulgarian Barrens." Above it, a skull and crossbones was hastily scrawled. Griffin scanned the coastline for the nearest town.

"There," he said. "It's toward the southwest a bit more. Firstport, it's called."

Kwint grinned. "Can't wait for my feet to touch the mainland." He sighed and watched the coast disappear behind him.

CHAPTER 32

Captain Genthus marched up and down the Seawall, disciplining his men when necessary. A young guard, no older than 15, his face dotted with pimples, called him over.

"Captain! There is something on the horizon, sir!"

"Let me see for myself," said Genthus, snatching a telescope from the guard's hand. He peered into the distance for a moment and then stepped back, startled. "A warship," he muttered, his mouth suddenly dry. "And flying a pirate flag!"

It had been years since a pirate vessel had come this close to Firstport, but Genthus sprung into action. "Men, ready yourselves for battle!" He turned to the young guard. "Lad, you must alert the council!"

The boy nodded. "I will at once!"

There was a brief pause. "Then why are you talking to me?"

The boy nodded again and took off running.

"Ready the ballistas!" Genthus bellowed. As soon as the command was given, dozens of ballistas were rolled onto the edge of the Seawall. "We hoped this day wouldn't come, but we've been preparing for it, men of Firstport! Like the

Demon Wars years ago, pirates arrive at our city once again. But have no fear, my brothers! This time we are ready!"

Genthus spun the telescope in his hand, looking down at it and admiring the fine craftsmanship. He then placed it against his left eye once more. "Ready! Fire!"

A wave of massive bolts flew into the air in a perfect arc, like an army of wooden seabirds diving in unison into the blue waters. *Let's see how these pirates treat their splinters,* thought Genthus.

A peaceful moment on the seas ended abruptly as a couple of wooden bolts thundered onto the ship's deck, knocking everyone off their feet. Large splinters of wood were catapulted through the air, one of them narrowly missing Naymeira.

"Why are they firing?" she shouted.

Griffin looked up and winced. A black flag showing a red fist of fire flapped in the wind atop the ship's mast. "We're flying a blasted pirate flag. We need to get it down. Now!" He began lowering the flag, but a large splinter of wood had caught in the pulley. The rope was stuck.

Griffin pointed up toward the flag. "Bo'cul, can you do it?" The minotaur nodded and began climbing. "Kwint," Griffin continued, "find a white bed sheet!"

As Kwint ran to the ship's cabin, Bo'cul began climbing the mast, muscling himself ever higher. Another wave of bolts soared toward them, a larger wave this time. Several bolts tore through the *Predator*'s sails, reducing them to tatters. A few more crashed into the ship's hull. One bolt whizzed past Bo'cul's ear as he climbed.

Kwint returned to the deck and handed the sheet to Griffin. He rolled it into a ball, climbed part of the way up the mast, and heaved the sheet up toward Bo'cul, who barely managed to reach down and grab a corner.

"Hurry!" shouted Naymeira. "One more wave, and the ship is sure to crumble."

With his last ounce of strength, the minotaur inched himself slightly higher. With one hand, he tore down the black pirate flag, replacing it with the white bed sheet. A white flag, a flag of truce.

Bo'cul slid back down, and the four companions waited. The only sound came from the wind whipping through their tattered sails. And they waited some more. Another wave of bolts did not arrive. Instead, soon after, two ships sailed up beside them. Men in chainmail jumped aboard and surrounded the misfit crew.

"Please," said Naymeira. "We can explain..."

Kwint's face grew red with rage. "We're not giving up without a fight!" he yelled, but he could barely do so as his hands were held behind his back.

A guard stepped forward. "By order of Captain Genthus Nyrn, you are arrested and are to be brought to the Council of Firstport for judgment."

Griffin sighed, but he said nothing as he and his companions were roughly escorted off the ship.

"From one cell to the next, eh Bo?" said Kwint.

The minotaur glared. They were all in a single cell, although it was a large one, much nicer than the prison on Galgavor.

"How did we get into this mess?" Kwint wondered. "We just angered a whole island full of demons. We should be welcomed with open arms, not tossed into a jail cell. And all because Griffin forgot to take down one little flag—"

"What do you mean *Griffin* forgot? You could have remembered the flag!"

"Oh, ya don't have to feel bad about it, Griffin. We've all made dumb mistakes…"

Griffin took a couple of lunging steps toward Kwint. "You're making one now, my friend. We were sailing a blasted pirate warship! Should I have used the bedsheet to cover that up, too?"

"Oh, so we're doing this now?" asked Naymeira. "If I had to blame anyone, it would be him." She pointed toward Bo'cul, and his red eyes widened. "By Droma, he's a demon! He's the one who should have known better. We almost got killed saving this bull, and now look at us!"

Naymeira, Kwint and Griffin began shouting at each other, and it went on for a while until Bo'cul released a deafening roar. The cell grew silent. The minotaur motioned to the cell's bars, and the companions turned to see a tall man who was watching them with interest. He removed his helmet, revealing long, blond hair. The man's face was stern and his posture that of someone in command. The guard eyed Bo'cul suspiciously and turned to Griffin.

"What's your name?" he asked loudly.

Griffin looked the man over. "Are you… Genthus Nyrn?" he asked softly.

Genthus nodded. "And I asked your name."

"He's the fool who ordered our arrest! Don't tell 'im anything!" Kwint shouted.

Griffin raised a hand to silence the dwarf. "Nonsense, Kwint. Let's be rational." He motioned to his friends, one by one. "The small dwarf with the big mouth is Kwint Kwinhollow. The minotaur is Bo'cul Strond." Bo'cul grunted. "And she is Naymeira... Naymeira..." He suddenly realized he had never bothered to find out the rest.

"Darkleaf," she said. "Naymeira Darkleaf."

"And I," Griffin gave an exaggerated bow, "am Griffin Blade."

"A very... unusual group you are," said Genthus. *Not very pirate-like,* he thought, *except perhaps the bull.*

"Aye," said Kwint. "What do you mean by it?"

Genthus shrugged. "A human, an elf, a dwarf, and a minotaur. Your story must be... unique."

Griffin stared at Genthus, as if judging him. Then he smiled. "Would you care to hear it?"

"No, Griffin! You cannot just tell him everything!" Kwint's face reddened.

"And why not?" asked Griffin. "The best course of action here is to tell the truth." He grinned mischievously. "As you know, I am a horrible liar."

CHAPTER 33

Griffin did, indeed, tell Genthus the truth—at least, most of it. He told him where they had been and where they hoped to go, but he left out the details about the gems. When he was finished, the Captain of the Firstport Guard remained silent for a while before speaking.

"I believe you," he finally said. "But others won't. You see, Firstport was originally part of the Southern Kingdom. Long ago, we were constantly attacked and raided by various pirate vessels from the Stinging Isles. The king refused to send any solders to aid us in our time of need, so the people of Firstport declared their independence from the Southerners, even adopting the Northern Tongue, just to spite them."

"What did you do about the pirates?" Griffin asked.

"We drove them off, but they returned, and then again, and again. We call those dark years the Demon Wars. Firstport was prepared for their final assault, however. We transformed our dam into a defensive wall that we call the Seawall, and we constructed a fleet of ballistas in an effort to drive the pirates away for good. And it worked. But we have begun to suspect that their return is imminent. The people of Firstport, including myself, still hunger for vengeance. And when you came along, well, we were ready. And in your case, I fear that a taste of victory and vengeance will be far more powerful than a sense of justice."

"So what will happen to us?" asked Naymeira.

"You will be brought before the Council. They will decide your fate."

"Then I suppose," said Griffin, "that we'll just have to convince them of our innocence."

Genthus shook his head. "You won't be able to. They have been waiting too long—we have been waiting too long to bring justice to the pirates who slaughtered our ancestors."

"Then all hope is lost," said Kwint.

Again, there was a long silence. "No, there is one way," said Genthus, as Griffin raised an eyebrow. "You have to give them what they want. Play the part of a nasty bunch of pirates."

"But they'll execute us!" cried Kwint.

Genthus simply smiled. "I will convince the Council to give you a crueler punishment—to send you away, back to the Stinging Isles as a warning for the demons not to return to Firstport."

"But we can't possibly go back there!" said Naymeira, and she was seconded with a grunt by Bo'cul.

"You won't. You said you wished to travel west, yes?"

Griffin nodded. "I... think so."

"You would be heading for an unforgiving place." He paused again. "But I will help you. I can provide you with enough rations to last a few weeks and send you in the appropriate direction."

"You can do this? You would do this?" asked Griffin.

"I would, and I think I can."

The four companions glanced at each other and shrugged. *We have to trust him.*

"Thank you for your kindness, but couldn't you just inform the Council of our innocence?"

Genthus sighed. "Maybe. But as I said, they probably wouldn't believe me."

"I sense a different reason," said Griffin.

The Captain of the Guard closed his eyes. "It is petty, perhaps, but you are correct. I ordered your arrest. I can't just go defending you. Think of how it will look to my subordinates! We rely on loyalty and leadership. Our lives depend on it."

It was Griffin's turn to sigh. "I think I understand. Very well, Captain Nyrn. We accept."

The men of the Council of Firstport appeared ancient. Wrinkles crisscrossed their faces like worn maps, and long gray beards grew from their chins like cobwebs. The Council Room was shaped like a huge slice of pie, and the seven council members were situated in a corner where two walls met, sitting in throne-like chairs on a platform raised a few feet above the floor. A large assembly of angry citizens filled the chairs in the remainder of the room, as it widened into an almost cavernous section.

Captain Nyrn guided Griffin and his companions to the center of the room, bound together by heavy chains. The citizens yelled and swore at them. The council members simply frowned down at the human, elf, dwarf, and demon in front of them. The leader, a rather short fellow named Hipthar, rose from his seat and slowly walked up to Griffin, using a wooden staff for balance. He raised it and pointed it at Griffin's head.

"At the end of my staff," he declared, quieting the room down, "stands a criminal, a dirty pirate who cares nothing for justice. He—"

"If I may interrupt you, councilman," said Griffin with a smile, "at which end of your staff?"

A handful of people in the crowd erupted in laughter, although far more responded with threats and epithets. Hipthar scowled and began to shout as best he could over the din, "These four rogues are accused of an attempted attack on the People's City of Firstport! How do you plead?"

"Guilty!" shouted Kwint, as he tried to step toward the Council. The guards responded, roughly pulling the dwarf back to his companions. Bo'cul roared when Genthus neared him, although the Captain of the Guard could have sworn he saw the minotaur allow a hint of a smile.

Hipthar grinned, revealing twisted, yellow teeth. "Their guilt," he said, speaking slowly, "is obvious and cannot be in dispute. They arrived at our city in a pirate vessel, flying a pirate flag, and with a demon on board!" He looked at Bo'cul and spat at his feet. "The question is... How are these criminals to be punished?"

"Behead them!" someone shouted.

"Send them to the bottom of the sea!" a woman cried.

"Do both!" a man yelled.

The crowd seemed to like that idea. Genthus coughed loudly and held up a hand to silence the crowd. "If I may make a suggestion..."

"Yes?" said a councilman who seemed even older than Hipthar. "Speak, Captain Nyrn."

Genthus cleared his throat. "Why not send them back?"

Nearly every person in the room gasped.

"What?" asked Hipthar, outraged.

"Hear my reasons," said Genthus. "What is our goal in Firstport? Is it vengeance, or is it peace and security? Let's send these vile bandits back to the Stinging Isles as a message to their fellow pirates, as a reminder of the impenetrable defenses we have constructed here, as a warning that no demon should come within leagues of Firstport."

"Are you saying we should allow them to live?" asked Hipthar.

"Nay," replied Genthus. "We all know what pirates do to those who bring them bad news." He placed his finger in front of his throat and made a slashing gesture, as the crowd murmured to each other. "I can assure you that the residents of the Stinging Isles can come up with far more brutal methods of execution than we can."

"You wouldn't!" Naymeira shouted. "No! Kill us! Drown us! But please... don't send us back!"

"Silence, demon elf!" shouted Hipthar, and then he turned back to Genthus. "How do we make sure they'll actually return? You don't contend that we should send them on their merry way and trust this pirate filth?"

"Some sailors and I will accompany them to a pirate outpost near the Mulgarian Barrens. We'll force them into a rowboat and leave them to their fate. They'll either die of starvation, which is a rather horrible death, or they'll be found by other pirates and wish they had died of starvation. Either way, we win."

Hipthar climbed back onto his platform and conferred with the other councilmen. Moments later, he banged the end of his staff three times on the marble floor.

"The Council of Firstport has agreed. You will set out in the morning. The faster we rid ourselves of this scum, the better."

The citizens cheered, and the Captain of the Guard led the foursome back to the cell. As the cell door clanged closed, Griffin whispered to Genthus, "The Mulgarian Barrens? I thought we agreed that you would help us find our way through the desert."

"It's the best I can do," said Genthus. "Frankly, I can't believe it worked. In your rowboat, I'll hide a few weeks worth of provisions and a small sack of gold pieces. You'll have to traverse the Barrens, but just travel west and you will eventually find the River Baj. Follow it northward. You may be able to find some assistance in one of the river towns."

Griffin exhaled, knowing he had no choice but to trust Genthus Nyrn. "If you're telling the truth, again I thank you," he said. "If you're lying… well, I hope you're telling the truth."

Genthus laughed. "I could say the same to you. This is the last time we'll be able to speak to each other, so good luck on your journey. May you find what you're looking for."

With that, he saluted and strode down the corridor.

CHAPTER 34

They watched from their rowboat as the Firstport ship disappeared into the fog. The thick mist combined with the continuous lapping of water to create an atmosphere both eerie and lonely.

Kwint broke the silence. "So, where do ya think Genthus hid the supplies?"

Griffin bent forward and knocked three times on the boat's floorboards. "It's hollow," he said, and he noticed a small metal ring protruding from a plank. Griffin pulled it, revealing a secret compartment. "There we are."

Inside were stored four large bags containing dried meat, bread, and a bit of cheese. They also found a handful of weapons and a small sack filled with gold pieces.

"He wasn't lying," said Naymeira, and Bo'cul nodded.

"Where's the gem?" asked Kwint.

Griffin reached in and retrieved a small leather pouch. Inside was the black gem. "He's an honorable man," said Griffin, replacing the floorboards. "Let's find a spot to go ashore."

The Barrens—it was an appropriate name. There was nothing for miles, nothing but sameness—a bleak, gray, rocky landscape. During the day they walked; at night, they found a place to sleep. They traveled west, as Genthus suggested. Fortunately, the Ungornem Gem seemed to be leading them in that direction, pulling them, almost magnetically. Everyone was quite curious about the odd gem, especially Bo'cul, who snuck glances at it when he thought no one was looking. They seemed to have enough food. They managed enough sleep to keep them going. Yet all four of them felt a constant unease. It was quiet. In the gray landscape the only sounds that could be heard were the crunch of their shoes on the ground and Bo'cul's heavy breathing.

The last night, they set up camp at the very edge of the Mulgarian Barrens. There, it seemed as if they were at the intersection of three distinct biomes. To the east lay the Barrens, as colorless as ever. To the north were the Southern Plains, an endless green and yellow grassland. And to the west was the Baj, a narrow but deep, twisting river. Beyond the river was another seemingly endless landscape known simply as the Desert of Waste. Griffin could sense that the gem was leading them in that direction. He stared toward the Plains, his eyes glazing over.

Naymeira watched him for a while and then moved closer to him. "What is it?" she asked. "Why do you stare?"

Griffin didn't speak for a moment, then he answered in barely a whisper. "That is where they took my father, where my life changed."

"And what of your mother?"

"I never knew my mother."

Naymeira let the silence sit for a moment. "My mother died when I was three, some incurable disease from the Far North..."

Griffin turned to face her. "And your father?"

"Never knew him."

They were quiet again for a while, each lost in thought. Finally, Griffin returned his gaze to the night sky. "Perhaps we are not meant to know what it is like to have a family."

Naymeira glanced for a moment at each of her three companions. "Perhaps."

With that, Griffin drifted off to sleep.

Bordertown linked two very different cultures, creating a distinctive culture of its own. Most of the residents wore clothing that was a mixture of simple Northerner fur and bright-colored, beautifully-patterned Southerner robes. Each building seemed to have its own unique architecture. Many had the sharp-peaked wooden roofs of the North, while others were square structures constructed from the sandstone bricks of the South. Merchants wandered the streets, pushing carts bearing items from all over Alastian.

Young Griffin ducked into an alleyway, avoiding all the new faces. He heard giggling coming from a building to his left. A single window was visible on that side of the home. He examined the alley and noticed a small box that was nearly empty, resting beside several rotten fruits and vegetables. Griffin quickly turned the box upside-down and pushed it under the window. Stepping up, he peered into the home.

A father and his young daughter were enjoying breakfast together. Nothing more, nothing less. Griffin watched with a blank expression. At least he thought it was blank until he felt a salty tear trickle down his face and into the corner of his mouth. At that instant a hairy hand grabbed him by the collar of his tunic, pulling him roughly off the box and onto the cold ground. A nasty-looking guard with a chipped front tooth glared down at him.

"What do you think you're doing, boy?"

Griffin began to sob. "Please, I didn't—"

"He's with me."

Griffin turned to see an odd man emerging from the shadows. His long black hair was combed back on his head—so severely that it almost looked painful. His mustache was dyed strangely red. Every few seconds his right hand twitched slightly. But his eyes twinkled with intelligence and determination, as if he were the only person in a tired land who was truly awake.

"Nifae! Blast it, you're involved with this little speck of trouble?"

The man glared. "Is that an impolite tone that I detect?"

The guard slumped his shoulders and released Griffin from his grip. "All right, carry on then. Whatever it is you were doing..."

The strange, twitching man watched the guard lumber away, and then he turned to Griffin. "What were you thinking, sneaking around an alley like that, peering into people's homes?"

Griffin didn't answer. Instead, he responded with a question. "Who are you?"

"I am uncatchable," Nifae replied, twisting an end of his bright red mustache. "The better question is who I'm not." He put a hand on Griffin's shoulder and led him out of the alleyway. "For instance," he continued, walking up to a portly merchant's cart confidently and swiping a bag half-filled with gold pieces, "I am not a rule follower."

Nifae opened the bag as they walked, tossed a few coins to a beggar slumped in a doorway, then placed the rest of the gold in the half-open satchel of a haughty-looking patrolling guard who was walking past them. Just then the stout merchant behind them looked around in a panic and shouted, "Who stole my bag of coins?"

Nifae thrust his hip into the guard's satchel, knocking it to the ground and spilling coins into the street. "Oh, I'm sorry. I—what's this? Why would a Bordertown guard have a bag of gold in his possession?"

The guard stooped to pick up the coins, as a crowd began to gather, shooting accusatory glances. The merchant pushed through them, towering over the unfortunate guard, and began shouting. Nifae grabbed Griffin by the elbow and slinked away.

"What I am," he said, "is a maker of chaos, an artist of anarchy, an architect of what the people see."

"What makes you... uncatchable?" Griffin asked, looking up at the man with newfound respect.

"Simple," he smiled. "I have all the power in the city... and the people don't even know it."

CHAPTER 35

Faveos was a sad, little village, a small collection of thatched huts strewn along the River Baj. It was far from civilization, and few there even understood the Northern Tongue.

"We need horses," said Griffin. "We cannot cross the desert on foot."

"Horses!" Naymeira laughed. "I think what we need are camels."

An older man with dark skin approached them. In a heavy Southerner accent, he explained, "You need scarabs."

Griffin thought he must have misunderstood. "I'm sorry, I don't—"

"Scarabs!" the man nearly shouted. He sighed. "Come. Follow."

He led them to what appeared to be a small stable, but the creatures inside were unusual and remarkable. They were great orange beetles as large as horses with heavy leather saddles strapped to their backs. The companions stood there, dumbfounded. Even Kwint didn't say a word.

"Scarabs!" the man grinned.

After a minute, Griffin spoke. "How much food do they need?"

The dark-skinned man shook his head. "No food. Only water."

"Where are we going to find that in the desert?" Kwint asked.

"They hold water. Store it. Like camels," said the man. "Will not need water for long time."

"We'll take four," said Naymeira before they could discuss it.

"Four?" asked the man, seeing only three of them. They had left Bo'cul at the outskirts of the village, hoping to attract as little attention as possible.

Naymeira held up four fingers and held out a handful of gold coins. The man nodded, his smile growing wider. To their surprise, he then opened the stable gate to allow four scarabs to scamper out. "Very calm. Well trained," he said. "Calmer than horses. Will not run."

Griffin and Kwint were hesitant about mounting the beasts at first, but when Naymeira boldly jumped atop one of them and the massive beetle seemed unruffled, they followed suit. They rode them around the stable for a few minutes, slowly gaining confidence. As they prepared to depart the village, Griffin asked the man about the Desert of Waste.

"Are there any sources of water? Any in the desert?"

"One that is known," came the reply. "In the desert's center. It is... oasis. We call it Mocon."

"Excellent," said Griffin, but the man shook his head.

"I warn you. There are stories. A creature." The three companions shared glances. "Beast of Sands."

"We will have one eye open at all times," said Griffin, grinning slightly as he thought of the gem he had retrieved from the *Cyclops*.

The man just smiled and bowed. "May scarabs serve you well."

"May our gold do the same."

During the day, they wished for the cold of night. When night arrived, they prayed for the heat of day. They were quite a sight, if there had been anyone there to see them—a human, a dwarf, an elf, and a minotaur riding upon bright orange scarabs. Over the course of the first few days, Griffin began to understand the desert's name. The Desert of Waste. A waste of space. The dunes seemed to roll in waves toward oblivion. A waste of beauty. The eastern portion of the Southerner country was filled with magnificent plains, lush woodlands, and quaint but often thriving towns. The western portion, however, was nearly uninhabitable. The companions saw no travelers besides the occasional group of tribesmen on pilgrimages north, most likely toward the Southerner capital of Bajuru.

"I wonder what they're heading there for," said Kwint, as he wiped sweat from his forehead. Bo'cul, who was riding alongside him, just shrugged.

As the days drew on and their water supply dwindled, Griffin began to wonder if the desert was also a waste of time.

They approached a particularly large dune, and he brought his scarab to a halt. He slumped forward, his head in his hands, as his companions' scarabs scampered alongside his.

"What are we doing here?" Griffin suddenly shouted, sitting straight up. "We could die of thirst in this forsaken place, and all for what? Do we even know where we're going? Or why? Or what will be there? Roland's in danger. He could be dead or dying. And what are we doing? We're riding beetles across this... waste."

"We've come this far, Griffin," Naymeira said softly. "We cannot give up."

"Oh? Watch me." Griffin launched himself from his scarab, landing knee-deep in the sand, then began to jog away, resisting the urge to look behind him. Naymeira prepared to follow him.

"Naymeira, no!" said Kwint. "He just needs a moment to calm 'imself."

The dark elf sighed. "Maybe Griffin's right. Perhaps we should not continue on..."

"No. We will go on." Kwint looked at Bo'cul and then back at Naymeira. "None of us 'as anywhere else to go, and ya know that."

Just then, the ground began to shake beneath them. Their scarabs began to look around in confusion, each digging into the sand as if to hide. But the shaking was coming from that sand.

"It's the dune!" Kwint shouted, and large fissures began to form in the sand.

"Griffin!" Naymeira screamed, just as the dune seemed to explode, launching them dozens of feet into the air. The scarabs landed on their backs, their legs moving frantically. Sand rained down on them like hailstones, half burying them. Through the swirl of grit, the travelers looked toward what had been a great dune, and their jaws dropped. A giant purple worm rose from the sand, eyeless but certainly not toothless, its cave-like mouth filled with dozens of sharp yellow teeth.

"The Beast of the Sands..." Kwint spat grit from his mouth.

Bo'cul roared, struggling to free himself from the sand, as the worm, longer than two pirate warships, turned its massive, grotesque head in his direction. He felt a hand beneath his arm, pulling him upward. It was Griffin, who whispered in his ear.

"I think it responds to sound instead of sight." He looked up at the bruise-colored serpent of the sands. "Don't even breathe loud. I have an idea."

He jumped into action, circling around the beast, running this way and that, screaming at intervals. Naymeira understood at once and began to do the same. Eventually, they both found themselves behind the worm, which was by now fully emerged from the sand. They did their best to stay at its back, shouting the whole time, and the grotesque creature began to move in circles, faster and faster, the circles growing smaller and smaller. Its gaping mouth grew ever closer and closer, chasing the two voices behind its twitching tail. When it was all too close, at the last moment, Griffin and

Naymeira each jumped to a side, and the worm clamped its spear-sharp teeth upon its prey. Crazed, it kept chomping and swallowing and chomping and swallowing.

Only it had caught its tail instead. By the time it slowed down enough to recognize—somewhere in its tiny serpent brain—the error of its ways, it was far too late. Its deafening roar faded into a moan, as a slimy, odorous mass of purple and red goo poured from its innards and stained the sand. Within minutes, the dead beast was already beginning to shrivel and bake beneath the desert sun.

Kwint stood wide-eyed for a few moments, and then he blinked a couple of times, as if trying to retain a grasp on reality. "Well, that just 'appened." He patted Griffin on the back. "Brilliant ploy, my boy."

Naymeira looked around. "Where are the scarabs?"

"Don't worry," said Griffin. "They're sand beetles. They'll probably just—"

The ground shook violently again, but this time a scarab gracefully crawled out of the sand, followed by three more. "They'll probably just do that."

CHAPTER 36

Just as the companions were beginning to doubt the existence of Mocon, Bo'cul spotted something in the distance. He pointed forward with a muscular, hairy arm and released a low grunt. As they drew closer, the travelers were stunned to see a grove of palm trees, green and inviting. The group had not seen any form of vegetation since Faveos.

Kwint was the first to jump off his scarab, and soon the others followed, sprinting toward the oasis, which included a large pool of water at the base of the largest palm tree. From a distance, the water appeared red as it reflected the desert sun, but up close it offered a blue-sky reflection. The foursome knelt at the water's edge and drank contentedly. The water was quite warm, yet endlessly refreshing. Their scarabs soon joined them.

After restoring their supply of water, they relaxed under the shade of the many palms that surrounded the pool. Griffin drew the Ungornem Gem from his bag and stood up. He held it in his hand, a curious look on his face.

"The direction it's leading us... I think it's changing."

"Which direction now?" asked Naymeira.

Griffin looked toward the sun and then back to the gem. "Almost directly north." He sat down again, resting his back against the trunk of a palm tree. "The fact that it's changing so rapidly suggests that the gem we're following is moving. And possibly with great speed."

"There are two gems whose whereabouts are unknown, correct? The Gem of Fire and the Gem of Light, yes?" asked Naymeira, running her fingers through the sand.

Griffin nodded, as Kwint raised his head from taking a sip of water. "Well, I sure 'ope it's the Hiamahu Jewel," he muttered. "I wonder who this bronze-fingered fellow is anyway... maybe the same person who snatched Roland."

"Perhaps he's just a common pickpocket," said Naymeira.

Griffin leaned his head back and closed his eyes. *Common pickpocket...*

Nifae allowed Griffin to be part of his street gang, and he made sure no harm came to him. The men of the gang were hairy thugs, and they didn't seem to like Nifae any more than the guards did. Like the guards, however, they couldn't and wouldn't do a thing about it. Nifae had contacts. He knew people. He understood how to exploit weaknesses, and he could be unmerciful when angry.

Griffin thought Nifae seemed kind enough, at least outwardly. He was easily amused and quick to laugh. A few days after their first encounter, Griffin grew curious about his skills. Ramyr Blade had been a pickpocket as a young boy and had reluctantly taught his son some of the skills. Nifae offered to elaborate further.

"What are the two most important elements of being a pickpocket?" he began.

Griffin thought for a moment. "Speed," he said. "And elegance."

Nifae looked impressed, briefly. "Right." The boy beamed, but Nifae continued, "If you want to be a common pickpocket, that is. Is that what you wish to be?"

Griffin's smile disappeared. "No."

"Good. Now, a talented pickpocket doesn't have to be fast. Speed can attract attention. Speed gets you noticed." Griffin nodded slowly. "Elegance is also unnecessary. Instead of quietly snatching something, there's nothing wrong with a good bump now and then. Be rough. Use their annoyance to your advantage. I often take what I want while apologizing. I'll show you. Watch closely."

Just then, a rather snooty-looking servant of some sort wandered by, his nose in the air and a bag of apples in his arms. Nifae rushed forward, straight into the servant, causing the bag to fall from his hands. Eight or nine apples bounced and rolled along the cobblestone.

"Watch yourself, street trash!" said the man.

"I'm so sorry," said Nifae, patting the servant on the shoulder. "Let me pick those up for you."

After gathering the apples and apologizing once more, Nifae walked back to Griffin. "Here," he said, tossing him an apple. "That wasn't the real treasure, though."

He held up an amulet and smiled. "Notice anything when I patted him on the shoulder?"

Griffin shook his head, biting into the apple.

"That is how it should be."

Sand flew into Griffin's face, wakening him from his daydream. He rubbed his eyes and scanned his surroundings, which were increasingly obscured by millions of grains of airborne sand that began pelting the travelers like tiny darts. In the distance, moving closer and closer, was a giant, brown sand tornado. It seemed to pick up more and more sand as it loomed larger. In the tornado's center, Griffin could spy some sort of dark shadow.

"Griffin!" Naymeira shouted over the wind. "Maybe the worm wasn't the Beast of the Sands!"

The palm trees swayed violently, their large leaves beginning to detach themselves and join the tornado's swirl. In only a few moments, the tornado was on the opposite side of the oasis pool, and there it suddenly stopped moving, hovering menacingly. There was a flash of red light from within, and then the sand exploded outward in a great circle. The companions covered their faces as waves of sand blew past them. When the sand cleared, all that remained on the other side of the pool was a man, or something like it.

His head and torso were normal enough. He had a tan, muscular body and fiery red hair streaked with gray. Below his waist, however, was just a floating swirl, a blur, a little cyclone where there should have been legs. His voice boomed from across the pool like a war horn.

"I believe you have something that is rightfully mine."

All was silent for a moment, as the creature's voice seemed to echo across the desert. He hovered for a while, then slowly drifted toward them, crossing the pool. The companions backed up to what remained of the large palm tree. Naymeira was the first to speak.

"We have nothing that belongs to you," she said.

"Not to me," came the booming voice, "but to my kind."

Kwint stood tall, as tall as possible, and cleared his throat. "And what kind is that?"

The creature's eyes flashed white, and he rose a few feet in the air. "I am a djinni! One of the djinn—seven immortal beings brought forth into this world!"

"A djinni?" said Kwint. "I've heard stories, but—"

"We speak for the land, and the land speaks to us," the djinni continued. "The gem you carry was entrusted to us by the land, and so it must be protected—until the land takes it back."

Griffin stepped forward. "The land entrusted it to you? What do you mean by that?"

The djinni lowered himself to ground level and sighed, and the companions felt a rush of hot air pass by their faces. "Thousands of years ago, seven djinn came into existence. To them was gifted four gems—the Sister Jewels, as they would later be called. At that time, the land had a soul, but the parts of the whole could no longer live in harmony. So the land separated its soul into four parts, and the power of its being was imbued in those four jewels. Its fiery passion was placed into the red gem, the Mizzarkh. Its cunning was placed into the blue gem, the Hiamahu Jewel. Its kindness and purity entered the white gem, the Anoelmenoh. Finally, no good can exist without its opposite evil, and that was placed in the black gem, the gem of darkness, the gem you currently have in your possession."

"Then why is it no longer in the possession of the djinn?" asked Griffin.

"Our mission was simple—to distribute the gems to the four dominant races of Alastian and to keep them as far apart as possible. The red gem was given to dwarves, the blue gem to humans, the white gem to elves, and the black gem to demons. But then, of course, some insolent fools had to go about creating organizations like True Shadow and Flame Web, as if they could possibly harness the power of the gems! Ha! One of the djinn, known by the name of Malamus, sided with True Shadow, and soon each djinni began picking a side. Two more joined True Shadow, and three supported Flame Web. The grand plan evolved into chaos."

Kwint counted on his fingers. "I thought you said there were seven."

The djinni hovered silently for a moment. "I am the last to decide. I needed to escape the chaos of civilization, and so I chose to flee to this forsaken place and have a nice long think."

"How long?" asked Kwint.

"Many of your lifetimes," he answered. The djinni's eyes flashed once more. "Now, I will have the gem, and you may continue on your way."

"And if we say no?" asked Naymeira, her voice shaking only slightly.

"Then I must take it by force."

Bo'cul stepped in front of Naymeira and roared, but the djinni merely flicked his hand and a gust of wind sent both the minotaur and the elf flying backward several feet. They landed with a thud in the sand.

"I am waiting for an answer."

"You've waited in the desert for centuries," said Kwint. "Ya can wait a bit longer."

The djinni glared down at the dwarf, and this time Griffin stood between them. "Let's calm down, all of us," he said. "What if we made an agreement?"

"No, not until I have the gem."

"Fine!" Griffin reached into his pocket and retrieved the black jewel. He held it out in front of him. "You can have the blasted gem!"

Naymeira gasped. Kwint moaned. Bo'cul looked particularly pained. But Griffin held his hand up to quiet them. The djinni had a curious look on his face.

"You are simply giving it to me?"

Griffin nodded, and after a moment of hesitation the djinni floated over and took it from his hand. He held it in his palm and observed it closely. "Yes. Yes. The Ungornem Gem. This has not touched one of my kind for a great many years." He returned his gaze to Griffin, his voice a bit softer. "You were speaking of an agreement?"

"Yes. The only reason we have the Ungornem Gem is because we are looking for the Hiamahu Jewel. We could use your help to find it."

The djinni studied Griffin's face. "Do you think me stupid? First, if I were to find the Jewel, I would take it for myself, as its rightful guardian. Second, I can sense that you are lying. I can see it in your eyes. What is it that you really want?"

"What I want is to keep the gems out of the wrong hands."

"No, that is what I want. What do *you* want?"

Griffin glanced at his companions and sighed. "What I want... what I want to do is find my friend. His name is Roland Silverbeard. He is a dwarf. He was taken by some shadowy figures in the Elder Forest, and I think the black gem will lead us to another gem and perhaps to him. Of course, I cannot be sure..."

For several moments, there was complete silence. Bo'cul brushed imaginary sand from his arms. Kwint slowly ran his fingers through his beard. Naymeira looked at the djinni, then to Griffin, then back at the djinni. Griffin merely stared at his feet, slowly lifting his eyes.

"Very well," said the djinni finally. "I would like to offer *you* a proposition. I will help you find your friend, but I—and I alone—shall decide the fate of the jewels." He looked at each one of them in turn. "I sense something about each of you. Integrity. Decency. Perhaps something more."

"I shall accompany you on your journey. You may call me Takal."

CHAPTER 37

The air began to cool as they made their way north. The djinni had no need for a scarab. He could match their pace easily enough. As they traveled, Takal and Griffin grew to trust each other, and Griffin revealed much of his tale—and those of his companions. After a couple of days they arrived at a disturbing sight—a small village of abandoned tents flapping in the wind, surrounded by lightly smoldering campfires. The sand crunched beneath their feet as they slowly made their way through the maze of tents.

"These are the tents of a Gocian tribe," said Takal.

"They sure left in a hurry," Naymeira remarked. "We saw some of these tribesmen traveling north before we arrived at Mocon."

As the companions left the tent village behind them, Takal said something to himself, though the others could hear him: "Something is about to happen. Chaos is brewing. I sense it in the wind."

By the next morning, the direction toward which the gem was taking them had shifted once more. Takal was leading them now. "We need to turn," he said, "toward the rising sun. To the east."

"East?" said Kwint. "By Hurverick, we're going in circles!"

"The gem-holders are moving east, and so shall we," said Takal.

As their travels continued, Griffin grew curious. "How did you know," he asked Takal, "that we possessed one of the gems?"

"The djinn are gifted with the ability to sense when one of the Sister Jewels is very near. It has to be very close, however, thus my powers are somewhat useless at the present—beyond what this gem is telling us."

"Who do you think has the gem? The Hiamahu Jewel, I mean."

"Almost certainly it is a member of True Shadow. Or Flame Web. They have fought over the gems for hundreds of years. I would imagine that one of them is in possession of your friend, as well."

"Might you have a guess?"

"True Shadow," said Takal, "is traditionally more sinister. I have mused on that often…"

"And might you suppose where they could be going?"

"Perhaps to the capital of the Southerners, to Bajuru. I have heard rumors that it is a True Shadow stronghold."

"And why would the Gocian tribes be traveling in much the same direction?"

"The answers to your questions," said Takal, "are unknowable at the moment. But do not concern yourself with the immediate. Time answers all."

"I fear," said Griffin, "that we are running out of time."

Later that afternoon, the desert ended abruptly at a lush, green expanse that proved a glorious relief from the parched desert. They had arrived at the banks of the River Baj. Bo'cul was the first to spot the city on the horizon, the late sun turning it into a great shadow. Tall towers and domes and minarets were surrounded by a seemingly impenetrable wall.

"Bajuru," said Takal.

As they drew closer, Griffin stopped suddenly. "Takal, Bo'cul, you will have to stay away from the city."

"No need for that," Takal replied. "The people of Bajuru are generally tolerant of others as long as they keep from causing trouble. A demon in the city is not as unusual as you might think."

"But what about a djinni?" said Kwint. "Surely, a creature who is half-man and half... swirl will attract unneeded attention."

Takal smiled and lowered himself to the ground, his sand tornado morphing into legs. A red Southerner-style robe appeared around him, along with leather sandals on his feet. "You were saying? Come, let us enter the city."

As the companions approached Bajuru's sandstone gate, a heavily-armored Southerner man shouted from the battlements above, "Halt! State your names and your business in the city!"

Takal cleared his throat. "I am Hilrak Vitali. The Northerner is Gonz Rackulb, the dwarf Laron Irontoe, the elf Cina Swiftdagger, and the minotaur Do'gink Mahun. We are a traveling band of mercenaries, hoping to find paid work in the city."

After a pause, the guard replied, "You can enter, but do not cause any trouble in my city. I have dealt with many mercenaries in my time."

The large gate creaked, and its two massive wooden doors opened to either side, revealing a city made almost entirely of sandstone and mud brick. The afternoon sun reflected off the buildings so that they appeared to gleam like gold.

"Bajuru is separated into four districts," Takal explained. "The area near the entrance is the Merchant District."

Shops and eateries lined the street, and the shouts of traders seemed to come from all sides. Kwint couldn't resist taking a peek inside every tavern that they passed along the way. Once or twice, Bo'cul had to grab his collar and stop him from entering. The sight of a demon might not have been all that unusual in Bajuru, yet many still seemed a bit uneasy in his presence. Several passersby hugged the other side of the street as he passed. Still, there were all types—elves, dwarves, an occasional goblin or ratman.

The vast majority, of course, were human Southerners, it being the Southerner capital after all. This became even more apparent as they started to explore the second district, the Residential District. It was much quieter, and the occasional glance from a resident wasn't particularly welcoming.

"Evening is approaching," said Takal. "We would be wise to find an inn, fill our bellies, and rest."

"Finally!" said Kwint. "Somethin' that isn't dried meat!"

They returned to the Merchant District and located a large inn. A small woman greeted them in the doorway. "Welcome to the Sunset Boar! Can I interest you in some rooms?"

Takal and Griffin shared one room, and Bo'cul and Kwint another, Naymeira took the third. They dined on fresh boar and then retired to their respective rooms. Bajuru's heat and exhaustion from their travels made it difficult to stay awake, and they soon found themselves in dreamless sleep. Well, most of them...

The very night sky seemed to shake with the footsteps of patrolling guards. Many carried torches with which to expel the darkness of Bordertown's many alleyways.

"What is happening?" Griffin asked Nifae, and the rest of the gang turned to hear his answer.

"I'll tell you," he said. "The guards finally worked up the courage to hunt us down! Fortunately, I saw this coming. There are fifteen horses at the stables, just about ready for riding. When the guards finally spot us, we will only be dots on the horizon."

Nifae sent them out in pairs, as inconspicuous as possible. He and Griffin formed the final pair. "I assume you're coming with us?" Nifae asked. Griffin nodded. "Good, because if you weren't I'd be forced to kill you."

Nifae pulled his hood over his head and led Griffin toward the main street. Guards seemed to be everywhere, running through the alleyways, forcing entry into various buildings. Amid the confusion, it was a rather simple task to stick to the shadows and slip by. They soon found themselves at the Bordertown Stables. The rest of the gang was already prepared to ride. Nifae tossed Griffin a saddle. "You'll ride with me. I'll be back in just a moment."

Nifae disappeared into the back of the stable, just as a large horn sounded. A good portion of the gang rode off in fear. Nifae reappeared, ran to his horse, and hopped into the saddle. He pulled Griffin up behind him.

"Ride west, boys! Let's see how much distance we can put between us and this place!"

They left only a cloud of dust, and Griffin didn't speak until they were, indeed, merely dots on the horizon. "Nifae, what were you doing back in the stables?"

He grinned. "Just leaving the guards a little message."

At that moment, the guards were storming the stables, looking high and low for elusive criminal elements.

"I found something!" shouted a younger guard, and he motioned the others closer, all of them staring at a message written on the stable's back wall.

The commander pushed through them. "Let me see this!"

There, in large black letters, was a simple note: FAREWELL, FOOLS.

CHAPTER 38

When he awoke, Takal was shaking him. "Griffin! Are you all right? You were trembling."

"Was I?"

Takal nodded. "That is not the only reason I woke you. The gem is in the city. I can sense it."

"Where?"

"I can never know exactly, but I feel fairly certain that we may find it in the Royal District, in the center of the city. I suspect the gem is somewhere in the king's court."

The companions assembled in the inn's foyer, and Takal explained the situation.

"It seems to me," said Naymeira, "that our only option is to enter the Royal District and exit with the gem."

"I am afraid it is not that simple," Takal shook his head. "We must use stealth, cunning. This is not some random jewel, not even a random priceless jewel."

"I stole it once," said Griffin. "I think I could manage it again."

They departed the inn just as the sun began to rise over the city walls, casting a pink light on Bajuru.

"Tell me about the King of the South," said Griffin to Takal.

The djinni thought for a moment as they walked. "I have kept to myself for many years, but I have had occasional encounters. And from what I have heard, he is a rash ruler, often making decisions in the heat of the moment without considering the consequences of his actions. His line has ruled for at least a century. However, he only took the throne very recently—nine years ago by your short-lived reckoning. After his father was killed, the son took over, increasing his power quite a bit.

"And his name?"

"Oh, of course. His name is Seretigo Va'hou."

Griffin stopped in his tracks. Dizzying images flashed through his mind. His knees buckled.

"Griffin, what is it?" Naymeira and Kwint ran to his side.

He couldn't stop his hands from shaking and his lips from trembling. "The man... the man who took my father..."

Griffin's face reddened. "I'll kill him. I'll KILL HIM!" He collapsed to the ground, whispering three final words before blacking out. "I'll kill him..."

"What are we going to do now?" asked Naymeira, as she looked toward Bo'cul, who was cradling Griffin in his arms as if holding a pile of firewood.

"We have to find the gem today. It could move at any time," said Takal. He glanced at Griffin and frowned. "We could have used his help. Bo'cul, Kwint, take Griffin back to the inn. Watch over him. Our task is a mission of stealth. You two strike me as more adept at brute force."

Kwint laughed sadly. "Very well, we brutes will play nursemaid. You 'ave fun tip-toeing through the castle."

They parted ways, and Takal and Naymeira started up the sloping and winding road leading toward the city center. Looming above them was a great castle built of red stone, its minarets spiraling toward the sky.

"The Scarlet Palace," muttered Takal, quickening his pace.

"You have a plan?" said Naymeira, matching the djinni's stride.

"A simple one," Takal shrugged. "But now as I think of it, we could use a boisterous fellow like Kwint. But you'll have to do, Naymeira."

She shot him a look, but he grinned and added, "You distract their attention. I discover their intentions."

"Will you attack them?"

"I cannot attack—unless I am attacked. It is part of the Oath of the Djinn, although I am afraid not all of my brethren hold it in similarly high regard." He dropped his gaze for a moment. "But I will watch and wait. My time will come."

As the large, wooden front gate of the Scarlet Palace came into view, Takal nodded to Naymeira and began to change form—into a humanoid shape, but one consisting entirely of swirling sand. He veered off, as the elf approached the gate, where four guards stood at attention, their eyes focused straight ahead.

"I have come to seek audience with the king," she announced.

One of the guards peered down at her and dismissed her request with a wave of his hand. "The king is concerned with more important matters than a meeting with a simple traveling elf."

"Simple? Simple! Do you not know who I am?"

The guard allowed a longer look this time before again turning his attentions straight ahead. "No."

"No, of course not. Why would a mere palace guard like yourself recognize royalty when he saw it?" As she spoke, she glanced to her right and watched as a whirl of sand began to climb the castle's massive outer wall.

The guard glanced toward each of his companions, none of whom seemed to want to be any part of the discussion. "Royalty, you say? Traveling alone in those rags?"

"I don't need any dim-witted guards surrounding me. And royal robes are for royal rubes." She noticed the sand-swirl passing over the wall and drifting toward a central tower. "I am Arfrindal, Queen of Gozreh Ekul, City of the Whispering Woods."

"City of the what?"

"The, um, Wandering Willows."

"I could have sworn you said something about whispers, Queen... what is it again?"

Naymeira hesitated as the cloud of sand disappeared into an arched window toward the top of a scarlet tower. "Queen... Arf... Alfrin..."

Another guard chimed in. "I believe you said Arfrindal, my lady." He gave an exaggerated bow, and the other three guards guffawed.

"I have no use for these questions. Will you announce my presence to the king?"

"What do you think, fellows?" said the first guard. "Should we call the trumpeters and the banner-bearers? Queen Arf Alfrin Arfrindal of the Whispering Wandering Willow Woods has arrived!" With another disdainful wave, he added, "Be gone with you, elf."

Takal hovered above a poorly lit room bearing only one very long, stone table. At its head, sat King Seretigo, a golden crown perched atop his bright red hair. To his left sat a shorter man, heavily tanned with a fat, twisted nose. To Seretigo's right sat a figure cloaked in black, his skin unusually pale, his fingernails sharpened like little daggers. Takal sensed something about him, something powerful and familiar. Toward the middle of the table on that same side sat a dwarf. He wore a fine orange robe and ran his fingers through his combed blond beard. In the table's center was placed a red gem, shining brightly in the dim light. The Mizzarkh. Takal's eyes widened, but he waited and listened. The short man spoke.

"The enemy approaches from the east, and you say we do nothing?" He rose from his seat. "This is war, your grace, not a game of hide and seek. Why would—"

Seretigo raised his left hand, and the man fell silent. "General Cairon, please, sit down." Cairon did so, immediately. "Indeed, General, this is war. And so we use war tactics. We appear weak. We appear desperate. And when they reveal their arrogance..." The king turned to the cloaked figure. "That is when we strike."

The figure in black chuckled. "That is when I strike."

Seretigo turned to face the dwarf. "Now, Ambassador Thrutch," he said, stretching out the word "ambassador" enough to make it slightly mocking. "Any news of the Gocian tribes?"

Thrutch, thought Takal, *where have I heard that name before?*

"They are on their way..." the dwarf began, but just then the doors opened, and two more figures entered the room—a man and a demon.

"Ah, Ranimus. Welcome to Bajuru!" *Ranimus, that name, too,* thought Takal. "How long ago did you arrive? I wasn't informed."

"Only just now," said the merman, and he took a seat beside Cairon.

"Gentlemen," said, the king, pointing to the man who had arrived with Ranimus, "this is Alnardo Fist. He has come to help us with our little... issue."

Alnardo bowed slightly and took a seat alongside the dwarf, who suddenly recognized him. "A pleasure to 'ave ya with us, Lord Fist."

The man smiled. Cairon raised an eyebrow. "Lord? What royalty do you belong to, if I may ask?"

Thrutch answered for him. "He is not royalty. In the north, he is known—respectfully, I might add—as the Lord of Lies."

Takal had heard enough. He had intended to sweep down and steal the gem, swirling his way out of the castle before a guard could lift a finger. But this gathering had shaken him to his core. If chaos was coming, here was a side well-pre-pared and ruthless. And Roland was nowhere to be found. The jewel would be his, but not now, not yet. He had chosen a side.

CHAPTER 39

The air was damp, and the young men's spirits were dampened, as well. Their horses grew silent as they traversed the Marshlands of the North, a maze of streams and swamps and shrubbery.

"The streams all lead to one place," Nifae explained. "Naran, the Lake of Frozen Tears." Griffin shivered behind him. "The men of old migrated from these lands long ago, to the northeast mostly. In fact, Quah was one of the largest of their new cities."

"We... we are close then? To Quah?"

"Yes, and the sooner we arrive, the better," Nifae nodded. "This chill makes me uneasy." When they arrived at the shores of Naran Lake, Nifae instructed the gang to halt. "We stop here for the night. Tomorrow we turn north to Quah."

As they set up camp, Griffin volunteered to collect firewood. It was difficult to find any suitable tinder amid the marshlands, the wood being either soggy or rotten, often both. With very little success, he emerged, ducking beneath the branches into a clearing. He had an almost perfect view of Naran, which looked like a flat, black plain with the stars and the moon dancing in its depths. Griffin dropped the firewood and wandered toward it.

Father loved the stars, *he thought*. He used to say they were the candles of the gods.

And then young Griffin cried, his shoulders heaving, his tears seeming to join the lake's waters. And the lake gratefully accepted them.

Griffin awoke with tears in his eyes and a dwarf's voice in his ears. "He's awake!" Kwint exclaimed. "Ya gave us quite a scare, Griffin."

He sat up and slowly rose to his feet, steadying himself and looking around. *We're back at the inn.* "What happened?"

"Ya passed out, my boy." Kwint handed Griffin a mug of water.

"Tastes a bit like wine," said Griffin after taking a sip or two.

Kwint shrugged. "Well, Bo may 'ave been using it earlier."

Griffin spit the water back into the mug. "Where is Bo'cul anyway? And the others?"

"Downstairs. I came to check on ya. I'll tell 'em to come up."

"No, I'll go down."

Griffin made his way across the room and down the stairs with Kwint following close behind. They found Naymeira, Bo'cul, and Takal sitting around a small wooden table in a corner. Kwint joined them.

"You're awake. Wonderful!" said Takal. "I was just about to reveal what I discovered in the castle..."

"You did it then?" said Griffin.

Takal nodded.

"You have the gem?"

Takal shook his head and offered Griffin his chair. "You may want to sit down."

None of the others said a word while Takal told them what his surveillance had uncovered, but the names simmered in their minds. Thrutch. Ranimus. Seretigo... Only when Takal finished did Griffin speak.

"And no word of Roland?" he asked.

"None," said Takal.

"Well, the others we know. Thrutch and Ranimus are no friends of ours, eh Kwint? Bo'cul? And Alnardo Fist was... well, I suppose you could say he was my employer at one time. He hired me to steal the Hiamahu Jewel. You all know what happened from there. Now it is obvious to me why he was so intent on obtaining the gem. He is working for... Seretigo. And that brings me to the king. I have not told you much of my past, and I do not wish to dwell there. But you all deserve to know this..."

While Griffin explained how his father had been taken from him many years earlier, his companions remained silent. He concluded by saying, "We know who our enemies are now."

"Yes," Takal spoke, and Griffin allowed a slight smile. *I'm glad to have him on my side.*

"We also know that we have allies," Griffin continued. "The enemy of our enemy is our friend, although in this case he may also be our enemy."

"What do you mean?" asked Naymeira.

"The man with the bronze finger must have known that I was stealing the gem on behalf of Seretigo, indirectly anyway. Therefore he seems to be Seretigo's enemy, correct?"

They nodded, and Griffin rose from his seat. "If Seretigo's enemy is indeed coming from the east, as Takal overheard, then that is where we should be going—east toward the Southern Plains. It is there, I believe, that we may discover what happened to our friend. And perhaps we may finally find the man with the bronze finger."

CHAPTER 40

Griffin hadn't set foot in the Southern Plains for fourteen years, not since he had left the village of Cana during the search for his father. The stable master at Bajuru generously agreed to exchange some of his horses for their scarabs. Southerner horses were a smaller breed of horse, less strong than most Northerner horses, but considerably swifter. It would have been nearly impossible for one of them to support Bo'cul's weight, so they were forced to pay extra for a large Northern stallion, which made the minotaur look quite imposing, indeed. They also purchased new rations for the journey ahead.

A day after they set out, they came upon the ruins of an old sandstone fortress. Remnants of stone pillars stood at various heights, and rubble decorated the ground below.

"We shall not stop here," said Takal. "This is an old Southerner settlement. Hellgrot was its name. Lost and abandoned in a war long ago. It is said to bring ill luck."

As they rode across the Plains, they often found themselves talking of Roland, alternately revealing hope and despair. Griffin told stories about him. Takal commented that he sounded like a fine fellow. Bo'cul grunted in agreement. Naymeira said she wished she had been able to meet him. Kwint smiled in silence. Finally, Takal pulled his horse beside Griffin's and said, "It is growing late. We should set up camp."

They unsaddled their horses and unrolled their bedrolls. Bo'cul and Kwint built a fire. As the flames began to fade into embers, Bo'cul's ears pricked up. Something was approaching. He roared in warning, but it was too late. Within moments, they found themselves surrounded by cloaked men wielding flails and riding giant spiders. Griffin and Kwint shared a glance. *The same riders who took Roland.*

The spiders were unusual creatures with piercing red eyes and hairy black bodies. But what surprised Griffin most was their utter silence. As they drew closer, two spiders parted to reveal a larger, slightly grayer arachnid. A tall man rode atop it. It was nearly impossible to discern any of his features in the darkness.

"Drop your weapons," he said in a low voice. They were outnumbered and out-armed, so they let their weapons fall to the ground. Takal simply spread his hands wide. No weapon necessary.

"You will saddle your horses. You will say nothing. You will then be... escorted by us. You will not ask where or why."

"How about who?" said Kwint. "Who are ya?"

The man jumped from his spider. "I told you to say nothing, dwarf. If you must know, I am Wayfere, djinni of the northern lands." Suddenly, Wayfere's legs were replaced by swirling winds. "It would serve you well not to make me angry."

Takal stepped forward. "Wayfere?"

Wayfere squinted in the darkness. "I know that voice, from a time long ago... Takal? Takal! By the gems, you have been gone for centuries! What are you doing traveling with this band of traitors?"

"Traitors?" Kwint started for his axe, but Naymeira grabbed his arm to stop him.

"You are scouts for True Shadow, are you not?" asked Wayfere.

"No, of course not," said Griffin. "But if your enemy is True Shadow, then you must represent..."

"Flame Web," said Takal. "Wayfere made that choice long ago."

"It was the right choice, Takal," said Wayfere, his eyes glowing red. "We are the light in the darkness. And you shall soon see the light, too, my friend." His eyes dimmed again. "Our camp is not far from here. If you are, indeed, our allies in this fight, it is good that you have arrived before the battle..."

"You are no ally of mine!" Griffin shouted, quite suddenly. "It was you who took a friend of mine, a dwarf named Roland. What have you done with him?"

Wayfere just smiled. "Roland is no longer with us..."

"You killed him?" Kwint screamed. "You blasted spider-riders killed him!"

"Wayfere," said Takal, "is this true?"

Unexpectedly, Wayfere began to chuckle. "All will be explained soon." He looked at Griffin. "You are Griffin Blade then, are you not?"

Griffin tensed. "How do you know my name?"

Wayfere's smile grew wider. "I thought so. I sense that you seek another—a man, perhaps?"

Griffin hesitated before speaking. "From the very beginning of my journey, I have been seeking a man. A man with a bronze finger."

This time, the warriors surrounding Wayfere laughed, too. "What is so funny?" Griffin asked.

The djinni did not answer directly. Instead he said, "You are in luck, Griffin Blade. The man you seek is nearby."

The companions were led at a slow trot. After a while, Griffin heard Takal's voice in his ear. "Wayfere is honorable, although he may seem otherwise. He can be... overbearing at times. But he can be trusted."

Griffin turned to find no one behind him. Takal waved from the back of the group.

The Flame Web camp was, indeed, close by. It consisted of a large cluster of tents of various sizes.

"We move often," Wayfere explained. "Nothing is permanent."

They climbed off their horses and spiders and entered the camp on foot. Although it was late, most were not sleeping. The group passed elves and dwarves and men of all kinds. Finally, they came upon a large, white tent in the camp's center. Wayfere pulled open its flap.

"You may wait in here," he said.

Griffin nodded and entered, followed by Naymeira, Kwint, and Bo'cul. Before Takal entered, Wayfere put a hand on his shoulder and leaned his head forward. Takal did the same, and the two seemed to share a bond, momentary yet ancient.

There were a few empty chairs in the tent, but none of the companions bothered to sit. Kwint paced back and forth. Bo'cul stood with his arms crossed and Takal with his hands upon his hips. Naymeira watched Griffin, who didn't seem to move a muscle. After what seemed like epochs, they heard a rustling outside and voices whispering low.

A hand reached into the tent to pull open the flap—a hand with a bronze index finger. In that split second, a memory returned...

Quah felt different. Different from what young Griffin remembered. He had taken his leave from Nifae and the gang, thanking them for all they had done to care for him, but telling them he had to find his own path now. Wandering Quah's cobblestone streets, he felt a cool drop of water run down his arm. He looked up. The sky was a deep gray. More drops fell, landing on his face, dripping into his eyes. Griffin didn't care. He didn't know why or how, but he knew at that moment that Ramyr Blade wasn't to be found there. His father was gone, and he would never return.

When the man with the bronze finger entered the tent, Griffin's first thought was, *This is not the man that I bumped into that day in Quah.* The man eagerly scanned the faces in the tent, his gaze settling on Griffin. Their eyes met. Griffin's second thought was, *I recognize him.*

The bronze-fingered man smiled and laughed, "You always had a knack for getting into trouble, didn't you, Griff?"

Griffin stepped toward him, speechless. He blinked. It wasn't a memory. He threw his arms around the man, weeping into his shoulder.

"Father," he finally said, and he cried some more before adding, "You and I both know I also have a knack for getting out of it."

Ramyr Blade is alive. Griffin stepped back and took a long look at his father. *Ramyr Blade is the man with the bronze finger.*

CHAPTER 41

"Griff, you have to understand. Everything I did... everything you think I didn't do... I did it for you."

"For me? For me! You've been alive all this time, and you never let me know! You never once came to see me!"

"That's not true at all—"

"I had to live without parents. Because of you. And then you steal the gem, the Hiamahu Jewel, from me. From your own son!"

Ramyr did not respond. Instead, he turned to Wayfere, who had entered the tent after him. "Griffin and I are going to take a little walk." He glanced at the rest of his companions. "Give his friends a proper welcome feast and explain all to them—preferably in that order."

He then exited the tent. As Griffin started to follow, he looked back at his friends, who motioned for him to continue. Sighing and closing his eyes, he turned and walked after his father, who was already making his way down a narrow path. Griffin caught up to him, matching his stride. They said nothing to each other. They entered a lush forest,

Ramyr leading him onward still, until they finally arrived at a clearing. Ramyr made his way to a tree stump and patted its flat top.

Ramyr Blade appeared much older to Griffin. When he had been taken by Seretigo, he had been in his late thirties. More than a dozen years later, streaks of gray danced in his dirty brown hair. His face was tired and wrinkled. A gleam of hope still existed, however, in his bright eyes.

"Sit," he told Griffin, and his son did so. "I am told you have been to this place before. This is Vi Celen Ve Pellentiri."

"The Forest of Regrowth," said Griffin. "How did you know I have been here?"

"Flame Web is very much a web of contacts and observers. Some might call them spies. One of them is a lady you may remember, Almitri Flamentari..."

Griffin's eyes lit up. "Miss Flamentari..."

"The one and only."

"I see. Are there any other... contacts I might know?"

"Just a few. Innkeepers Algra and Garuf in Dunalar. My gnomish friend Know in Gnarvik. A councilman or two in Firstport. Oh, and Lord Scadnik, the fellow from whom you stole the Hiamahu Jewel in the first place. But that is not important right now, Griffin. I am going to attempt to explain the last fourteen years of my life... and yours."

And so he began. For Griffin, it was like learning about his own life through a window, from a perspective distant yet intimate.

"I will begin at the point when I was taken away by Seretigo," he said, almost spitting the king's name. "I was taken west across the Southern Plains to Bajuru, where I was jailed. At the time, I had begun working in secret for Flame Web. Just little tasks. Stealing plans and letters, conveying misleading information, and so forth. The King of the South then was Neogagon Va'hou, an evil and short-sighted piece of filth. You see, he was also the secret leader of True Shadow, intent on dominating Alastian. I was kept in a cell for days, then weeks, until they realized my... importance."

Ramyr had been pacing the entire time he was telling the story. He stopped and stared toward Griffin, whose eyes were locked on his. "I know you have learned about the people of power, those who can control the Sister Jewels. Griffin, I am one of them, and so are you."

Griffin's first response was confusion. "What?"

"Our line, our blood, we can control the Hiamahu Jewel. When King Neogagon and his minions discovered who I was, I became exponentially more valuable to them. They figured they could convert me to their side, the fools. They only thought of power and money. The king gave me my own room in a castle tower and invited me to all of his royal banquets as an honored guest. For nearly four years, I was treated like a duke, like a prince. I wasn't deceived. I was still a prisoner. They never let me contact you, Griff. It tore me to pieces. Seretigo said you were dead, but I knew you would find a way to survive."

Griffin thought he heard a catch in his father's voice, as if he were about to dissolve in tears. But Ramyr cleared his throat and went on. "Slowly over time, however, I realized that I was succumbing to their lies. I feared that my own will wasn't strong enough. There was only one thing I could do to prevent them from using me for their purposes." He looked down at his right hand, instinctively rubbing his bronze finger. "One night I snatched a knife from the banquet table and retreated to my room. It was one of the hardest things I've ever had to do. In one quick chop, my index finger fell to the marble floor. I was no longer a person of power. A person must have all five fingers on his dominant hand in order to be able to draw power from one of the Sister Jewels. For the next week or so, I wore gloves at all times. I knew that if they discovered my secret I would become useless to them, hanged without a second thought if I was lucky. So I opted to risk it all. I planned my escape, but not before I killed the king."

Griffin sat there with his mouth agape. "You... you cut off your finger to prevent the king from manipulating you? You killed the king?"

Ramyr nodded. "Yes, and in a manner I perhaps should not have chosen. It was foolish of me. I put myself in danger. More importantly, I put you in danger. King Neogagon had a tendency to drink too much at his feasts, the gluttonous pig. I stayed longer than usual—until the king and I were the only two remaining. Luckily, Neogagon had a rule about guards not being present during banquets. Royalty only or some such nonsense. He had nearly passed out, so it was a simple matter of sneaking behind him and strangling him with a coil of rope. But then I made a rash and arrogant decision. I left my dead finger on a plate in front of him. That was a mistake, a mistake I never should have made."

He rubbed his bronze finger again. "My escape wasn't as difficult as you might think. I bribed a young servant with some gold that I had found on the king's person. The boy hid me in a crate that was to be taken to the stables. From there, I slipped out of the city and found my way back to Flame Web. Seretigo was the first, we believe, to discover his father's body. He was also one of the few who understood the significance of that finger I left behind. He knew that I was no longer a person of power. Sadly, Griffin, that made you a prime target for True Shadow. Seretigo is wiser than his father was, if even more ruthless. He figured, based on my behavior, that it was unlikely that you could be convinced to join them. And if they couldn't have you, they would see to it that Flame Web couldn't either. For the first few years, after Seretigo became King of the South and leader of True Shadow, he made it his goal to hunt you down. Fortunately, you instinctively gravitated toward the shadows, Griffin. Perhaps it's a family trait. Seretigo finally assumed you had, indeed, perished... until recently, anyway."

"But why didn't you come back to me, father? You were free. I was in danger..."

"That's just the point, Griff. I wanted more than anything to talk to you, to explain everything, to tell you how proud I was of the man you were becoming. But the leader of Flame Web at the time, Hurk Redlaw, cautioned against it. And he was right. It was for your own safety. True Shadow has spies everywhere. I couldn't risk my presence alerting them to you, although it pained me greatly. I continued in my service to Flame Web. I devoted myself to the cause. You see, Griffin,

True Shadow has only one goal—power. And how do they achieve the power they so desire? The Sister Jewels. Flame Web wants exactly the opposite. It isn't that we want the gems for ourselves. We simply do not want True Shadow to obtain the power that the gems contain. It is a noble cause, perhaps the noblest. It is not power we seek, but rather the prevention of too much power."

Griffin nodded. His instincts were much the same. Ramyr continued, "I gained respect quickly as a member of Flame Web, in part for the sacrifices I made. I was given the responsibility of tracing the gems' whereabouts, discovering who possessed them and if they were friend or foe. On one of my trips to Dunalar, I stopped by the forge there. What is it called? Ah yes, Briskhammer Forge. I had been invited by the dwarven king to one of his councils—King Rindivor is a supporter of Flame Web. Hurk had instructed me to forge a silver key. I later learned that it opened one of Know's books. But I was also in Dunalar for my own purposes. I requested a finger to be made of bronze. The first of its kind, I was told."

Ramyr walked over to Griffin and put a hand on his shoulder. "I was watching you always, Griff. But I couldn't directly contact you. If anything happened to you... because of me..." His voice trailed off and he was silent for a moment. "But now that I hope you understand that, let me explain more recent events. Hurk got word that Seretigo had been corresponding with Alnardo Fist in Quah. He knew that Quah was where the Hiamahu Jewel was located, although most only thought it was a priceless gem, not realizing it was far more than that. If Seretigo was getting help from a master of thieves, that meant trouble. I had done some work for the Lord of Lies once or twice. I'm not necessarily proud of it. Hurk knew this well and asked me to travel to Quah and prevent the blue gem from shifting hands. I accepted the mission, of course, because it gave me an opportunity to be close to you. I've spied on you several times before, always in disguise. You never would have recognized me. I became a rather convincing old man, I must say. And so I waited in an alleyway, watching over the treasury of Lord Scadnik. I suspected that I would encounter a thief. I never dreamed it would be you—working for the Lord of Lies and thus Seretigo himself, though you did not know it. The universe does queer things. I found it quite remarkable, actually, that Alnardo Fist never knew how valuable you really were. How valuable you still are. I couldn't let you bring the Hiamahu Jewel to him, of course, so I stole it back."

As Griffin rose from the tree stump, Ramyr sighed. "Griff, I understand if you feel—"

Griffin embraced his father once more and held him close. Tears leapt freely from his eyes. "I'm sorry," he kept saying, over and over again. "I'm sorry."

Ramyr couldn't help but laugh. "Griffin, my boy, my son... you're not the one who should be apologizing." They held each other in silence, as if making up for years of unwanted distance.

The trees began to thin as they walked toward Flame Web's camp. Griffin inquired about how they were able to keep the peace among so many different races and strong personalities.

Ramyr smiled. "Some of our people are beginning to call it Camp Cauldron. Many different ingredients, all mixed together. No, we're not as different as you might imagine. We have developed our own culture here."

Suddenly, Griffin stopped dead in his tracks. He felt immediately ashamed that he had spent the night thinking only of himself, his worries, his past and future. "Father, where's Roland? What have you done with him? Why did you take him?"

"Take him? No, Griff, we saved him." Griffin raised an eyebrow. "My men believed that he was alone, but Roland later informed me that he was with you and Kwint."

"I don't understand."

"It was a True Shadow party that originally attacked your dwarf friend. Flame Web received word of their plan and arrived to stop them just in time."

"So your men were riding the spiders..."

Ramyr nodded. "You see, True Shadow had been told by their spies that Kwint Kwinhollow was in the area. They were looking for you, as well, but we drove them off. In the chaos, everyone apparently mistook Roland for Kwint."

"But why would they want..." And as soon as he began to ask, he realized the answer. "Of course! Kwint is a person of power, too, isn't he? The Mizzarkh!" He shook his head and allowed a laugh.

"Yes, the gem of fire. Like the Sister Jewels themselves, people of power have a tendency to... find each other, and the gems tend to find the powerful—although we are yet to determine the other two bloodlines for the other two gems."

"But you still haven't answered me, father. Where is Roland?"

"After we explained ourselves and our purpose to him, he wanted to rejoin you. We couldn't permit it, of course. Far too risky. So instead, he joined Flame Web. Currently, I believe he is out scouting somewhere northwest of here..."

Griffin nearly jumped out of his boots. "So you're saying he's alive?"

"Oh, very much so. He's a feisty one, that Roland."

Griffin laughed again. "That he is, father. That he is."

When they entered Camp Cauldron, Griffin asked his father one more question. "When will I be able to meet this Hurk Redlaw?"

"You did. On one dark night in a cottage located in the forest we just exited."

Griffin stopped walking. "There was a man in black. In Miss Flamentari's cottage..."

Ramyr nodded. "He could not risk revealing his identity, but he wanted to make sure you were well cared for." He sighed. "I'm afraid you cannot meet him a second time. He was killed just a week after I left for Quah. Ambushed by True Shadow. He was more than my leader. He was my friend."

"Oh, I'm sorry."

His father tilted his head and looked toward the sky. "It's nearly morning. Get what sleep you can. We have a big day ahead of us."

Griffin yawned. "Goodnight, father."

"Goodnight, Griff."

Ramyr began to walk away, but then he turned back around. "Oh, and Griffin..."

"Yes, father?"

"I am Hurk's replacement. I am the leader of Flame Web."

Griffin's friends were asleep in the tent when he returned, even Takal, who preferred to sleep in human form. *Thousands of years old, and he's curled up like a baby,* thought Griffin. He found a bedroll and stretched himself out on top of it. Although it was late and Griffin was exhausted, his mind raced, and he found himself going over all the information he had just learned.

My father is alive. My father is the leader of Flame Web. Roland is alive. Kwint is a person of power. I am a person of power.

When he finally drifted off to sleep, there were no dreams, no images from his past, no recollection of his travels. Griffin slept peacefully until morning arrived.

CHAPTER 42

When they awoke late in the morning, they were summoned to a council meeting. The companions were told to come to the tallest hill overlooking Cauldron. There they found a large, round stone table. A map of Alastian was carved into the stone, and on the map were placed three painted pebbles—one red, one blue, one black. Surrounding the table were many faces that were new to Griffin.

"Good, you are here," said Ramyr, as the companions arrived. His eyes brightened at the sight of his son. "Let me introduce you to a few of Flame Web's most important members." He pointed to a pair of tall figures with short black beards and intense red eyes. "Ragnar and Lagnar, I'm sure you have..." Before he could finish, Takal rushed over to the pair and enveloped them in a hug. "My fellow djinn! How long has it been? A few hundred years, it seems!"

"At least," said Ragnar.

"Indeed," added Lagnar.

Ramyr nodded toward a dwarf with a long black beard who was standing to his left. "Ambassador Ralun from the

Kni Hmun Mountains." The dwarf gave a slight bow, and it seemed to be directed toward Kwint. Griffin noticed that his friend stood just a bit taller at that moment.

Ramyr then patted the shoulder of another man standing next to him, his blond hair tied in a ponytail, his beard flecked with gray. "And this is Flame Legion Commander Salek Myon…"

"Pleasure to make your acquaintance!" he boomed. "You folks have had quite a journey to get here."

A swirling cloud slowly drifted toward the table, forming into the djinni Wayfere as it touched the ground.

"We have now assembled," said Ramyr. "Commander Salek…"

Salek cleared his throat and began, loudly, "We stand here today to confront an incomparable evil, a shadowy society with a lust for power that would lead Alastian toward a state of ruin. This coming war is not fought over conquest. This war is not fought over resources. No, my friends, this war is a battle over four precious treasures—treasures far more valuable than the land and its bounty. The Sister Jewels. Two of those treasures are with us today."

He nodded toward Takal, who hesitated slightly and then produced the Ungornem Gem from his sleeve. He placed it on the table with a low thud.

Commander Salek turned to Ramyr. "Sir?" From his breast pocket, Griffin's father removed an object wrapped in parchment tied with a simple string. After untying it and placing the long awaited Hiamahu Jewel on his end of the table, he looked up at Griffin and winked.

The two gems, reunited, glowed and pulsated as if they were long lost friends who finally found each other again amid the random pathways of their lives. The gems then returned to their original state.

"Your friends informed us about how you obtained the black gem," Wayfere told Griffin. "Remarkable. I never knew a mortal—especially a human—who could accomplish such things."

Griffin scowled. "I'm not sure what you mean by that…"

"I simply—"

"He meant nothing by it," Takal interrupted, and Wayfere simply allowed a slight nod of apology.

"Gentlemen!" said Commander Salek, and then he remembered Naymeira. "And m'lady. It's time we talk war."

"Tactics?" asked Ragnar.

"Strategy?" added Lagnar.

"Precisely," said Salek. "My plan, I hope, will be effective. We cannot rely on strength in numbers. The enemy has gathered a superior force, a combination of both the army of True Shadow and that of Bajuru."

"That and the various Gocian tribes that have allied with them, as well," Wayfere muttered. "They may be primitive, but they are great in number."

"So that is why we saw so many tribesmen traveling north!" exclaimed Naymeira. "I suppose we were fortunate they paid us no heed."

"Takal," Salek continued, "would you mind repeating what you discovered while spying…"

"Observing!" Takal interrupted.

"... while observing Seretigo's secret council."

"What I found most interesting," said Takal, "was Seretigo's statement that True Shadow's strategy was to appear weak."

"Then let us assume at all times that they are stronger than they appear," said Ramyr. "Please continue, Takal."

The djinni sighed softly. "There was a hooded man sitting beside Seretigo. Mysterious fellow. I could not see who he was, but he seemed familiar. He said something about a... special attack." Takal glanced at Wayfere, then turned back to Ramyr. "A special force of some sort. I really do not know."

Commander Salek nodded. "Thank you, Takal, and may I say that we are glad that you have finally chosen to support Flame Web's mission. We are grateful—and relieved. Now, as for the battle itself, it looks as if our force and the enemy's will converge in the vicinity of the Ruins of Hellgrot..."

"Cursed place!" shouted Ragnar.

"An evil omen!" added Lagnar.

The council members began to murmur to one another, and Ramyr, sensing their unease, raised a hand to silence them. "Perhaps the place is cursed. Perhaps the location is a portent of evil," he said. "But ask yourself this, my friends: To whom will this so-called curse befall?"

The council members murmured once more, a few of them nodding this time.

"Well," said Salek, "perhaps we can discuss how to use the ruins to our advantage..."

The council went on to speak of elevations and positions and fortifications, counter-offensives and choke points and flanking maneuvers, much of which Griffin didn't understand. As the discussion continued, he found himself more and more inclined to fix his stare upon the Hiamahu Jewel, which sat on the table's opposite side. He was roused from his trance only when he heard his name.

"Griffin," said Ramyr, loudly but gently. "You may be most interested in this."

Salek continued, "You and your friends will play a vital role in this battle. If you are willing, that is."

Takal looked at Naymeira, who turned to Bo'cul, who glanced at Kwint, who grinned at Griffin.

"We're willing."

"We will focus on the larger battle," said Commander Salek. "Your mission is of a more specific nature, but no less important. And by no means simple. You are to retrieve the Mizzarkh, the red gem."

Ramyr spoke, and as he did so he looked straight at his son. "We have received information that Seretigo—typically, given the ego of the man—wears the Mizzarkh on a chain around his neck at all times. Which means—"

"Which means we have to find Seretigo during the battle," Griffin interrupted.

"And in all likelihood kill him," said his father. And then he added, "It is a deed I would have liked to have saved for myself."

Commander Salek pointed to the red pebble on the stone map. "You have surely already surmised that these pebbles represent the three gems—"

"Three?" asked Naymeira. "What about the fourth?"

"The white gem has been lost for years," said Ramyr.

"Decades," said Ragnar.

"Centuries," corrected Lagnar.

"No one, as far as we as we know, is aware of its whereabouts," said Ramyr. "Not us. Not True Shadow. And we would prefer to keep it that way. But let us focus on Seretigo."

Salek motioned toward the red pebble, which was placed just west of Hellgrot. "Seretigo is a proud man. Dishonorable, greedy, merciless, but proud. So we believe he will participate in the battle. However, don't expect him to be on the front lines. Which means you will have to make your way past—or perhaps around—a wave of enemies first. We will help you strategize as best we can, but are you willing to take on this task?"

Griffin nodded, as did his companions. He looked toward his father and thought for a moment that he saw concern in his eyes.

"Last but not least, our allies," said Salek, "are unfortunately few."

"The dwarves are pledged to assist ya in the battle," said Ambassador Ralun. "The question is whether or not they will arrive in time. It is a long journey from the Kni Hmun Mountains."

"And what of the Northerners?" asked Salek. "Will they join us?"

Ragnar glanced northward, then shook his head. "Doubtful," he said.

"Unlikely," added Lagnar.

"The Northerners and Southerners have not exactly had good relations over the years," said Wayfere, "but they will not embrace the opportunity to join someone else's fight. Even if the dwarven forces do arrive in time, we shall still be greatly outnumbered."

Naymeira stepped forward. "What about the elves?"

Wayfere scoffed, "What of them? The light elves are a bunch of arrogant fools who care about no one but themselves."

Naymeira's eyes narrowed. "And the dark elves?"

"We have not asked for their assistance," Commander Salek answered. "Of late they have shown no interest in the world beyond their lands. They are factionalized, wary of others, distrustful even among themselves."

"Then let me try." Naymeira looked Salek directly in the eyes. "Someone must try to unite the dark elf clans under one cause. If the fate of Alastian is at stake, then perhaps I can convince them that isolation is no longer an option."

Salek looked toward Ramyr, who glanced at Griffin as if to ask, *Do you trust her fully?* Griffin's eyes told him yes.

"I suppose there is no harm in trying, but I fear the time has grown too late. The battle will begin any day now," said Ramyr. "This is my horsemaster." He turned to a broad-shouldered man standing behind him. "Entian, give her the swiftest horse you can find. Naymeira, you must leave at once."

The dark elf smiled. "I will not disappoint." She turned to her companions. "Goodbye. We shall meet again soon."

As she turned to leave, Griffin put a hand on her shoulder. He tried to speak, hesitated, then said only, "Will you make it in time?"

"If all goes well," she replied. With that, she was gone.

Moments later, the council members left the clearing, too, until only Griffin and his father remained. Ramyr picked up the black gem with his left hand and the blue gem with his right, the hand bearing the bronze finger. "Griff, take the Hiamahu Jewel. Use it cautiously. Use it wisely. You will need its powers in the coming war."

"What will happen to the Ungornem Gem?"

"It will be kept in Cauldron, heavily guarded, so True Shadow cannot get to it."

Griffin said nothing. Ramyr approached him. "Good luck in the days ahead, my son." He slipped the blue gem into Griffin's hand. "Keep it safe," he said, and he walked away.

Griffin found himself alone, the jewel in his hand glowing, vibrating slightly, sending a spark that seemed to move from his fingertips to his arms to his torso and to his very soul. He looked down at the stone map of Alastian, and his eyes fell on the blue pebble that represented the very jewel he was holding.

A smile danced upon his lips.

CHAPTER 43

Naymeira traveled east from Cauldron on horseback, a portion of her journey that took longer than she would have liked because of the countless hills that dominated the human and elf borders. She pulled at her horse's reigns as the Elder Forest came into view, and she breathed in the forest air.

I am nearly home, she thought, and she was surprised at the feeling of comfort that came over her. She had rarely felt that way when she was actually home.

She rode onward, north this time, following the forest's edge. When she spotted the Northern Plains to the west, she knew it was time to enter her homeland. She knew, too, that while time was short, her timing was also fortunate. Every three years the leaders of each dark elf tribe assembled at the sacred shrine of Larr to pay their respects to the Unseen Gods. According to custom, no violence could occur at Larr, lest it anger the gods. It was there that Naymeira intended to confront them, hopefully to unite them.

For another few hours, as daylight dwindled, she made her way through the forest. When night fell, she fought sleep and continued. Every time she would begin to nod off, she would be awakened by the sound of a crackling twig or the brush of a branch against her shoulder. She had no time to set up camp and close her eyes for a while. By the time morning arrived, Naymeira had come to the banks of the River Syl. She followed it northward until she reached Lake Sylvania. She gazed upon its placid waters, so different from the frothy sea of the south. The lake and she became partners in the quest. Whenever Naymeira glanced at it, her determination was reinforced, and she pushed onward. Naymeira would not rest.

On the third day, just as her mind was beginning to register exhaustion, she arrived at a row of trees, each carved with a different elvish symbol, leading to a small clearing. She blinked a few times, just to make sure she wasn't hallucinating, then followed the path.

Larr appeared to be a simple shrine, a large stone cube inscribed with ancient runes, their purpose being to ward off those who arrived with violent intentions. Surrounding the cube were eleven small pillars that represented the Unseen Gods. Next to each pillar sat tribe leaders, their black cloaks blowing in the winds like the dying leaves clinging to the trees around them. All were silent, even as Naymeira approached. They would not dare interrupt their vigil for fear of inviting the wrath of the gods. Naymeira waited, and the dark elves showed no sign of movement. She continued to wait as patiently as she could.

When the sun began to set over the tops of the trees, the eleven tribe leaders finally stood, turning toward her one by one. They did not move from their positions alongside the pillars. The nearest leader, a dark elf with blue eyes and long, brown hair braided down his back, spoke in a low, solemn voice. "I am Raygaul of the Vensaguard. Who are you, and why do you intrude upon our sacred ritual?" The other leaders watched her silently.

"I am Naymeira Darkleaf, a member of the Dromaguard."

"Impossible," said a silver-haired elf a few pillars away. He was Tuliv, Dromaguard's leader. "Naymeira was killed in an attack by a human and a dwarf from the west."

"I am the very same," she bowed. "As you can deduce, I was not killed. Indeed, you could say the human and the dwarf saved my life."

"Why have you come here, Naymeira Darkleaf?" asked Yaruf of the Jiguard.

Naymeira breathed deeply. "There is a threat in the far west. It is coming and coming soon. I have traveled three days without sleep to warn you of it and to ask for your assistance in fighting it. The Southerners have allied with a force known as True Shadow. If they are victorious, if they succeed in their aims, they will have Alastian on its knees."

"Then let Alastian fall!" shouted Pyreln of the Anoguard. "Ano believes in supremacy over others. If the gods desire change, who is to stop them?"

Naymeira raised her voice, but only slightly. "We will, of course. The tribes could be unified as they once were. We can fight under one banner and save our way of life. If we choose not to ally with the forces of good, are we not enabling the forces of evil?"

"Nonsense! And blasphemy, as well!" barked Xelon of the Quilaguard. "Imagine how we will look to others if we disregard so many years of devotion! Quila, lord of vanity, would frown upon us."

"Blasphemy? No, just the opposite," Naymeira continued. She motioned toward Raygaul. "Vensa is the master of fear, is he not?" Raygaul nodded. "Then we shall strike fear into the hearts of our enemies." She turned to Pyreln. "Ano's message will be upheld as well. We shall declare supremacy over True Shadow and the ruin it would bring." And to Xelon she said, "How would it appear to Quila, lord of vanity, if our way of life was humbled into submission?" Finally, Naymeira bowed again to Tuliv. "And Droma, his ever-reaching maw shall be opened once more in the coming days. Our forces shall greedily hunger for enemy kills until the Southern Plains are dyed crimson."

For a long while, the dark elf leaders said nothing. They looked toward one another, almost as if seeing each other for the first time. Finally, a tribe leader who was by far the eldest, his hair gray and his eyes a deep green, spoke in a voice like the whisper of the wind. "I am Kaas, leader of Nuelguard. The ways of Nuel, lord of fate, are a puzzle—even to the greatest of minds. But a belief in fate does not mean a choice of inaction. In the times of old, we were a powerful nation, joined as one... and still we crumbled. It was because we were not strong enough to fight against the disease that divided us. We were not courageous enough to stand as one and thus we fractured into many."

He rose from his seat. "The balance of power in our lands is delicate. If we are to unite once more, someone must lead." Kaas glided toward Naymeira and studied her face for several moments. The other leaders did the same. "We shall not choose," he said. "An ancient artifact will choose for us."

The elderly dark elf strode up to Larr's center and ran his fingers over the runes carved into the stone cube. Closing his eyes, his hand on the cube, he mouthed what appeared to be a prayer in an ancient tongue. For a few seconds, all was still. Then, suddenly, there was a loud crunch, like snow being crushed underfoot. The cube's sides fell to the ground, and its top flew into the trees. What was revealed brought the leaders into an even quieter silence.

On the remaining slab of stone was a white crown, simple yet so dazzling that it seemed to cast a bright light onto the entire forest. Naymeira gasped in wonder. The elvish legends were true. The Radiant Crown existed.

In the center of the crown was a single white gem.

CHAPTER 44

The sense of impending war grew by the hour. A mutual unease strengthened as the armies of Flame Web and True Shadow approached one another. Flame Web's army was an impressive array, riding swiftly across the yellowing Southern Plains upon their steeds and spiders. After a day spent mustering forces at Cauldron, they had traveled west for another two days, stopping only to sleep long enough so that fatigue didn't become a weak point in their armor. Still, exhaustion and anxiety hung like nooses around the soldiers' necks.

"We are six thousand strong," Commander Salek told Griffin, who rode beside him.

"Are we enough?" Griffin asked.

Salek grunted. "Undoubtedly, no." He lowered his voice. "If allies do not arrive, we are likely riding to our deaths."

Griffin said nothing, glumly taking a swig of water and staring ahead.

"Do not let that diminish your intent," said Salek. "We are also riding for the salvation of our realm. If we fall, then we fall as heroes."

"Heroes, yes," muttered Kwint, who rode behind Griffin. "And failures as well."

Ramyr Blade suddenly appeared beside them, as did Bo'cul and Takal. "Do not forget," he said, "we have a person of power among us."

"Two persons of power," Kwint corrected.

"Your gem," said Ramyr to the dwarf, "is worn around our enemy leader's throat. Until the day comes when that gem is ours, your powers are not of use."

Just then, horns blew as the ruins of Hellgrot came into sight—the remnants of a once great fortress cast down by the legions of time. A couple of nights earlier, while sitting around a campfire during a brief rest, Ramyr had told his son what he knew of Hellgrot's hazy history. It was as if he were telling him a bedtime story to make up for the years they missed together:

"Many theorize that it was built by Southerner ancestors. Or it was an ancient elvish outpost. Whatever the case, it is not generally a place where a man wants to find himself. As for the curse, it seems to have begun during a war long ago. During that time, there was a very powerful djinni—Malamus was his name—and he sided with True Shadow. He came to be known as the Dark Djinni, although he is no longer a true member of the djinn, not after breaking his kind's oath and attacking without provocation. He was relentless and unpredictable with his attacks. He laid entire villages to waste. In that age, Flame Web was much larger in number. Its leader at the time, Nateniel Strongarc, directed his efforts toward defeating Malamus. Their final battle took place at Hellgrot."

Griffin's father had not concluded the story that night because soldiers had arrived to inform Ramyr that Flame Web was ready to move on toward Hellgrot. But now, as they approached the ruins themselves, Griffin asked him to finish the tale.

"Malamus and Strongarc fought alone upon its ruined tower," said Ramyr. "Flame Web's leader was nearly defeated until he managed one final, desperate swing of his weapon, and the Dark Djinni toppled over the tower's side, landing... landing..." He squinted into the distance and then pointed. "Landing there, actually." There stood a lone sentinel alongside the ruins, a tall tree, a dead tree. Its long, gnarled branches made it look like a hand, perhaps the hand of a giant corpse who had suffocated in Hellgrot's soil.

"The Dark Djinni's body was never recovered. His fate remained a mystery. It may be that he simply disappeared from Alastian. Or not. A djinni's power is tied to his health. And just as they can live forever, their physical recovery can take ages, too. Regardless, many say a curse was placed upon this land that day."

"And what do you say?"

Griffin's father sighed. "I suppose we will find out soon enough."

Just then, Entian, the horsemaster, rode up beside them. "Very sorry to interrupt," he said, "but Griffin, I believe you would like to see what we have found."

Griffin followed him through a maze of soldiers on horseback until he was startled by a familiar sound—a rather annoyed horse's neigh. And there was Fuss, his old horse, whom he had been forced to leave behind.

"But... how?" said Griffin.

"We found him roaming free in the Northern Plains. Looks like he escaped from a stable somewhere near the dwarven lands," Entian explained. "One of our spies recognized him as yours. Put up quite a fight, that horse of yours."

Griffin leaped from his horse and ran to Fuss, patting him gently. The horse neighed contentedly, and Griffin returned—atop his old horse—to his father's side.

The horns blew a second time. The enemy had been spotted. A man rode up and whispered into Commander Salek's ear.

"Gocian scouts," Salek told Ramyr, and he rode forward, disappearing into the waves of soldiers.

War cries could now be heard from the hill where Hellgrot was situated. Gocian tribesmen emerged from the ruins wielding long spears. Their mounts were creatures Griffin had never seen before—great lizards of a sort, purple and green in color, with rows of gnashing yellow teeth. Large, spiked balls of iron were tied to the ends of their flexible tails. The Gocians' cries grew louder, and they shook their spears.

Ramyr watched the scene, then his eyes opened wide. "No. They're taunting us. They want us to charge. Men! Hold your positions!"

He rushed toward the front lines, but it was too late. Led by Commander Salek, Flame Web charged, a wave of spiders turning the hill black. The Gocians waited, then BOOM—men screamed as they were hurled into the air. Out of nowhere, a giant purple tail at least ten times larger than the others smashed a massive spiked ball into the ground, crushing and scattering Flame Web's forces. With a guttural roar, an enormous lizard revealed itself, towering over the others.

"The mother," whispered Griffin. He thought he was talking to Takal, but at that moment the djinni was leaping from his horse and transforming himself into a cyclone of sand. He flew toward the beast, but even amid the chaos of war the lizard saw him coming. The beast swung its deadly tail in his direction, narrowly missing the mark. The sand cyclone darted back and forth, and the lizard's large reptilian eyes followed it, almost with amusement. Suddenly, Takal flew into the ruins, and the great beast followed. Soon, both disappeared from view.

"Griffin!"

Kwint pulled Griffin from atop his horse, and as he fell toward the ground, he felt the breeze of a Gocian spear passing by his ear.

"Ya 'ave to pay attention," said the dwarf. "I can't save ya all the time."

In the confusion after the mother lizard's emergence, the Gocians had pushed forward, driving deep into Flame Web's lines. *We are being pushed back,* Griffin thought. *We have to take the ruins.* Kwint watched as Griffin removed the Hiamahu Jewel from his satchel.

"Do ya even know how to use it?"

"My father said its powers should bend to my will."

"And that's all ya need?"

A Gocian tribesman charged toward Griffin, who raised the gem above his head. A blast of blue light escaped from his palm, sending his attacker reeling backwards, twisted into a lifeless heap. He looked at Kwint and shrugged, almost apologetically. The two persons of power shared a momentary grin.

Griffin sent wave after wave of light against their foes, and for a while the Flame Web warriors managed to stay their ground. But then the enemy's true army arrived—row upon row of men in black cloaks riding stallions as dark as night. They rolled through Commander Salek's legions like water rushing past rocks in a stream.

"Fall back!" Ramyr shouted from afar, and Salek echoed his call.

A gap began to grow between the armies, and one of True Shadow's generals rode forward. He halted the enemy's front lines, trotted in front of them, and lowered his hood. "What do we have here?" cackled Ranimus, loud enough that both armies could hear him. "A force armed with a gem that can rival the power of the gods themselves, yet retreating like cowards." The merman raised his long sword. "We are the ones with power—the courage to crush our adversaries! The weak will be trampled beneath us!"

Legions of True Shadow warriors cheered and raised their swords. It was a strange pause in the battle, as if each army was sizing up the other. At that moment, Bo'cul jumped from his horse, strode forward before both armies and roared. He spit in the direction of the enemy. Ranimus only laughed, and his soldiers followed suit. The minotaur kneeled down and snatched a spear from the hand of a dead Gocian warrior. He stood up as the laughter died down, smiling slightly as he broke the spear in half like a twig. True Shadow grew silent. Although Bo'cul had no words, his message was clear to all:

The war has only just begun.

CHAPTER 45

The True Shadow army arranged itself in a defensive position around Hellgrot. Griffin and Kwint found Ramyr and Salek kneeling in the dust, drawing up plans with their fingers in the dirt. As they strategized, Griffin's father grew ever more frustrated until finally he threw his hands into the air.

"No! No! That is no path to victory!" he exclaimed, and he rubbed his temples.

But the frustration was only temporary. He raised his eyes in surprise when the sound of an unfamiliar horn echoed in the distance. As the sun set, throwing a red haze on the horizon, he glanced to the north. Over a hill, their armor glinting in glorious colors, came a wave of shortish soldiers wielding largish axes—weapons nearly as big as themselves. Then the sound of a single horse's gallop was heard, and the Flame Web ranks separated to allow the rider through.

"I, King Rindivor, have arrived!" he said, raising his axe toward the heavens. "And with me I bring the Dwarven

Legion and the blessings of the Nine Gods!" The dwarves behind him cheered and pounded their armored chests, and soon the soldiers of Flame Web did the same.

Griffin turned to say something to Kwint, but his friend had already made his way toward the king's horse. Kwint stood there for a moment, blinking nervously, then awkwardly bowed to his king.

"King Rindivor, sir. I am Kwint Kwinhollow from—"

"Oh, I know who ya are," said the king sternly. Then he leaped from his horse, surprisingly gracefully, and stood in front of Kwint. He placed a hand on his shoulder. "It will be an honor to fight beside ya, Kwint Kwinhollow."

As the king made his way to confer with the Flame Web leaders, Kwint just stood there, dumbfounded.

Griffin scanned the vast numbers of King Rindivor's army. *It seems the tide may turn in our favor,* he thought. He followed the king and arrived just as he was greeting his father and Salek.

"Ramyr, me old friend, today is a glorious day," said the king, his hands tightly gripping his axe handle. He noticed Griffin. "And this must be yer lad, the one ya can't stop boastin' about." He shook Griffin's hand. "Well done, my boy. Maybe now that I've met ya in person yer father will stop braggin' about ya."

Griffin looked at his father curiously. Ramyr simply tried to change the subject.

"King Rindivor, if we may, the battle is far from over. True Shadow's army has not even fully arrived yet. We must prepare."

Ramyr, Salek, the king, and the king's most trusted general spent the next several moments strategizing. But in the end, the plan was simple.

"So Flame Web will circle to the south of the enemy while the dwarves charge from the north. The hope is that they will have nowhere to go."

"An ancient dwarven tactic, that is." Rindivor actually winked at Griffin when he said it.

"And what about Griffin?" asked Ramyr.

Commander Salek looked toward Hellgrot. In the torch light, he could see row upon row of men silhouetted. Large, wooden stakes had been driven into the ground around them. "True Shadow's northern force has become more heavily defended since the dwarves arrived. Until we discover Seretigo's position, I think Griffin should fight with the dwarves."

Griffin stepped forward. "What? Why? My apologies, King Rindivor, but Flame Web's force is weaker. It would benefit us all if—"

"No, Griff," said Ramyr. "Commander Salek is right. You are needed for the charge."

"But what if... one of you is injured. I won't be there to—"

"Someone else will be there," said Ramyr. "We'll be fine."

He said it with as much conviction as he could.

They attacked at midnight. Earlier that evening, the crescent moon above had seemed like a bemused smile, but it soon disappeared into the darkness as ominous clouds rolled in. Cold rain began to fall, and soon all torchlight was reduced to smoldering sticks. The only light that could be seen in the darkness was a faint blue glow. It eminated from the Hiamahu Jewel, which Griffin gripped firmly in his fist.

With cries of "Rindivor!" and "Duna!" the dwarves charged into the night. Griffin quickly grew overwhelmed. Amid the chaos, he was a glowing beacon, but also a target. He sent countless blasts of light at his aggressors, but he was soon surrounded. The circle of enemies began to draw in closer and closer until a single figure stepped forward. Griffin held out his gem, but before it could produce a burst of power, it was knocked from his hand by the swift strike of an iron flail. Just before the light dimmed, the man drew back his hood. For a few moments, Griffin laid eyes once again on the face of Alnardo Fist. Then there was darkness.

"And so we are together again," said the voice of the Lord of Lies. "I see you finally have my gem. But my deadline has long passed."

Griffin fell to his knees and searched around frantically in the darkness, attempting to recover the jewel. But he found only trampled mud. He heard the jangle of a chain, as Fist raised his flail again.

"A shame really," said Fist. "You had such a bright future, and now you are to die in the dark."

Still searching for the gem, Griffin closed his eyes, waiting for the final blow. But it never arrived. Instead, there came the ear-shattering shriek of a great beast—a bird, it seemed, but more. Griffin heard the flapping of wings and the tearing of flesh and the screaming of men. And then a moment of quiet. He tentatively opened his eyes, and there stood before him a dream, a phantom. Was it a memory?

The voice of his father reverberated in his mind: *"It is the symbol of justice, luck and victory—a griffin. It is the source of your name. And, perhaps, the course of your destiny."*

Meanwhile, Takal was bating the great lizard, leading him farther and farther from Hellgrot. When he finally materialized into his original form by the banks of the River Baj, the beast growled in displeasure. Its tail swung back and forth violently, as if searching the air around it for the now familiar cloud of sand. The lizard turned back to the djinni and opened its jaws wide, revealing its many rows of yellow teeth and releasing the stench of death and decay. Takal drew his sword as the lizard's spiked tail swung in his direction. The djinni's bottom half turned to a whirl of sand in an instant. He flew upward to avoid the blow.

Now it was his turn to attack. Takal aimed his sword at the lizard's left eye and sped forward in a blur. The beast wailed and shook its head in pain, as Takal fell to the soft earth, the sword still protruding from the lizard's eye. He landed on his back, looking up at the lizard's purple, scaled midsection. The beast collapsed, hoping to smother Takal under its weight. But the djinni was faster, transforming into a sand storm and splitting into two halves, which flew around the lizard's body and rematerialized behind the great lizard.

When the beast's enormous body hit the soil, large chunks of earth began to crumble and fall. Just as Takal began to understand what was happening, the two of them fell, too, toppling into the River Baj and disappearing in the fast-moving waters.

CHAPTER 46

As the rising sun began to color the sky, the griffin offered Griffin a remarkable view of the battle below. They were doing well. Griffin had found the Hiamahu in the soft mud of the battlefield, and he and the dwarves—with the help of the great flying beast's deadly talons—had pushed hard into True Shadow's defense, and a large portion of their army was nearly cut off. Flame Web held their ground in the south. The enemy was nearly surrounded, an exception being a weak point to the east. Griffin directed his flying creature to glide down in that direction. It was only then that he found time to ponder the griffin's existence.

Have I gone mad? Am I dead? Is my corpse down there with the others, sinking into the muddy grass? Suddenly, he remembered the wooden statuette that Know had gifted to him atop the massive library tree in Gnarvik. *It can't be. No, that's ridiculous. It was lost with the wreckage of the Flamentari.* But then he noticed something peculiar about the griffin's eagle head. It was difficult to see at first, but as the morning light arrived, it became obvious. Amid the white feathers were brown ones, and they spelled out an unmistakable letter "K."

Griffin landed atop an ill-fated True Shadow warrior, and his heart leapt as he discovered Kwint and Bo'cul fighting side by side nearby. He launched a beam of blue light in their direction, sending their enemies flying and flailing. Kwint turned to face Griffin, and his mouth dropped open at seeing his friend riding atop the great beast of lore—part eagle, part lion, all real.

"Is—is that...?"

Griffin nodded. "Any word from my father? Or Salek?"

Kwint turned and repelled a warrior's attack, then Bo'cul finished him off with a slice of his two-handed axe.

"Bad news, I'm afraid," said the dwarf.

"What happened? Is my father all right?"

"No, no, nothing like that," said Kwint. "It's the black gem."

"It's guarded at Cauldron," said Griffin.

"No," Kwint replied. "It's gone. Taken."

Griffin's heart sank. "I must find my father." He prepared to take flight aboard the griffin.

"Wait!" shouted Kwint, and then his eyes met Griffin's. The dwarf started to speak, but for once he seemed tongue-tied. All he could spurt out was, "Good luck."

Bo'cul grunted in agreement. Griffin nodded. "And the same to you."

His friends soon became dots on the battlefield, an expanse increasingly littered with the blood and bodies of both sides. Griffin soared high into the sky and headed straight for Hellgrot. He flew over the enemy's front line, bombarding the fighters with blasts of blue light as he did so. He glided in circles, lower and lower over the field of battle, until he spotted his father fighting alongside his soldiers.

Flame Web's leader stands and fights, Griffin mused proudly. *Why is it that Seretigo is nowhere to be found?*

The question would soon be answered. Griffin landed in front of Ramyr, trampling two True Shadow soldiers. His father was so surprised that he nearly dropped his blade. And then he laughed.

"The Curio's magic is a marvel, indeed. I am grateful that little gnome is on our side." The great griffin let out a gentle squawk. "But Griffin, something horrible has happened at Cauldron..."

"The gem was stolen. I know. Kwint told me."

"Cauldron was laid to waste—by a force I can't explain," said Ramyr, as low drum beats could be heard from the east. "Not only that, Wayfere was killed. And the enemy's main force, the Southern Cavalry, is soon to arrive. Seretigo leads them."

Out of the chaos of the battle, the djinn Ragnar and Lagnar emerged, breathless, and rushed toward Ramyr.

"We must tell you something," cried Ragnar.

"Important and terrible," said Lagnar.

Ramyr shook his head. "No need. I hear Seretigo's drums."

Ragnar frowned. "No, not that. The enemy..." he began.

"... has a greater power," Lagnar finished.

Suddenly, a blast of wind came from Hellgrot, confusing both armies and all but stopping the fighting temporarily. The sky grew dark. The battlefield grew quiet. A great black vortex came spiraling from the ruins, followed by two smaller, gray whirlwinds.

Ragnar shuddered. "Malamus lives again."

Lagnar's body tensed. "And the Dark Djinni has returned with a vengeance."

Ramyr took a moment to absorb the information, but only a brief moment. "Griffin, I need you to attack Seretigo's force," he commanded. "And Ragnar, Lagnar... is there still no sign of Talak?"

"None," they said in unison.

"One of my powerful assets, and he disappears before the main battle has begun." He ran his fingers through his hair in frustration, then pointed toward the black and gray cyclones growing ever nearer. "I'm afraid you will be outnumbered."

Ragnar's eyes widened. "Three djinn against two?"

Lagnar's jaw dropped. "And one of the three defied death itself!"

"We are out of options, my friends. Go. Now."

And so two great pillars of yellow sand rose and began to swirl furiously, sending blasts of warm air all around them. They traveled toward the dark tornados wreaking havoc on the Flame Web armies, aiming for a confrontation.

Griffin directed his great flying beast toward another target—the new host of True Shadow warriors, cavalry, and Gocian lizard-riders. As he glided over the army, he gasped at its size. The griffin soon landed with its beak open wide, snatching a soldier from his horse, shaking him, and dropping his lifeless body to the side. Griffin spotted Seretigo in the distance. The man was difficult to miss, as he was surrounding by waving banners and upright guards on elegant horses. But soon the chaos of the battle obscured even the self-importance of the king.

A Gocian and his lizard leaped toward Griffin, who simply opened his palm wide. Instantly, the lizard was catapulted backward by a shaft of blue light. He was doing his part, but as he scanned the battlefield he realized that the enemy was slowly advancing, charging into Flame Web's weaker defenses, gaining every advantage it could.

The battle is no longer in our favor, Griffin thought. *We are losing.*

CHAPTER 47

There was an empty clearing in the center of the battle-field, almost like the eye of a hurricane. It was there that the djinn converged. Their cyclones suddenly ceased to spin. The drifting colors of sand changed slowly into new forms—feet and legs, arms and torso, head—until four humanoid sand giants stood face to face. The fifth, the Dark Djinni, stood taller than the others, nearly matching the height of Hellgrot itself. His eyes burned bright red with aggression centuries in the making.

Ragnar, in his sand-giant form, made the first attack, sending a thundering fist into Malamus, creating a massive hole where the djinni's chest used to be. Malamus had no reaction. His chest simply reformed around the hole, and he kicked Ragnar's legs out from under him, sending the djinni's giant form toppling to the ground. The sands that formed the Dark Djinni's face twisted into a cruel smile.

As Ragnar's legs began to recompose, the two gray djinn began to move toward Lagnar. Each grabbed one of his arms, pulling on either side until they separated from his torso and scattered into the wind. One of the djinn curled his hand into a fist and prepared to thrust it toward Lagnar's head. But suddenly a sound came from the east, and while the gray djinni was distracted, Lagnar head-butted him, sending him crashing backward.

Men say war can feel like an eternity, Lagnar thought. *Djinn combat is that and then some.*

Griffin turned his head. *What is that sound?* It came again, louder this time. *Are those horns? Gongs?* Hovering above the battlefield, he first noticed a bright, white light coming from the east, almost as if the sun were rising again. He closed his eyes for a moment, then reopened them. A wide smile crept over his face.

A procession of elves was cresting a hill—male and female, riding horses of silver and gray, armed with blades and bows. At the head of the legion were the leaders of each of the eleven elvish tribes. Each leader rode atop a black stallion. The dark elves had arrived.

In the middle of the front line, atop a magnificent stallion as black as coal, was Naymeira herself, a throwing dagger in each hand and a magnificent white crown atop her head.

"For the Eleven!" she cried, and the gem affixed to her crown glowed fiercely.

"For the Eleven!" her army echoed, many hundreds of voices strong.

Naymeira tilted her head skyward, and a beam of white light shot into the heavens, the crown somehow channeling the power of the gem. The dark elves cheered and charged into Seretigo's forces, decimating a large number of True Shadow's warriors. The enemy was surrounded—Flame Web to the south, the dwarves to the north, and the dark elves to the east. True Shadow was slowly being pushed back, westward, into Hellgrot's ruins.

Griffin directed his winged creature to land just behind Naymeira, just as he sent a blast of blue light toward her nearest foe. She turned to see where it had come from and smiled, not appearing the least surprised to see him riding a beast that was half-eagle and half-lion.

"Nice bird," she said.

"Nice crown," he replied.

"The crown is fine," she agreed, as white light shot from her forehead, knocking a Gocian lizard onto its side. "But the gem is better."

"How did you do it?" asked Griffin, as he leaped from the griffin and finished the lizard off with a blaze of blue power. "How did you unite them?"

"It seemed impossible at first," she said, twirling and tossing her daggers behind her head, landing them in the neck and torso of an enemy soldier. "But then each tribe leader placed the Radiant Crown atop his head. If the legends were true, the crown would choose the long-awaited dark elf leader. It chose none of them. But then it was placed atop my head, and it chose me. Or at least the Anoelmenoh Gem did. All I have to do is... focus."

"Quite a sensation, isn't it?" said Griffin, as he directed a blast of light into a charging group of soldiers, sending them toppling end over end and falling in crumpled heaps. "My father was right when he said that people of power have a tendency to find each other."

Naymeira laughed. "I'm glad we did."

"But Naymeira, for now we are the only ones. The black gem was stolen. The red gem is theirs. Keep pushing forward." He climbed aboard his griffin once more. "Good luck. I'm going to look for Seretigo and his generals."

The griffin flew off toward the setting sun, which was just beginning to dip below the horizon. The second day of all-out war would soon come to an end. As Griffin glided toward the ruins of Hellgrot, he noticed the unusual dead tree that his father had pointed out just before the battle had begun. A few moments later, he landed his griffin on the palm of the tree's gnarled, grasping hand.

Griffin dismounted and drew his sword.

CHAPTER 48

Exhausted and drenched in his humanoid form, Takal sputtered and spit water from his mouth. He had been carried southwest by the river's current. He knew not how far. As he bobbed amid more placid waters, he struggled to clear his head and recall what had occurred. *The great lizard is dead.* The djinni clearly remembered the beast's carcass strewn across sharp rocks at the river's edge. He considered himself fortunate not to have experienced the same fate, especially when he rubbed his head and arrived at a large, painful welt, an odd sensation. *Very fortunate,* he thought. Slowly, he willed himself out of the water and looked around. Hellgrot was nowhere in sight. Neither were the armies of Flame Web and True Shadow.

"Wonderful," the djinni muttered to himself. "And Ramyr was relying on me..."

For a while at least, he was in no condition to whip up a whirlwind and find his way back to the fray. He turned his attention back to the flowing waters of the River Baj, and in the early morning light he spotted something in the distance, approaching from downstream. A boat!

Takal squinted. Not a river-pirate. This boat's sails had diagonal stripes of blue and white. Not reinforcements from Bajuru either. *Their colors are crimson and gold.* As the vessel drifted toward his position, Takal lowered himself back into the water, hiding much of his appearance so the sailors wouldn't be frightened.

"Help!" he shouted when the boat came close. Dozens of men struggled with their oars, pushing the vessel forward against the current.

The sailors rushed to his aid, lowering a rope ladder. Takal climbed to the deck, wet and tired, and was immediately wrapped in a wool blanket. The boat's captain approached him.

"Who are you? And how, may I ask, did we find you bobbing alone in the River Baj?"

The djinni rose to his full height and let the blanket fall to the deck. "I am Takal. I am a djinni. And I was carried by the currents away from a great battle being waged upstream. Perhaps the greatest battle. It is being fought at Hellgrot."

The sailors glanced at one another, their gazes mixed with fear and resolve. "We are aware of the battle," said the captain. "But I must ask you: On which side are you fighting?"

Takal looked him in the eye and answered truthfully. "Flame Web."

The captain's expression changed. His eyes seemed to smile. "Then we are here to help." He motioned toward a fleet of riverboats coming upriver behind them. "I am Captain Genthus Nyrn, and we are the men of Firstport."

Naymeira was hopeful. *Victory draws near,* she mused. They had nearly pushed True Shadow back into Hellgrot. *Once we take the ruins, the battle is ours.* She scanned the area around her and spotted a group of enemy soldiers. A perfect target...

Thwack! An arrow plunged into the back of her leg. Naymeira fell to the ground, the Radiant Crown falling and landing unceremoniously in the mud. Pain exploded from her left leg. She reached forward, but a boot heel landed on her forearm.

Naymeira looked up to see a short man, his nose bent like a crooked branch. General Cairon smiled over her. He picked up the crown and placed it in his satchel. Then he swung his foot, his boot connecting with her jaw. She fell unconscious into the mud, and he lifted her body onto the back of his horse.

As Cairon rode toward Hellgrot, he chuckled to himself. *This will bring us the last piece of the puzzle. King Seretigo will be pleased.*

Kwint's mighty axe seemed like an extension of his arm. He swung it wildly, always a step ahead of his enemies. *I was once dismissed as a beggar,* he thought. *Now I am a warrior.* He looked around, frantically trying to locate another opponent. The gods gave him one.

Their eyes met first. He wore an orange robe and a sinister grin, as he stepped forward to meet Kwint in combat, a war hammer in his hands. "Ah, my not-so-loyal gem guardian! I seem to recall our last meeting at a tavern." His smile faded. "I do not recall it fondly."

Kwint balanced his war axe in his hands. "Funny, Thrutch. It's one of my favorite memories." He aimed for Thrutch's knees. But his former captor slid to the side, and the axe missed its mark.

"That's Ambassador Thrutch to you, maggot." He swung his hammer, but Kwint ducked, narrowly missing being bludgeoned.

"You are no ambassador. You are a coward, a pathetic excuse for a dwarf."

Kwint swung once more, eyeing Thrutch's throat this time. But Thrutch blocked the blow with his hammer, sending a jolt through Kwint's arm.

"Pathetic? When we met, you were a lowly beggar. We could 'ave been a powerful pair—yer gem-wielding, my strategy. Yer a fool, Kwinhollow. I gave you riches. I gave you purpose."

Kwint had to roll sideways to avoid the next hammer blow. "You gave me a prison," he spat. "I am no beggar, just as you are no ambassador."

Thrutch just laughed and raised his hammer above his head and brought it down. This time, it was Kwint who blocked the attempt, rising to his feet just as the hammer lowered.

"I'll aim for yer legs," said Thrutch. I'll break 'em both. When we defeat Flame Web, you will live out yer days on the streets o' Bajuru as a wretch, a pitiful creature. Filth. You will spend yer days begging for scraps o' food, Kwinhollow. I will be sure of that."

Thrutch attempted another blow, aimed at Kwint's left leg. But with reflexes that his enemy wasn't counting on, Kwint sidestepped the hammer, grabbed Thrutch's arm, and used his momentum to toss him to the ground. Thrutch's heavy war hammer fell from his grasp, Kwint stepped on his chest to hold him in one place.

"Wait! Mercy!" shouted Thrutch.

Kwint lifted his axe "Who's begging now?"

A head went rolling toward the ruins, its sinister grin having been replaced by abject fear.

Men. Dwarves. Elves. Blades. Blood.

Bo'cul felt the air shift behind him. He turned just in time to glimpse a mace heading toward his skull. The minotaur ducked, yanked it from his attacker's hand, and sent it flying into the man's face. The man was down in an instant.

Where is he? Bo'cul thought. He sniffed the air. *Fish. I smell fish.*

And then there he was, his black horse trotting toward the minotaur. Bo'cul laughed as the scars from jellyfish stings became evident on his face.

"Why do you find me so humorous, bull?" Ranimus snarled. "Is this how you prefer to confront death?

Bo'cul roared, spittle flying from his mouth. *No,* he thought, *this is how I confront the soon-to-be dead.*

Ranimus's horse whinnied and attempted to gallop away. As he tried to restrain the animal, Bo'cul roared even louder, and this time the horse bucked Ranimus off, sending the merman and his sword into the tall grass around them. The stallion neighed joyfully with the weight lifted from its back, trotted into nearby tall grass and began to chew contentedly. Ranimus simply rose to his feet, his albino eyes red with fury, a curved Jagamaurian blade in his hand. But compared to Bo'cul's gigantic double-sided axe, it looked more like a dagger than a sword.

"Do you like it?" Ranimus hissed. "The demons of Jagamaur certainly make sturdy blades. Sharpest in Alastian, they say. But I have added a little something of my own." The merman tilted his sword so that the sun caught a black liquid that seemed to line the edge of the blade. He began to walk toward Bo'cul. "There is a rare plant located near the top of a select few mountains on the Isle of Eag. Those who know its secrets can transform it into a most deadly poison. Slow Death, it is called in the Far South. When it enters your bloodstream... well, why spoil the surprise?"

Not wasting a moment, Bo'cul charged the demon, and steel met steel. The clank of axe and blade could be heard from afar. Again. And again. And again. Bo'cul was stronger, yet Ranimus was swifter, dodging, leaping, counterattacking. As the sun began to grow low, and the sky turned into a lavender haze, the darkening surroundings mirrored a growing anger in Bo'cul. He remembered the days he had spent alone in his cell with only his tears as company. He recalled how he had been seconds away from execution, from a most horrible death. And he turned his rage into a weapon.

When axe and blade met once more, the clash was so mighty that Bo'cul's axe flew from his hands. Ranimus was knocked to his knees, and his blade shattered. Bo'cul felt a small shard of metal plunge into his left shoulder, but he felt no pain. The merman eyed the metal protruding from the minotaur, and this time he began to laugh.

"The poison should already be spreading through your body! You are marked for death, bull!"

So are you, Bo'cul thought. He pulled the shard from his shoulder and stabbed the merman through the heart. Ranimus fell dead on the spot.

Bo'cul dropped to one knee. It was growing difficult to breathe. The battlefield began to blur around him. He collapsed on the ground beside his enemy.

CHAPTER 49

The riverboats of Firstport dropped anchors, and sailor–soldiers streamed out, wielding swords and crossbows. Takal morphed into sand and watched from above, as the men approached Hellgrot from the west. He saw that the battle had transformed while he was away. The dwarves and dark elves had joined their cause, and True Shadow's forces were ever so slowly backing up to the ruins. He saw, too, great whirls of sand and wind darting and charging with tremendous speed and power.

Takal's eyes narrowed. *And so, like in the days of old, the djinn shall face off once more.*

He counted five djinn, not including himself. As far as he knew, Wayfere was still alive, but still guarding the black gem at Cauldron. That could only mean...

"Malamus has returned," he muttered to himself.

Takal was off in an instant, fearlessly blazing off toward his fellow djinn until he reached the center of the storm. To the rest of the participants in the battle, it was just a blur of shifting and thrusting cyclones. But time slows down for the djinn. It was obvious who had been winning the conflict. The yellow djinn, Ragnar and Lagnar, were riddled with holes, repairing themselves ever more slowly. The gray djinn were struggling, too. The black djinni, Malamus, seemed by far the strongest.

There must be a significant shift in power to end this combat, thought Takal. With a deep breath, he closed his eyes. Fierce winds whipped around him. Power coursed through his soul. When his eyes opened, they were as red as the setting sun. He formed a cyclone of white swirling sand.

He knew what he had to do first. Takal drifted toward Malamus and hovered directly in front of the Dark Djinni. Malamus did not hesitate. He charged forward, aiming for his enemy's head, and Takal exploded into a great cloud, rings of sand vibrating outward from his original position. A cruel laugh seemed to eminate from Malamus, echoing across the Southern Plains.

But Takal drew his power from his righteousness. And his right was greater than Malamus's might. *Malamus attacked first. My oath is intact.* In an instant, the circles of sand retracted inward again, converging on the Dark Djinni with such force and pressure that there was no escape. The black, swirling sand giant wobbled, then grew suddenly motionless. The Dark Djinni's body fell with a thud and then began to dissolve, as if melting. The once mighty and feared Malamus had been reduced to a stain in the sand.

Takal drifted alongside Ragnar and Lagnar and turned toward the two gray djinn, who had long ago taken the side of True Shadow, choosing conquest over their oath of protection. The three of them charged forward with fists of wind and fire, but the gray djinn raised shields of sand and rock, deflecting the attack.

So that is the game, thought Takal. *Humanoid form and weapons.* His hands morphed into two jagged white swords. Ragnar did the same, creating a flail. Lagnar transformed his arm into a spear. The gray djinn responded with weapons of their own. Slash, dodge, slice. The djinn trio forced the evil djinni duo slowly backwards. Swipe, slide, swing. They soon had the gray djinn backed up against the ruins of Hellgrot's tallest tower. Lagnar hurled a spear at one of them, pinning him to the tower. His limbs flailed wildly. Athough there was no blood, the djinni was evidently in a great deal of pain. The other djinni, struck directly in the forehead by Ragnar's flail, fell to the ground. The two gray djinn locked eyes and then nodded to one another, defeated. In the blink of an eye, they morphed into gray clouds of sand and zoomed into the distance, beyond the horizon, not to be seen again for ages to come.

Ragnar and Lagnar cheered lustily, raising their weapons high. Takal allowed a tired smile and looked up to see a winged beast nearing the top of the highest tower. *A griffin? Where in Alastian did that creature come from?* He then grinned when he recognized the man riding the creature. As Takal stared up in fascination, Griffin stared down. Their eyes met, but then Takal noticed the Griffin's eyes seemed to widen in fear. He was looking right behind Takal. Drop by drop, layer by layer, black stain transformed into black sand, and the black sand sculpted itself into the giant humanoid shape of

Malamus the Unending. There were countless daggers at his fingertips.

Takal turned just in time. He swung his great sword in an arc, just as his enemy threw the daggers. And just as suddenly as Malamus had returned, the Dark Djinni fell for the final time, countless grains of black sand wafting aimlessly with the winds, most of them drifting to the Far South, where they were enveloped by the great ocean.

But the Dark Djinni's daggers had been thrown. Takal's world seemed to spin. He attempted to take a step forward, but found himself on the ground, gazing toward a sky that seemed to be darkening rapidly.

CHAPTER 50

Griffin feared for Takal, but he had to focus on the task at hand. Minutes earlier, he had landed beside his father on the battlefield. He had jumped to the ground, and they had shared a brief embrace.

"More good tidings, Griff? Several of Seretigo's generals have been defeated. Our armies seem to have them trapped. The power of the white gem has been brought to Flame Web..."

"I'm afraid not," Griffin had interrupted. "Naymeira was injured. Most of the men believe she was captured, as well— she and the Radiant Crown. It seems the white gem is theirs."

Ramyr looked stricken and said, his voice now quiet, "That leaves only yours."

Griffin had nodded, then climbed back aboard his flying companion. "We need that gem. We need Naymeira. And I'm going to find her."

"Griff!" Ramyr had shouted. "You cannot try it alone!" But by then his son was already too far away to hear and too determined to listen.

When the battle had begun to shift in Flame Web's favor, Seretigo had retreated into the stone towers and pillars of Hellgrot's ruins. Griffin had a notion where the king might be found. *Seretigo is an arrogant man,* he had thought. *Arrogant men always want to look down on everything else.*

While veering toward Hellgrot's tallest tower, which was almost entirely intact, Griffin had peered down to see the last moments of the djinn battle. *I may possess the gem,* he thought. *But there is no rival to the powers of the djinn in this world.* Was Takal going to survive? He desperately hoped so, but he also knew that his actions could determine the survival of Alastian as well.

Griffin spotted four figures atop the tower. Without a second thought, he landed among them, sword drawn. Almost immediately, he feared that he might have made a fatal mistake.

Seretigo stood to the side, stroking his bright red beard. His other hand held the Ungornem Gem. The Mizzarkh sparkled on a band around his neck, and the Radiant Crown sat askew atop his head. All three gems—red, white, black—glowed intensely, united once more.

Naymeira was nearby, gagged, with both her hands and feet bound. On one side of her stood a man with a grotesquely bent nose. Griffin figured him for a general. Next to him was a burly younger man, a Southerner who carried two blades on each side of his belt. There seemed to be worry in his eyes.

As Griffin landed, the general immediately seized Naymeira and placed a blade—twisted like his nose—to Naymeira's throat. Seretigo showed no surprise.

"Ah, you have come, as expected, Griffin Blade."

Griffin began to reach into his pocket for the Hiamahu Jewel, but the general only drew his dagger closer to Naymeira's throat.

"Dismount that ghastly bird of yours and hand me the gem," Seretigo demanded, "or this so-called queen of the elves will bleed royal red. I long ago grew impatient at the trouble you have caused me, Blade."

Griffin battled to control his anger. "You brought it upon yourself," he said, through clenched teeth, "the day you took my father from me."

"Mind your tongue, Blade. You may temporarily hold power, but I have the power to end your friend's life with a simple nod." He took a step forward. "Ramyr Blade was a criminal, a traitor to the crown. I urged my own father to kill him. He didn't. He was weak. And now my father is dead and yours lives. Now, is that justice?"

The king began to walk slowly toward Griffin. "It was then when I truly understood what drives True Shadow. The strong live. The weak die. At first, after my father's death, only one thing truly mattered to me—your demise. Revenge. I searched everywhere for you, yet you eluded me, thief that you are, living in the shadows like some sort of insect. I figured you were dead. You had to be. I was satisfied. But then you returned, like a ghost from my past, intent on causing me nothing but grief." Seretigo shook off the thought. "Grief is for the weak. I am strong. True Shadow is mighty."

He eyed the griffin like he was seeing it for the first time, and he chuckled. "It could not be more fitting. The legends

claim that the griffin is a symbol of victory in battle. And yet…
hold your bird at bay, Blade, or General Cairon here will slit
your friend's throat. Kelgy! Put that filthy thing in chains."

"Yes, sir," replied the younger, broad-shouldered man.

Reluctantly, seeing the fear in Naymeira's eyes, Griffin
did as he was told. He kept the griffin from attacking, while
the man grabbed a long, rusted chain that had been un-
touched for ages atop the ruins and wrapped it around the
beast's talons. The distraught and confused griffin's screech-
es and caws could be heard across the battlefield below, a
noise the man ended by wrapping another chain around its
beak. Both chains he tied to one of the large, iron spikes that
protruded from the edges of the tower's roof.

"It's a wonderful metaphor, isn't it?" Seretigo smiled.
"Victory being chained by the forces of True Shadow."

"But it is a false premise," said Griffin.

"Oh? And why is that?"

"Because we have won. Your forces are overwhelmed. You
could kill both Naymeira and me, if you choose, but the victory belongs to Flame Web."

"That is where you are wrong," said Seretigo. "The strong
survive. The weak wither. You are holding the Hiamahu. I
hold the other three. All four of the Sister Jewels have not
been reunited since the ancient ages. I trust you are aware
of what occurs when one person holds all four of the gems."

Griffin's eyes darted back and forth, as he searched for
any advantage. He kept his voice steady. "I have heard stories."

"Yes, it is wondrous, if the ancient texts are to be believed.
When all four gems are in one man's possession, he inherits

all the power. My power shall be supreme, unstoppable. I will wreak havoc on my enemies, starting with your pathetic family and friends. Power is strength, and the strong live on, Griffin Blade." He held out his right hand. "Now give it to me."

Griffin hesitated, then released a sigh. He slowly reached into his pocket and removed something from it. He extended his arm and, revealing what was in his hand, he smiled mischievously. Sitting on his palm was a blue pebble, snatched days earlier from the stone map at Cauldron.

"You are playing a dangerous game, Blade. I will give you one more chance. Hand me the Hiamahu Jewel, and I promise the elf will live."

"Your promises are as valuable as your courage, Seretigo. And I'm afraid I don't have the jewel with me," said Griffin, as the king glowered. "I cannot help but find it funny that you were searching for me all those years when I wasn't really hiding in the shadows at all. I was right under your nose—not in name, perhaps, but in person all the same. In fact, I worked for the Lord of the Lies. I was the very thief whom he sent to steal the gem in the first place."

Astonishment registered on Seretigo's face. "You worked for..." he began, and then he muttered, "I'll have Fist's head for this."

"No need. My griffin handled that on the battlefield."

The leader of True Shadow grew quiet. He balled his hands into fists, and his face grew as red as the gem that hung from his neck. "Cairon!" he shouted, and then he added quietly, "kill her."

Naymeira and Griffin locked eyes briefly, as the general's dagger was lowered to her throat. But suddenly, a large black creature scrambled to the top of the tower. It was a giant spider. Atop it rode a dwarf, and he was brandishing a flail. With one well-timed swing, he knocked the dagger from the general's hand and sent him flying backwards—right onto one of the roof's protruding iron spikes. He lay limp, never to rise again.

Seretigo stood shocked for a second, then he quickly ducked out of sight through an archway too narrow to allow the spider to follow. Griffin quickly rushed up to the man called Kelgy and held his sword to his throat. He then turned to face the dwarf, who had dismounted from his spider and was smiling through an umistakable silver beard.

"Roland!" Griffin nearly dropped his blade in excitement.

"The one and only." The dwarf hopped from his spider and rushed up to Griffin, hugging him tightly around the waist. "Do you remember," he added, stepping back, "what you asked when our journey began? You wondered what a dwarf's silver beard represented. It's loyalty, Griffin. And you have mine."

The dwarf bent down to free Naymeira and then rushed to the archway where Seretigo had disappeared. "He's gone," said Roland, "but we'll find 'im."

"For now, watch him," said Griffin, removing his sword from the burly soldier's neck and instead quickly unchaining the griffin. Cornered by Roland's spider, the soldier found himself backed to the edge, the heels of his boots hanging over a long drop to the ground below. Griffin turned his attention back to the man and walked toward him.

"You look oddly familiar to me. How is that possible?"

"You... you probably don't remember me," said the soldier, his voice quavering. "My true name is Saiof Kelgen..."

Griffin gasped. He suddenly remembered the stableboy from Cana, the boy who had been so helpful during his desperate search for his father so many years before.

"Saiof..."

"Hello, Griffin." The man tried to smile, but a single tear formed in the corner of his eye.

"You were so kind to me. You... you were kind." Griffin could find no words.

"We were children," said Saiof. "Our paths diverged long ago. You chose what was right for you. I chose what was best for me. I have been corrupted by True Shadow. I see that now. But it was my choice."

Griffin moved closer. "But it is not your fate. You still can choose..."

Saiof held up a hand to stop Griffin and shook his head, the tears streaming freely now. "No," he whispered, "my path ends here."

With that, Saiof Kelgen stepped backwards from the tower, plummeting to the earth below.

CHAPTER 51

His mind reeling, Griffin solemnly unchained his bird, which screeched and stretched its wings joyfully. Griffin hopped on and turned to his friends. "I'm going to find my father. And we're going to find Seretigo."

Roland and Naymeira looked up at him. They both seemed to want to say something, but couldn't find the words. Roland nodded. Naymeira just smiled.

Minutes later, atop the griffin's back, Ramyr and Griffin Blade were soaring far above the battlefield. Convinced that Seretigo was fleeing with the three gems, they scanned the grass plains below.

"It seems that we were destined to end this war together," said Ramyr.

"At the moment," Griffin replied, "I'm just concerned with ending Seretigo."

"And the Hiamahu Jewel?" asked his father. "We can't risk all four falling into Seretigo's hands."

"It is safe, father." Just then, Griffin's eyes lit up. He pointed westward. A lone horseman rode toward the setting sun as his black cloak billowed behind him. "There he is! We can stop him at the river."

Their hair whipped behind them, as the griffin dived sharply toward a stretch of the River Baj frothing white and littered with sharp boulders. Crossing was impossible. Seretigo heard the griffin before he saw it. He pulled at the reins of his horse and turned to face the oncoming beast. The king, still stubbornly adorned in the Radiant Crown, crouched low in his saddle.

"What is he doing?" Ramyr wondered.

The griffin dived lower, its talons outstretched. When it was mere feet away from grabbing the man, Seretigo leaped forward off his horse with a dagger in each hand. He managed to stab each dagger into the griffin's flesh, as the creature shrieked in pain and feathers drifted to the ground. The beast veered violently, its wings flapping frantically. Griffin managed to wrap one arm around its neck to prevent himself from falling, but Ramyr lost his grip and tumbled to the side, saved only by his son grabbing his hand at the last instant.

Ramyr Blade and Seretigo Va'hou found themselves staring face to face, only a few feet apart, one clinging desperately to his son and the other to his daggers as the griffin twisted and ascended, heading back toward Hellgrot. With his free hand, Ramyr fumbled for his sword. Seretigo let go of his right hand and unsheathed his own blade. It was then that the final fight between Flame and Shadow began.

Ramyr drove his sword forward, but Seretigo barely drew his blade in time to deflect the attack. For the next several moments, they traded thrusts and parries while dangling precariously above the Southern Plains. Meanwhile, Griffin was losing his grip on his father, and Seretigo's hand was beginning to slip from his long dagger handle. With one final attempt, Seretigo knocked the sword from Ramyr's hand, and it fell a few hundred feet to the ground below. The king grinned, but before he could finish off his opponent, Ramyr swung his legs and let go of his son's hand. He used his momentum to leap and grab hold of the griffin's long lion tail. Seeing that Ramyr was out of range, Seretigo created his own momentum and clambered atop the creature. He reached down, pulled the dagger from the beast's side, and plunged it deep into the griffin's back, eliciting a screech of pain.

They were circling Hellgrot's ruined tower now, as the griffin cawed and shrieked, craning its neck to see what was happened behind it and atop its back. As Griffin grasped its neck and Seretigo gripped his dagger, the two men glared at each other, swords in their free hands.

"Your legacy of failure will live on after you die, Blade," said the leader of True Shadow.

Griffin didn't reply. At that moment, amid the chaos, he glanced at his father dangling from the griffin's tail and suddenly recalled his fight with Thrutch in the Giggling Goose at Dunalar. It seemed so long ago. *I imagined myself facing off against Seretigo in the place of my father. Now I do it to save him.*

He lunged at the king, but it was a feeble, off-balance attack, easily dodged.

"After I run my sword through you," Seretigo said, "this disgusting creature will serve as a reminder of your failure." He raised his weapon high. "It will be tortured..." Seretigo swung. Griffin blocked. "It will be tormented..." Seretigo sliced toward Griffin's midsection, and their blades met again. "It will be made to suffer..." His blade arced toward Griffin's neck, but was again repelled.

And then Griffin laughed. "You think I worry about my legacy? You should be more concerned with your own."

Griffin let go of the creature's neck and balanced himself, at one with his griffin. "You will be remembered as a coward..." He raised his sword. "As a gluttonous son of a gutless father." As Seretigo focused on the long blade, Griffin swiftly reached behind his head and grabbed a throwing dagger from a sheath attached to his upper back.

The last words that he spoke to Seretigo were a whisper. "... as the king who fell..."

Seretigo's eyes widened. He looked down at his chest to find the hilt of a dagger buried deep in his heart. A red stain expanded around the dagger. His eyes grew cloudy.

"The strong... survive," the king gurgled.

With that, Seretigo Va'hou, King of Bajuru, Supreme Commander of True Shadow, toppled and fell. The world seemed to freeze as his body descended. The Radiant Crown lifted from his head and spiraled downward. Even the gods were watching, it seemed, for with a thud and a sickening crack Seretigo landed on the very tree where Malamus had supposedly perished so many years before. But there was no uncertainty about this death.

The cursed tree—a gnarled hand, clawing desperately at the day's fading light—was from that day forward known as the Hand of the Fallen Shadow.

The scarlet sun passed beneath the horizon, and dusk began to blanket the plains. *The gods like their little jokes, don't they?* Griffin mused. *Darkness envelops the world, just as darkness is routed from this realm.*

CHAPTER 52

Griffin and Ramyr stood solemnly on the Hand of the Fallen Shadow. The wind whispered like a chorus of a thousand hushed voices. Seretigo had fallen on his back. He seemed almost peaceful, staring up at the star-filled sky—a stare only dead men can achieve.

Ramyr leaned over and tugged at the chain that decorated the fallen king's neck, breaking the Mizzarkh free. He examined the red gem for a moment and then sighed with relief. Griffin withdrew the Ungornem Gem from Seretigo's breast pocket and placed it gently in his own. At that moment, a horseman pulled his steed to a halt below them, stood tall in his stirrups, and raised a dazzling white item in his hand.

"Nearly landed on my head, sir," he said.

Ramyr reached down to retrieve the Radiant Crown, the Anoelmenoh Gem still sparkling from its center. He turned to face his son, who noticed that years of weariness seem to have vanished from his face. "That leaves one more, Griff. Where is it?"

Griffin grinned and pointed toward the tree's thick, contorted branches—the fingers of the hand.

"What of them?" asked Ramyr.

"Look at the index finger," said Griffin. "Where the knuckle might be."

Suddenly, his father understood. The second of the five twisted branches bore a large knot, but upon closer inspection it was now only a covering of sorts. Ramyr looked at his own index finger, the bronze now battle-worn, caked with blood and dirt. Then he chuckled and removed the knot from the branch. Sure enough, the Hiamahu gleamed like a blue eye amid the dark notch in the tree, shining brighter than ever before.

"I had to make sure Seretigo wouldn't find it, no matter what happened to me," said Griffin. He shrugged. "I suppose he came closer to it than I expected."

Ramyr glanced down at the king's corpse, then at the jewel once more. "Perhaps a trade."

"What do you mean, father?"

Ramyr pressed down on where his bronze finger attached to his hand. With a small pop, the bronze mechanism separated and landed in his palm. He retrieved the Hiamahu Jewel, leaving the bronze part in its place.

"A new finger for the Hand."

"Griffin, come quickly!" a voice shouted from below.

He would recognize that voice anywhere. Kwint sat atop a horse, one arm bandaged, the other holding the reins. *Thank the gods he survived.* "What is it, my friend?"

"It's Bo," said the dwarf, and even in the moonlight Griffin saw the concern on his face.

He turned to his father, who nodded. "Go."

Moments later, they arrived to find a cluster of people whispering to each other in a circle. Ragnar and Lagnar were there, propping up Takal, his head bandaged, but his eyes still bright. Roland stood alongside Commander Salek. The dwarf looked up as Griffin approached and smiled to see his friend alive, but the smile was tinged with sadness. Naymeira leaned on a longbow, using it as a crutch, keeping her weight off her injured leg.

"Are you all right?" Griffin asked the elf.

"I am not the one you should be worried about." Her eyes were red. He had never seen her cry.

Bo'cul lay shaking in the grass, his breathing heavy and labored. The corpse of Ranimus was sprawled only a few feet away. Firstport Captain Genthus Nyrn kneeled over the minotaur, inspecting his wound.

"I know the smell of this poison," he told Griffin as he neared. "From the Isle of Eag." He shook his head. "There is no stopping it."

Griffin kneeled beside the bull. He grabbed one of the minotaur's meaty hands. Kwint grabbed the other. "I promised, Bo'cul. I said I would get you home. Please let me keep that promise," Griffin whispered. The minotaur looked at him, golden teardrops in the corner of his eyes. "We've done it, Bo. We've done it! Seretigo is dead. Malumus, too. Flame Web has all four of the Sister Jewels for the first time since their creation."

Griffin reached into his pocket and pulled out the Ungornem Gem, holding it in front of Bo'cul's face. "You see? Look, Bo. We've won."

The minotaur's eyes began to flutter. His breathing slowed. His eyes closed.

"No, Bo'cul!" shouted Griffin. He pressed the black gem against the bull's chest. "Fight!"

The minotaur's breathing stopped entirely. For a moment. But then the gem began to glow so intensely that it caused the surrounding group to avert their eyes. How could the Dark Gem be so bright? Suddenly, life returned to Bo'cul's face. His heart beat once more. His eyelids opened and he released a breath that seemed to come from deep within.

"Bo?" Griffin seemed startled. "Bo, let me take you home to your family."

The minotaur's mouth actually widened into a sharp-toothed smile. "This... is... family," he said.

The surrounding group gasped and cheered. Bo'cul wrapped his enormous hand around Griffin's, clutching the black gem.

"He can speak?" said Naymeira, laughing through tears.

Kwint just sat back in the grass, bowed his head, and chuckled softly to himself. He looked up at Naymeira and winked. "I suppose there is a first time for everything."

Commander Salek stepped forward and stared at the gem shining fiercely in the night. "Does this mean..."

"I believe it means," said Takal, "that our friend Bo'cul is the fourth person of power."

"The Sister Jewels," said Griffin, helping Bo'cul to a sitting position. "They found each other." He scanned the faces of each of his friends in turn. "So did we."

EPILOGUE

The war was won. The few remaining True Shadow soldiers had fled to the west soon after Roland's scouting party and the troops of Firstport had arrived. They were scattered, divided. As if a hammer had been flung against glass, their once mighty army was shattered.

All members of Flame Web congregated on the outskirts of what remained of Cauldron. The four people of power carried their respective Sister Jewels. Naymeira Darkleaf held the Anoelmenoh, the Gem of Light, in both hands. Kwint Kwinhollow brandished the Mizzarkh, the Gem of Fire, waving it high above his head. Bo'cul Strond stared down at his own jewel, the Ungornem Gem. The power the Gem of Darkness held was tempting, yet the minotaur would not submit to the lure. Finally, there was Griffin Blade. He let the Hiamahu Jewel, the Gem of Water, rest in the center of his palm. Griffin's original aim had been to retrieve the magnificent jewel. Now it was moments away from once again slipping from his grasp—this time, certainly for good. But the decision to let that happen had been unanimous, and that included his consent, too.

Behind the four people of power were a number of familiar faces. Roland stood up as straight and tall as he could and stroked his silver beard. Salek scanned his soldiers and smiled with pride. Genthus Nyrn was in a cheerful mood, joking and laughing with the dwarven King Rindivor. Takal, Ragnar, and Lagnar hovered to one side and discussed what the future might hold. Ramyr Blade stood behind his son, his four-fingered hand on Griffin's shoulder. Even Fuss neighed nearby, in an unusually cheerful mood.

The now-healed griffin watched from above, its glistening eagle eyes seeing all. Four black-cloaked riders galloped toward the group and dismounted their steeds. Each knelt before a person of power, their heads bent low and their hands held high. One by one, each rider received one of the Sister Jewels. Griffin hesitated for only a moment before sighing and handing over his gem. After a loud trumpet blast, the black-cloaked men departed, cheered by all, followed by none.

The first man rode for days on end until he reached the perilous woods and swamps of the Far East. He sent his horse off with a hard slap and made his way on foot, navigating mazes of low-hanging branches that seemed to grab at him, slogging through murky bogs that tried to swallow him whole, even fending off a small pack of swampcats. After he was satisfied with his distance, he placed his Sister Jewel amid some overgrown weeds in an unexplored marshbed far from civilization.

The man then made his way even farther into the wilderness, threw a thick rope over a tree branch, tied a loop in its end, stood atop a rotting log, and slipped his head into the waiting noose. He took a deep breath and let the log roll away.

The second rider galloped toward the distant horizon of the Far South, to where the land came to an end at the open sea. He boarded a sailboat and steered his vessel through the Isles of Confusion, stopping for provisions at the sparsely-populated ports of Kyne and Kalac, keeping his head hidden beneath the hood of his black cloak. He sailed across the green Sea of Ye'vel until he entered largely uncharted lands. There, he came upon a tiny island, no more than a spit of land in the sea. He beached his sailboat, made his way inland a few dozen feet, and looked around to make sure nobody was watching, even though there wasn't a soul within many days' travel. He buried his Sister Jewel deep in the sand.

The man climbed back onto his boat, bringing with him the heaviest rock he could lift from the island. He sailed until there was no land in sight, tied one end of a rope tightly around his ankle, and secured the other end to the rock. Then he looked skyward, one last glance at a cloudless sky, and pushed the rock into the sea.

The third rider passed through the endless rolling hills of the Far West, pushing his horse to exhaustion. He stopped only to hunt for his food and to sleep briefly beneath a bright canopy of stars, his hand always gripping the Sister Jewel in his possession. When his horse could go no further, he let his own legs carry him until he, too, reached his physical limit.

He stumbled forward until he came to a great gorge that had been gouged through the landscape as if a giant had dragged his sword behind him. He found a sharp rock and gouged out a small hole of his own in the dry dirt near the edge of the gorge. He placed the gem gently in the hole and then covered it once more. From a distance of a few feet, it was impossible to tell that the ground had been disrupted in any way.

He wiped the dirt from his hands, rose to his feet, closed his eyes, and walked a few steps forward before falling into the dark abyss.

The final rider climbed the frigid cliffs of the Far North, past spiraling ruins that were once ancient dwarven strongholds. His horse soon succumbed to the bitter cold, leaving frostbite and hunger as the man's only companions. When the cold grew too fierce, he knew he had to stop. Just before his fingers became too numb to grip it, he tossed his Sister Jewel into a snowdrift. The small indentation was soon filled in by blowing snow.

The man unsheathed his dagger and raised it towards his throat. He hesitated. His hand trembled. He shouted toward the heavens and cursed the gods, then he hurled the dagger into the mist. Perhaps the journey had weakened his mind, or the cold had eaten away at his spirit, but he did not have the resolve to finish the act. The four riders had volunteered to take their own lives to assure that the locations of the gems would never be known. If just a single gem were to be found, it would eventually lead to the others. They are the Sister Jewels. The man had failed. A dark shadow loomed over him.

Watching from above, the griffin had known this would happen, even as the four riders had departed. *There will always be men with a desire for power, and there will always be power for the men to desire.* With a caw and a screech, the griffin soared into the distance—gone, but perhaps not forever.

Made in the USA
San Bernardino, CA
08 December 2014